Krisanne Blessing knew instantly who was on the other end of the line. After almost seven years, his voice still had the power to make her pulse quicken.

"I was thinking of driving over next weekend," she answered.

"Can you make it this weekend?"

A knot of anger began to form in the pit of her stomach. Some things never changed; neither did some people. "Let's try again," she said, struggling to remain calm. "Why should I come to Coyote Springs this weekend?"

"Something's developed, Kris. But I don't want to discuss it over the phone. Will you come?" He paused, and this time his question sounded like a sincere, almost desperate, request. "Will you come, please?"

She breathed out slowly. It must be serious for him to call her like this. "All right," she replied. "But can you at least tell me—"

"I'll explain tomorrow. See you then." He hung up.

Had that been a call from an old lover—or was it from Drew Hadley, her brother's lawyer and best friend…summoning her home without an explanation?

Either way it was not good. Not good at all.

Dear Reader,

A few years ago my father-in-law passed away. He was in his mid-eighties, had lived a full life and quietly and courageously accepted the fact that his time had come. Standing by his bedside in those last hours was difficult, but it was also incredibly rewarding. In a mysterious way, being allowed to help him "cross over" was his final gift.

Life, as we all know, is an endless stream of experiences, each of which influences who we are and how we react to the events that come after them. Falling in love. The birth of a child. The marriage of a friend. The death of a loved one.

Krisanne Blessing, the heroine in my story, must face all of these situations. And like all people, she must discover her own values, her own emotional base and the source of her happiness.

This book, like my first, is set in the fictitious West Texas town of Coyote Springs. Needless to say, what the characters go through could be experienced anywhere.

I love to hear from readers. You can reach me at: P.O. Box 4062, San Angelo, TX 76902.

K.N. Casper

Books by K.N. Casper

HARLEQUIN SUPERROMANCE
806—A MAN CALLED JESSE

HER BROTHER'S KEEPER

K.N. Casper

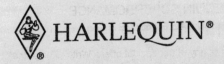

HARLEQUIN®

TORONTO • NEW YORK • LONDON
AMSTERDAM • PARIS • SYDNEY • HAMBURG
STOCKHOLM • ATHENS • TOKYO • MILAN • MADRID
PRAGUE • WARSAW • BUDAPEST • AUCKLAND

ISBN 0-373-70839-4

HER BROTHER'S KEEPER

Copyright © 1999 by K. Casper.

Look us up on-line at: http://www.romance.net

Printed in U.S.A.

This is a work of love that extends to the many people who helped me along the emotional path of its writing. Mentioning their names doesn't say enough. It's only one very small way of acknowledging a debt of gratitude for all their help, advice and encouragement.

To these ladies I can only offer my heartfelt thanks.
Janet Branson
Barbara Jennison
Lori Kerr
Connie Marquise
Starla Criser
Linda Cope
and of course,
Mary Casper.

And to all hospice workers who guide us through those final moments of love.

This book is dedicated to the memory of
T. G. Hutchinson, Sr., who left us a legacy of
tears and laughter.

CHAPTER ONE

"Is DAVY GOING to be all right, Doctor?"

Krisanne Blessing didn't have to see the tears streaming down Nelly's face to know the little girl was frightened. Hearing the halting sob in her whispered question was enough to melt Krisanne's heart. Nelly had found the starving, half-drowned kitten after a major rainfall six weeks earlier.

"Looks like a refugee from Davy Jones's locker," Krisanne's sailor neighbor had commented when he brought his daughter and the foundling to her door. The fact that the orphaned animal was a female hadn't changed Nelly's resolve to name it Davy.

Krisanne had helped Nelly dry and clean the shivering creature, then taught the eight-year-old how to feed it from a bottle. When it had grown strong enough, she'd brought shots home for the meowing fur ball. Now Nelly and Davy were back. Davy seemed determined to use up another of her nine lives.

"She's going to be fine," Krisanne soothed the worried child. "It's a bad cut, but we're going to fix it. A couple of stitches and she'll be climbing trees again in no time."

One glance at the bloody cat cradled in the child's arms convinced her that delaying her trip to Dallas for a couple of hours wouldn't matter. The child trusted her. With Nelly's mother's permission, Krisanne brought the girl and kitten to the closed clinic for treatment, leaving behind the suitcase she'd only half filled when Nelly had come beating on the door. Checking out new business opportunities in Big D would have to wait a little longer.

"I'll give Davy a shot to take the pain away," Krisanne explained, as she placed the frightened pet on the treatment table. "Then I'm going to sew up that nasty cut. I can use your help to keep her calm." It wasn't really necessary. The injection would sedate the young cat, but petting and soothing the woozy kitten would make Nelly feel better.

The little girl's expression was a mixture of compassion and alarm. Krisanne remembered her own initial revulsion at the thought of using a needle and thread on living tissue. But Nelly's hesitation didn't last more than a heartbeat.

"I'll do anything just so Davy'll be all right."

"Good girl." Krisanne smiled. If her hands had been free, she would have hugged the girl for her bravery. "Davy's going to be fine. I promise."

Ten minutes later she was tying the last tiny stitch when the phone rang.

"Nelly," Krisanne said, as she snipped the hair-thin filament, "would you press the button on the phone that says speaker, please?"

With an anxious backward glance, the girl darted over to the instrument on the white-tiled wall, examined it a second, and gave the gray button a determined push.

"Lesko Veterinary Clinic," Krisanne called out.

All he said was "Hello, Kris," and she knew instantly who was on the other end of the line. Her hands froze. After almost seven years, his voice still had the power to make her pulse quicken. Why was he calling her?

"I'm glad I found you. Can you come to Coyote Springs tomorrow?" Drew Hadley asked.

Krisanne cut a length of gauze and started wrapping the sutured wound. "I was thinking of driving over next weekend."

"Can you come this weekend?"

A knot of anger began to form in the pit of her stomach. "I wasn't planning on it."

"So you've said. That's not what I asked," he persisted. "Will you come tomorrow?"

She snipped off a piece of adhesive tape, applied it gently to the bandage, and shook her head. Some things never changed, or some people. Drew had always been focused, assertive. His strength was one of the qualities she'd loved about him.

"Let's try again," she said, struggling to sound calm. "Why should I come to Coyote Springs this weekend?"

"I'm sorry, Kris," he said after a brief pause. "I didn't mean to be so—"

"Bumptious?"

He hesitated. "Bumptious. Yes." There was no mistaking the smile in his voice.

Damn it. Why had she used that word? Their word. Full of meaning and innuendo—and images....

"Something's developed, Kris. But I don't want to discuss it over the phone. Tomorrow will be soon enough for explanations...if you can make it." He paused again, and this time his question sounded like a sincere, almost desperate, request. "Will you come, please?"

She breathed out slowly. It must be serious for him to call her like this.

"All right," she replied and finished binding the kitten's paw. "If you really think it's important. Can't you at least tell me—"

"Do you know where my office is?"

"In Law Tower. But—"

"Kris, I'll explain everything tomorrow. Around noon?"

"Well, I guess so, b—"

"See you then," he concluded and hung up.

After a moment of stunned silence Krisanne asked Nelly to hit the button again to disconnect.

A call from an old lover...or was it from Drew Hadley, the lawyer...summoning her home without an explanation. Not good. Not good at all.

She and Nelly left with Davy a few minutes later and drove back to their apartment complex. Krisanne commended Nelly to her mother for her help and gave them instructions on caring for the injured animal. As soon as she was back in her own apartment, Krisanne retrieved her personal phone book from the desk. Flipping to Drew's name, she tried to call him at the office, but it was Friday and well past normal business hours. All she got was an answering service.

She hung up and dialed her brother Patrick's private number at his laboratory at Blessing Pharmaceuticals. No answer. She tried him at home. No luck there, either.

Patrick had given her Drew's home number last year when Blessing hired Pruit and Hadley as their corporate attorneys, but the baby-sitter for his young son said Mr. Hadley wasn't at home, and she couldn't say when he would be. Krisanne glanced at the mantel clock on the sofa table. Almost seven o'clock. Can't be too big a crisis if he's out wining and dining, she thought, or dancing.... He always liked to dance. It was the Bump they'd learned at a 70s party and then practiced alone late one night that had led to their first lovemaking. It gave bumptious a new meaning, a code word they could use in public.

"If he returns before midnight," she told the woman at the other end, "please ask him to call me at home. Here's my number." Fat chance it'll do any good, she told herself as she hung up.

She dialed Patrick's home number again, this time leaving a message on his answering machine for him to call her if he got in before midnight. Something told her the effort was futile.

By eleven o'clock, she was so frustrated and bursting with curiosity, she tried to call Celia, her stepmother. "Mrs. Blessing is out for the evening, Krisanne," the housekeeper informed her. "May I take a message?"

What is this? Party night in Coyote Springs? "No, no message."

Midnight came and went. No one had called.

Perhaps, she thought, Blessing Pharmaceuticals was in some sort of trouble. A lawsuit? Why would Drew call her about a lawsuit? They had reserves to cover product liability, not to mention the prestigious firm of Pruit and Hadley to represent them. Financial problems? Patrick hadn't mentioned any cash flow concerns, although the company hadn't paid any dividends in the three years since Celia's big expansion and building program. Was it worse than that? Could they be bankrupt?

Damn, damn, and double damn!

Just when she'd finally made up her mind to leave

Dr. Lesko's veterinary clinic and open one of her own! She would have preferred to stay and enlarge his practice, maybe even buy him out, but the old man wasn't interested in expanding or retiring.

So she'd decided to move out on her own. But not in Austin. She didn't want to compete against her old employer. Dallas was the place to be. The problem was capital. It would take at least a half-million dollars to open the animal care center she envisioned. She certainly didn't have that kind of money in a savings account, or any other account for that matter. What she did have was her quarter interest in Blessing. But if the family business folded, she could forget about opening her own clinic in the foreseeable future.

She turned off the bedside lamp around one o'clock. She'd practically worn a rut in the carpet with her pacing. Nighttime TV bored her. Reading meant sitting still.

Damn Drew's hide! *All he had to do was tell me what's going on.* Why did men do things like that?

Darkness didn't help. It conjured up too many memories.

She'd been a junior in high school when Patrick brought his freshman year roommate home from the University of Texas for Thanksgiving dinner. Drew Hadley was brawnier than her brother and taller by a couple of inches, dark-haired, and he had a healthy, outdoor manliness that could make her feel giddy just being near him.

She'd sat across from him at the dining room table, entranced by the dimpled cleft in his chin, the squareness of his jaw. Her father had been impressed with him, too. Hadley was smart. They'd talked about drug laws and the legalization of certain substances. But she'd found herself less attentive to his words than the mellow resonance of his voice, and the perfect way his big hands fitted the oversized holiday sterling silverware. When he'd caught her staring and smiled at her, her face had grown hot, and she was sure she was going to die.

Drew hadn't invited her out on their first date until exactly two years later when he was again at the Blessing's House for Thanksgiving dinner. By then she was a freshman at Texas A&M U. and he was talking about staying on at UT to go to law school. He'd asked her to go dancing with him on Saturday night. Her heartbeat had stuttered, but she'd dallied, pretending to give it a moment's thought—she'd considered herself more sophisticated by then—before accepting. On the appointed night, she'd felt like Cinderella with Prince Charming when he'd held her on the dance floor. The evening had ended with their first kiss.

Over the next four years they'd traded visits, she going up to Austin one weekend a month, he coming down to College Station two weeks later. They spent their summers together, too. He worked at Blessing with Patrick and her father, while she volunteered at the local animal shelter. He was her first lover, her only lover. They hadn't actually set a wedding date, but she'd assumed that after she graduated from vet school and he passed the bar…

Then came the engraved announcement in the mail, just before her graduation. He'd married Lisa Turner.

DREW HADLEY SAT back in his office chair and pinched his fingers across the bridge of his nose. His secretary was gone for the day, and he'd been tempted to answer the phone when it rang a few minutes after his call to

Austin. Figuring it was Krisanne calling back, wanting to know what was going on, he'd forced himself to let the answering service pick up after the third ring. Tomorrow would be bad enough. Hearing her voice again tonight would only add further to his discomfort.

He put the papers concerning Troimaline back in the file folder and shoved it to the edge of his desk. A complex issue, but one he would worry about Monday. Now it was time to go home.

He locked the office and took the elevator down to the lobby. The unrelenting west Texas wind ruffled his hair, as he walked to his Mercedes-Benz in the Law Tower parking lot. With the sun setting, it was chilly, too, even though it was spring.

Maybe returning to Coyote Springs had been a mistake. Lisa had objected to coming here, with good reason. She knew what he and Krisanne had once meant to each other. Working for Blessing, where Krisanne might show up at any moment, only increased the tension in his already tumultuous relationship with his wife.

Now Lisa was dead, killed in a car crash less than two months after they'd settled in. Friends suggested he start dating, but the one woman he wanted would never have him. She'd never trust him again, nor could he blame her. He'd told Krisanne to get on with the rest of her life and she had, apparently putting him completely behind her. She'd never called him, never written.

Still, he'd kept track of her over the years—thanks to her brother. Krisanne had graduated from vet school at the top of her class, worked at an animal shelter in Beaumont for a while, then joined Dr. Lesko in Austin. From all accounts, she was doing well.

Drew also knew there'd been occasional men in her life. Patrick had made no secret of them, or of his conviction that the relationships wouldn't last. It made Drew wonder, sometimes, if what he'd done seven years ago had undermined her trust in men, her confidence in herself and her willingness to commit. He hoped not.

Tomorrow he'd see her. The sound of her voice this evening had awakened memories he didn't want to think about, feelings he had no right to pursue. He owed it to her to keep his distance, but then, she would undoubtedly make sure he did.

He moved his son's bicycle away from the steps to the back door and let himself into the house. The place was too quiet, too peaceful for the home of a six-year-old boy. Mrs. Chambers came around the corner into the kitchen.

"Good evening, Mr. Hadley."

"Hi. I'm sorry I'm so late. Where's Trav?"

"In his room watching *The Lion King* on his VCR."

"Has he eaten yet?"

"I offered to fix him some macaroni and cheese a little while ago, but he wanted to wait for you."

Drew felt a sharp pang of guilt mixed with pride. He remembered all too well the loneliness of childhood. His own parents were rarely home. Once in a while his fashion-conscious mother would visit the kitchen when his nanny or some other servant was feeding him, but only to watch. Drew couldn't recall her ever sitting beside him and sharing a meal. As for his father, Drew wasn't sure the distinguished judge even knew where the kitchen was. Later came boarding school and college. Going on to law school had been ordained rather than elected.

Drew vowed early on that his own children wouldn't suffer that kind of benign neglect. Lisa, unfortunately, had hardly been a homemaker. Becoming a single parent hadn't been hard, Drew realized. He'd been one from the minute Travis was born.

"If you don't need me anymore, Mr. Hadley, I'll run along."

"Thanks, Mrs. Chambers. Trav and I will get along just fine on our own."

"Oh, a Dr. Blessing called. She asked you to call her back. Her number's on the pad."

After seeing the sitter out the front door, Drew returned to the telephone table in the hallway and stared at the note by the phone. Call her? He shook his head and backed away.

I won't take the easy way out this time. Tomorrow I'll see her, tell her what has to be said face-to-face. She deserves that much from me.

KRISANNE LEFT AUSTIN before dawn, restless and gritty-eyed. There was no point in delay. Besides, by arriving early she'd have a chance to see her brother before keeping her appointment with Drew.

A couple of hours later, she exited Route 87 east of Coyote Springs. The downtown streets were deserted, and the old house on Coyote Avenue loomed huge and dark against the early morning sky. She turned into the driveway, drove to the back of the house and parked in front of the three-car garage. Letting herself in by the back door, she flipped light switches, and climbed the carpeted stairs. After dropping her suitcase in her old room, she went across the hallway to Patrick's door.

"Good Lord," she muttered to herself, as she lifted

her knuckles to the paneled oak. "He'll be furious if he's not alone." Her bachelor brother loved his work and put in long hours, but he was far from being a dull boy. He liked to party, and he had a definite fondness for female companionship.

There was no response to her timid first tap or her more aggressive second knock. Already embarrassed at the thought of what she might find, she turned the knob and inched the door open. The pale light oozing through the corner window blinds revealed a pristine bedroom with its corniced ceiling and sleigh bed. He wasn't there. Nobody was.

She clucked to herself. So he didn't come home last night. Who was he with? Was it serious this time? After all, he was almost thirty, time to think about settling down and starting a family.

He'd laugh if he found out she'd crept into his room like this. But he'd do the same thing if their roles were reversed. They'd been taking care of each other ever since their mother died when Krisanne was thirteen and Patrick fifteen.

She went down the winding stairs at the back of the house that led to the kitchen, desperately wanting a cup of coffee, but too restless to take the time to make it. Slipping behind the wheel of her car, she set out for Blessing Pharmaceuticals, stopping at a drive-thru on the way for her shot of caffeine.

The last time she'd visited the family-owned business was six months ago when they'd opened the new plant. The landscaping had been incomplete then, the emphasis on the modern equipment and stylish executive offices.

Hourly employees didn't work on Saturdays, so the company parking lot was nearly empty. She was a little surprised, however, to see her brother's red Bronco in its reserved parking space. She chuckled softly, remembering he hadn't gone home last night. Obviously he was burning the candle at both ends.

Parking near the main entrance, she walked down the path of geometrical paving stones between rigidly trimmed hedges. Songbirds chirped in redbud trees, lifting her spirits. She pushed open the smoked-glass double doors.

"Good morning, Dr. Blessing," the uniformed guard greeted her. He was in his late fifties or early sixties, a little on the portly side, with a shiny bald pate rimmed with a gray fringe. His eyebrows and mustache were salt-and-pepper.

"Hello, Mr. Connors." She clipped the badge he gave her onto the left pocket flap of her blue chambray shirt. He'd sign her in on the log himself.

"I'm real sorry about…" He twisted the pen in his hand. "How's your brother handling things?"

Her mood plummeted. Her hunch must be correct— the business was in trouble. Celia was the company's CEO, but when the chips were down, it seemed everyone turned to Patrick.

"I don't have all the details yet, but we managed to deal with the turmoil when my father died. I'm sure we'll get through this, too. You know Pat. He'll find a way to handle it."

Connors compressed his lips and nodded, but his averted eyes said this time she was whistling in the wind. She could understand his personal concern. If Blessing went out of business, he'd be out of a job, and as close to retirement as he probably was, that could mean disaster. How safe were the company's retirement funds, she wondered, and how many other employees were in the same precarious position? She'd seen enough "downsizing" to know how devastating it could be.

She started along the main corridor.

"Your mother isn't here," Connors called out. "Left a little while ago, said she was going over to Springs General—"

My stepmother, Krisanne nearly corrected him and felt a familiar jab of guilt. Her father's second wife had always been pleasant enough, but Krisanne had never warmed to her. Polite and distant seemed to characterize their relationship.

"That's all right," she replied over her shoulder as she continued down the hallway. "I didn't come to see her, anyway, at least not right now."

Even if the company were in trouble, why would Celia go to General, Krisanne asked herself, then shook her head. Speculation was pointless.

She took the first right. Patrick's laboratory was located at the far end of the brightly lit corridor. A relatively small enterprise in the world of pharmaceuticals, Blessing's bread and butter was in patent medicines, generic drugs and over-the-counter cold remedies. Most of Patrick's staff worked on routine quality testing of existing products. They didn't have much invested in drug research, certainly not on a level likely to make a breakthrough in conquering cancer or AIDS. But as a biochemist and registered pharmacologist, Patrick insisted on carrying on a certain amount of basic research himself. It was good business, he pointed out.

Entering the outer office, Krisanne spied Nadeen Thomas slumped round-shouldered at a computer terminal in the far corner. Patrick's assistant was alone.

The tall, lanky woman straightened at the sound of the door opening and swiveled on her stool.

"Oh, Kris." She hooked a stray strand of brown hair behind her left ear. It looked as if she had a galloping case of spring allergies—her amber eyes were so red and puffy. "I didn't expect to see you here. I figured you'd go directly to the hospital."

Krisanne's breath caught in her throat. "Hospital? Why should I go there?"

Nadeen bit her lip. "You mean you don't know?" Her hand reached for a tissue from the box on the corner of the workbench. "That's where Pat is—Springs General, room 408."

Krisanne's stomach muscles clenched. Patrick was there as a patient? Her mind pounced on the aggressive way he drove. But the Bronco was parked in its usual place outside, apparently without a scratch.

"Did he have an accident on his motorcycle?"

The young woman shifted uncomfortably on the round seat, grabbed another tissue from the box at her elbow and wiped the tip of her raw, runny nose. Dropping her hands in her lap, she explained, "He collapsed here in the lab Monday morning. We figured he was just run-down…" she trailed off.

"He passed out?" Krisanne exhaled with relief. At least she could dismiss the image of her brother encased in a full body cast, suspended from cables and pulleys. "But you said on Monday. Are you telling me he's been in the hospital all week and nobody called me? What's wrong with him?"

"They've been running a lot of tests."

"What kind of tests?"

Nadeen's congested voice quavered, her fingers shredding her soggy tissue. "I really don't know—"

Krisanne's exasperation increased. "Room 408, you say?"

Barely seeing the lab assistant's nod, she spun out of the room and raced down the hallway, her heart pounding. Connors's mouth opened at her approach, but he said nothing as she slapped the badge on his desk, barged out the front door and ran to her car.

Patrick passed out at his desk? She worried her lower lip with her thumb and forefinger as she waited for a light to change. Why hadn't Drew simply told her Patrick was in the hospital? Why all the mystery?

Krisanne's tension mounted higher when, fifteen minutes later, she strode into the gleaming white medical center. Out of nervous habit, her fingers twirled a lock of hair above her right ear as the elevator crept up to the fourth floor. The door finally opened. She stepped out, swung right, rounded a corner—and found herself facing Drew Hadley.

Her pulse, already racing, slammed into overdrive and a half-forgotten tingling coursed through her veins.

He stood at the nurse's station, head thrown back as he shared some joke with a heavyset woman in blue scrubs. His thumbs were hooked casually in the belt loops of worn jeans slung low on his narrow hips. Even from a distance, the intoxicating richness of his laughter threatened to undermine her resolve not to be affected by his presence.

Drew turned at her involuntary gasp, the joviality instantly vanishing from his tanned face. A hospital patient, towing an IV stand, crept in slow motion across their path, breaking Krisanne's trance. She shivered in the refrigerated air and reminded herself that concern for her brother was what had brought her to this place. Drew stepped toward her.

"Kris, I didn't expect to see you here."

Her eyes roamed over his face, noted the worry lines at the corners of his mouth, the neatly trimmed thick dark hair. Even in the harsh fluorescent glare, his hazel eyes sparkled with the golden specks she'd always found so fascinating. But there was a sadness in them, too, that frightened her.

She marched past him on her way down the corridor.

"Please wait a minute," he begged, trailing along beside her. "We need to talk first."

Anxiety quickly slipped into anger. She stopped and pivoted to confront him. "We could have done that last night, Drew. Why the hell didn't you tell me Pat was in the hospital?"

"I…" He hesitated, just as he'd done on the phone the evening before. She lost what little patience she still possessed and brushed past him. He followed her into room 408.

Her brother was sitting up in the raised bed, looking forlorn in one of those hospital gowns that seemed fiendishly designed to fit no one. He smiled a little awkwardly and reached out his arms for an embrace. He smelled faintly of rubbing alcohol and medicinal soap.

"Cute threads," she teased, trying not to be disturbed by the memory of her father in a similar setting after his first heart attack three years earlier.

Patrick grinned mischievously. "De Sade originals."

"Nadeen said you collapsed Monday, that you've been here all week." She turned to face Drew. "You should have called me then."

"I asked him not to," Patrick interjected and shifted uncomfortably in the bed. He'd always been wiry. His compulsive athleticism—tennis, swimming, jogging, skiing—kept him that way. But he'd obviously lost weight in the three months since she'd seen him over the Christmas holidays.

"Pat, what's this all about?" Krisanne's worry bordered on panic. "What's going on?"

Her brother's pale blue eyes flickered with uneasiness. This, too, was unlike him. He was always so sure of himself, the rock she could count on under any circumstance.

Drew dragged an upholstered metal chair to the side of the bed. "You better sit down, Kris."

"Thanks, but I'd rather stand." Instinctively, however, she crossed her arms under her breasts in a self-protective stance. Her stomach churning, she tried to ignore the feeling of dread that was making her heavy-limbed and lightheaded at the same time.

Patrick reached over, filled a glass with water, sipped, and settled back on the thin hospital pillow. "I've been feeling a little run-down lately, Sis—"

"You never said anything when we talked two weeks ago."

They were in the habit of phoning each other every Sunday evening. Last Sunday, however, she'd driven to Dallas for a continuing education course in small animal dermatology. Not her favorite subject. She would have preferred one on equine surgical techniques.

"I thought it was the flu or a bad cold. It didn't seem worth mentioning."

Considering where he was and how long he'd been here, she knew it had to be more serious than that.

"So what is it?" she asked. "And why didn't you call to tell me you were here?"

"They wanted to run some tests first," Drew explained. "We didn't see any point in worrying you until the results were in."

"We?" She glared at him. "What's this got to do with you?"

"Drew's my friend," Patrick interceded.

"And I'm your sister." She took a deep breath, trying to calm the agitation foaming within her. She hated feeling left out, unsettled, especially in the presence of the man she'd once loved—the man who had betrayed her. "All right, so what's the matter?"

"We got the results yesterday," Patrick explained. Then he paused so long her heart started thudding. "I've got acute lymphatic lymphoma."

CHAPTER TWO

KRISANNE COLLAPSED INTO the chair Drew had offered her a minute before.

Lymphoma. A form of cancer that affects the lymph nodes that produce the white blood cells—key elements against infection in the body's immune system.

Her brother was dying.

"That's impossible," Krisanne whispered.

She stared at the man in the bed, but he offered no qualification, no extenuation. She saw only an uneasy submission. Her heart hammered in her chest. She jumped up and hugged herself to ward off a chill that was suddenly creeping through her bones. Turning back, her spirit wept at the anguish on his pallid face. She moved to his side, pressed her hand into his and looked up at the sculpted features of Drew Hadley standing on the other side of the bed.

"This can't be true," she muttered. "It's got to be a mistake. Surely they can't be certain yet. There must be more tests they have to do."

Patrick smiled wryly. "I wish there were, Sis, but that's one of the perks of having a strong-willed stepmother. They've been thorough and quick in running every test known to man and medical science. There's no doubt."

A tap on the door broke the tense silence that followed. Krisanne glanced around and saw a middle-aged man, small in stature, enter the room. Her first impression of the horn-rimmed glasses and nondescript face was of a petty bureaucrat. Only the white smock and the picture badge fastened to his left lapel, told her otherwise. He carried an aluminum clipboard in his right hand.

"Dr. Chaffee," Patrick greeted him, "this is my sister, Krisanne Blessing."

"Miss Blessing."

"It's Doctor," Drew pointed out. "She's a vet."

Chaffee shook her hand.

Patrick said, "And you've met Drew Hadley."

The two men nodded.

Krisanne addressed the physician. "My brother tells me the diagnosis is lymphoma. Can you tell me what stage it's at?"

"Four."

"Four?" Her mind reeled and her knees turned to jelly. She clutched the back of the chair. Four was the highest and last stage of the disease. It meant all the major lymph nodes above and below the diaphragm were affected, and the cancer was spreading to non-nodal areas.

"I guess it's been developing for some time," Patrick mumbled. "I just wasn't aware of it."

"That's not unusual," Chaffee told him, then turned to Krisanne. "As you know, the symptoms are not very specific. He hasn't experienced any noticeable swelling in the neck, armpits or groin. There's been some fatigue and weight loss, but those are easily attributable to other factors."

"Has it gone into the bone?"

"Sis, if you're thinking of a bone-marrow transplant," Patrick interrupted, "forget it."

"But…Pat, there's a good chance we'll be a perfect match."

He shook his head. "It doesn't make any difference."

"We don't know that yet." She looked again at the doctor. "How soon can I be tested?"

Drew moved around the foot of the bed and came up beside her. "You're not listening, Kris." His voice was compelling with a note of intimacy she remembered so well. Maybe he was trying to comfort her, but his being here, now, only made her edgy, defiant.

She glowered at him before addressing Dr. Chaffee. "When do you start chemo? Since it's this advanced, I know you'll have to be very aggressive with it, and I assume you're also considering radiation."

"Sis," Patrick bellowed in exasperation, then lowered his voice to almost a whisper when she looked at him. "There isn't going to be any therapy."

She froze. "What are you saying?"

"Mr. Blessing has refused treatment," the doctor informed her.

She raised a hand to her forehead. "This is just a bad dream," she mumbled to no one in particular. "This can't really be happening. In a moment I'm going to wake up." She looked back at her brother. "I expected you of all people to—"

"Now you know why I couldn't tell you on the phone last evening," Drew said. He placed a hand gently on her shoulder, but she squirmed out from under his contact. He jerked his hand away as if he'd touched a hot stove and stepped back, giving her space.

"I urge you to reconsider, Mr. Blessing," Chaffee said to his patient.

"Believe me, Doctor, I have considered and recon-

sidered all the options very carefully. I know what con-
coctions you use and in what quantities. And I know
they won't work at this stage. It's too advanced for a
cure.''

"Maybe not a cure," Chaffee agreed, shaking his
head, "but with chemotherapy some remission might
be possible.''

"What about the side effects?"

"We can control any nausea or other physical discomfort with medication.''

"So, in effect," Patrick concluded, "you would poison me, then give me drugs to alleviate the side effects
of the poison.''

Chaffee's expression remained totally bland. "It
might give you a little more time.''

"Quantity at the price of quality? No thanks, Doc.''

Krisanne looked back and forth between the two
men.

"You're giving up?" She gaped breathlessly at her
brother, trying to control the underlying panic.

"No, Kris, I'm facing reality.''

The hurt on his face made her instantly wish she
could retract her words. But she couldn't let him die
without a fight.

Chaffee looked from Krisanne to his patient. "If you
change your mind, let me know and we'll set up a
regular program. Just don't wait too long. The sooner
the better.'' He scribbled a mark at the bottom of a
form on the clip board. "You can get dressed now.
Someone will be by in a few minutes to take you downstairs.'' He again offered Krisanne his hand. "If you
have any questions, Dr. Blessing, give me a call.'' With
that he left the room.

Krisanne watched him go, then drifted trancelike to

the narrow window on the far side of the bed. The bright sunshine, the delicate green of spring, the yellow daffodils and purple pansies laid out below in neat rows mocked the desolation in her soul. She couldn't imagine a world without her big brother.

She felt Drew watching her. Resentment burned like an acid in her stomach. Patrick should have confided in her this past week. Instead, he'd chosen the man who'd humiliated her to be by his side.

"I'm sorry," Patrick said quietly, as if reading her mind. He'd always been able to do that, ever since they were little kids. "I didn't want to worry you, until we knew the test results."

"Sorry?" She felt helpless to suppress the turbulence surging inside her. Her rage wasn't against him or even against Drew, but against death—all-conquering death that stole from her the people she loved.

It took an act of sheer will not to give in to the bitterness fraying the edges of her sanity. But willpower couldn't suppress the tears sliding down her cheeks. "You've got nothing to apologize for, Pat. Sorry? I'm the one..."

He held out his arms and she threw herself into them. Her big, strong brother couldn't be dying. He couldn't. She wouldn't let him.

"We'll find someone, a doctor, a specialist. They're coming out with new drugs, new treatments all the time. We're going to beat this."

"Kris, listen. I know something about this disease and what drugs can do for it." His voice took on an edge. "I also know what they can't do."

"But there must be something," she cried, knowing in her heart that her words were spoken in vain. Patrick

wouldn't change his mind about taking treatment he
knew was useless. He'd accepted his fate. She should
admire him for his wisdom and courage. Her throat
constricted as new tears fell. How often had she told
clients that she was sorry, but there was nothing more
she could do for their pets, that they must accept the
inevitable? Now it was her turn to accept a harsher
truth. But how could she? Why did the truth have to
be so painful? Her irritation with Drew seemed so triv-
ial now, faced with the death of the person closest to
her.

Patrick tightened his grip, and Krisanne sensed he
was holding himself back from mingling his tears with
hers. Then, just as quickly, he released her.

Easing herself away, she groped for a tissue from
the dispenser on the bedside table in a futile attempt to
dry her cheeks.

"He's going to be well cared for," Drew promised.
"You don't have to worry. I'll make absolutely certain
he gets the best of everything."

She looked from one man to the other. "What are
you talking about?"

"Drew's helping me find a good nursing home," Pat
explained.

A cold shiver ran down her spine. "You're not going
to a nursing home."

"He can't stay here in the hospital," Drew reminded
her. "Not if he's refusing treatment."

She brought up her chin. "He's going home."

"Kris, I haven't got much time left," Patrick said
from his bed. "A few months, six at the very most.
They tell me I'm going to need around-the-clock attendance pretty soon."

"Then that's what you'll get," she said with quiet intransigence. "From me—at home."

"Kris," Drew said with equal firmness, "we're not talking about companionship. Pat's going to need nursing."

She shot her most withering glance at him. "I may be only a vet, Drew, but I know a little about medical care and what it entails. And I don't appreciate your interference—"

"I'm not the enemy, Kris. The disease is."

Shutting her eyes, she exhaled, then glared at him. "My brother is not going to some faceless, heartless nursing institution where he's just another bedpan to be emptied. He's going home—with me."

"Well, I guess since everybody else is arranging my life for me," Patrick lashed out, "all I have to do now is lie back and die."

The two combatants turned to him, jaws slack in shock. They'd been talking past him, as if he weren't there. How often had Krisanne been excluded from professional discussions, because she was a woman? The realization added shame to her already growing jumble of emotions.

"Is that what you want, Pat?" Drew asked, the quiet plea in his question suggesting his own embarrassment in patronizing his friend, "to go to Austin with your sister?"

The question made her fume. He was making it sound as if she were kidnapping her own brother. "Austin? Who said anything about Austin? I'm talking about here in Coyote Springs—Patrick's place. The house we grew up in—our home."

Relief brightened the sick man's blue eyes, and all at once she understood he'd hoped she'd do this all

along, but he didn't want to ask. Krisanne slipped her
hand over his.

Drew touched her shoulder. "Can I speak with you
outside for a minute?"

"Go ahead," Patrick said, smiling for the first time.
"I've got to get dressed."

Krisanne moved silently into the sun-filled corridor.
She stood by one of the large plate-glass windows, instinctively wrapping her arms around herself. Drew
closed the door behind them, separating her from her
brother.

"I'm sorry," Drew said.

She barely nodded. He'd said the right words, but
they didn't mean anything—or she was too numb to
comprehend them.

Coming up behind her, he placed his hands on her
shoulders to begin a slow, gentle massage, the way he
used to when she was tense. Instead of leaning into his
hands, she recoiled.

"Are you all right?" he asked, backing off.

"Oh, sure, I'm fine," she drawled sarcastically.
"I've just been told my brother is dying, but sure, I'm
fine, perfectly fine." Her voice broke and she veered
away, unwilling to let him see the flood of tears she
seemed powerless to check. Blindly, she stared out the
window.

Drew stood beside her. "I'm sorry I was so abrupt
on the phone last evening. But under the circumstances
I thought uncertainty was better—"

"Than knowing my brother was dying?"

She turned her head and looked up at him. Even at
an angle she could see concern lining his clean-shaven
face, glimpse pain in his eyes, catch just a whiff of his

woodsy aftershave and the scent that was uniquely
Drew.

An awkward silence grew between them.

"What about your job?" he finally asked.

"I'll take the time off," she said. "Dr. Lesko can
get along without me for a while, or he can hire someone else. I don't care. I have only one place now, and
that's with my brother."

"I'm glad you're doing this for him," Drew said
with an uneasiness that had her looking into his golden-
brown eyes, wondering how long the sadness had been
there. "Pat means a lot to me, Kris. This last year…"
He cleared his throat. "These next few months are going to be very difficult for him—for all of us."

"He's my brother. We're family. This is my responsibility and I can handle it."

"He's also my friend, Kris. For his sake, please
don't cut me out." He looked into her eyes. "No matter what happened between the two of us, I'm still his
friend, and I can be yours…if you'll allow me to." His
tone, already soft, took on an imploring quality. "You
don't have to go through this alone. Let me help."

A nurse's aide pushed a wheelchair past them into
Patrick's room.

Krisanne wiped her cheeks with the back of her
hand. Drew dug into his hip pocket, shook out a white
handkerchief and handed it to her.

"I never meant to hurt you, Kris," he said, in a voice
as soft and tender as she remembered it on her pillow,
so many years ago.

Her chest muscles tightened and for a moment she
couldn't breathe. He wasn't talking about her brother
anymore. Panic rippled through her, a sensation as
acute as pain, as sweet and bitter as burnt sugar. She'd

been waiting for seven years for some word from him, for an explanation. Now she was afraid to hear it.

She bit her lip against the pounding of her heart. "Why, Drew? Just tell me why."

He took a deep breath and looked down at his fists. "It's so simple and so complicated." He paused, closed his eyes and rubbed his chin.

She knew the story of what had happened at the big celebration after the last football game of the season. Drew had never been much of a drinker, but that night the former star quarterback had gotten caught up in the rounds of tequila and beer. Afterwards, he'd fallen into bed with Lisa Turner, a senior at the college. A one-night stand—until she showed up two months later, pregnant with his baby.

Her brother had told her about it, but Krisanne wanted to hear it from Drew. She needed to see his face when he told her she hadn't been enough for him. Yet even now he wouldn't give her that satisfaction. He stared out the window. "Lisa said she was going to have an abortion unless I—"

"Unless you married her," Krisanne finished for him.

Drew stuffed his fists in his pockets. "Yeah." He turned to look at her, his expression searching for some hope of understanding. "I had to, Kris. You must see that."

Oh, I see fine. Her eyes fixed on his. How much she wanted to hate him. "Pat explained it all to me."

"I tried to…"

Her eyes burned—not with anger—she'd managed to get past that a long time ago. At least, that's what she'd told herself. It was the sense of humiliation she'd never been able to completely conquer—the sense of inadequacy. She'd loved him, given her soul as well as her body to him, and neither had been enough. Being drunk was absolutely no excuse for betrayal.

"You guys ready?"

They spun around. Patrick emerged from his room in a wheelchair, pushed by the aide. In the elevator going down to the lobby, Drew stood beside her, the atmosphere between them charged like static electricity ready to spark.

Krisanne remembered the short note he'd scrawled on the back of his wedding announcement. He hoped she'd wish them well and get on with the rest of her life—no explanation, no apology, no regrets. She'd stained the expensive vellum with tears, then torn it up in a rage. But it was all in the past now. She wouldn't dwell on it anymore. Her sole concern now was Patrick.

The doors opened, and the aide rolled her brother across the flagstone lobby and out through the automated glass doors. Krisanne hurried ahead to her Honda.

The two men were talking when she pulled up to the curbside loading area. They fell silent when she came to a stop beside them. Their behavior renewed her sense of isolation and loneliness. Drew opened the passenger door and stood aside while Patrick got out of the wheelchair and into the waiting car. He slid the front seat back to accommodate his long legs and belted himself in. Drew closed the door.

Patrick smiled through the open window. "Thanks."

Krisanne pulled away from the curb, leaving Drew standing there.

"Celia was by this morning," Patrick commented as he rested his arm on the window frame. "She wants us to join her for dinner at the country club this evening.''

Krisanne reached the end of the parking lot and glanced in her rearview mirror, but Drew had moved away from the entrance. She put on her direction signal. There was very little traffic in this part of town on Saturday mornings.

''I don't know—'' she started as she negotiated a left turn.

''I told her we'd meet her there at seven.''

Krisanne would have preferred being asked rather than told. ''Okay,'' she said.

''Stop by the plant,'' Patrick instructed her when they reached the loop. ''I want to pick up the Bronco and take it home.''

''Should you be driving? I can get someone—''

''I'm not dead yet,'' he snapped. ''Just drop me off at the damn lab.''

She was jarred by his bitterness, though she knew she shouldn't be. ''I'm sorry. I didn't mean—''

''I'm sorry, too,'' he replied stiffly, sounding annoyed with himself. She tried to imagine what he was going through. Young men didn't die. They were immortal—or thought they were.

''I shouldn't be biting your head off. I appreciate your staying with me, Sis, more than I can ever tell you.'' He was silent for a minute. ''But I don't want you hovering over me. I know my limits. So relax. I'm not planning any long trips, just a short one across town from the lab to the house. I promise you, I can drive that far safely.''

Biting her lower lip, she recognized the undercurrent of fear in his voice and understood that his anger wasn't directed at her. She also knew there'd be other outbursts like this, moments when he would want to fight back—at whomever or whatever happened to be handy.

He was more like his old self a few minutes later. "Drew said you told him you were planning to drive over here next weekend. What's up?"

"Can't I visit my brother?" she teased, knowing her attempt at the light banter they so often enjoyed was falling flat.

"Sure, and I love it when you do. But Easter's only two weeks away, and I know your work schedule. You don't drive two hundred and fifty miles on a whim. There's got to be a pretty darn good reason." He took a deep breath. "Come on, Kris, out with it. I'm tired of games and evasion."

She owed him honesty, now more than ever. "I've decided to open my own vet clinic."

He nodded his approval. "I'm glad to hear it. What finally convinced you? Are you having trouble with Dr. Lesko?"

"Not really." She pulled around a mud-spattered dump truck straining to make it up a gradual slope with a heavy load. "He's a great old guy with a heart of gold."

"But…"

"He's good at what he does, but he's also set in his ways and can't see any reason to change. Frankly, I think he's intimidated by some of the new technology."

She turned off the loop when they reached the intersection with Highway 87. "I'd like to do more than give shots and neuter house pets."

Patrick brushed a lock of sandy brown hair off his forehead. "Sure sounds like time for you to move on."

"I want to work with large animals, too."

"What are we talking about here? Sheep, goats, cattle?"

Even out of the corner of her eye, she could see the mirthful grin on his face. He already knew the answer.

"Horses."

He laughed. "Gee, what a surprise."

Krisanne loved horses, ever since her father had given her a pony for her sixth birthday. She'd owned an Appaloosa mare through high school and college, but after Honey Babe died of old age, she didn't have the money to buy and board another horse, or the time to train and care for one.

"The problem," she said, "is that I need capital."

"And you were hoping I'd buy your share of Blessing."

Leave it to Patrick to zero in on the heart of the matter. Maybe that was what made him such a good research scientist. She glanced over at him. He looked meditative as he contemplated his hands, palms up.

"Unfortunately," he said, turning his attention to the road before them, "you've waited too long, Kris. If you'd come to me sooner, before I was diagnosed, I could have arranged a loan to buy you out. That's not an option anymore."

Timing again…and irony. A month or two earlier he could have borrowed from the bank using her shares as collateral. The note would have been insured, so that if he died it would be paid off. She would have had the money free and clear and kept her stock in Blessing, as well. Now there was no way he could help her, nor was there any way she could dispose of her share of the company—except to sell to their stepmother.

In his will their father had broken up his single proprietorship into three shares: one quarter to Krisanne, another quarter to Patrick, and the remaining half to Celia. By not giving any of them complete control, he'd hoped to draw them together. It had been a calculated risk, one which might just as well have split them irrevocably apart. Their father had also added the proviso that none of them could sell their interest in the company to outsiders without giving the others first option to buy.

"It's about time you got involved in the business, Kris. Who knows, you might like it."

But she'd never been interested in the pharmaceuticals industry when her father was alive, even less after Celia took over following his death.

"How is the company doing?" she asked, pausing to swallow in an attempt to ease the burning in her throat. "It hasn't paid a dividend in three years—not since Dad died."

"The new building and high-tech equipment we've installed cost us a fortune. If you'd looked at last year's balance sheet, you'd know we're operating pretty close to the edge."

She'd received the report over a month ago but had barely given it a cursory glance. Numbers and statistics didn't interest her. She'd relied completely on Patrick's judgment.

"Plus, I've been practically browbeating Celia into putting more capital into research," he added.

"I'd like to have seen that." She chuckled, unable to imagine anyone, even her brother, pressuring Celia Maddox Blessing into doing something she didn't want to do.

"Obviously," he bragged with feigned pomposity,

"she's seen the merit of my argument. Investment in research now will earn big profits later."

Krisanne produced a little laugh. "I'll probably go ahead and sell my share to her."

They were nearly at the entrance to Blessing Pharmaceuticals before Patrick responded. "I wish you wouldn't, Kris."

"Why not, for heaven's sake? It's the logical solution for what I want to do." And the only way she was going to raise the money to open her clinic.

"I'm going to leave my quarter of the business to you, Kris. That means you and Celia will be equal partners. Grandfather always wanted a member of the family to be active in running the company. Celia's a Blessing in name only. If you sell to her, she'll be sole owner and free to sell to anyone she wants. Blessing won't belong to a Blessing anymore."

The full impact of what he said rolled over her with paralyzing force. She'd always known time would bring change, but she'd never expected these changes. After Drew left, she'd slowly come to realize that Patrick—this man who would make a perfect father— might be the only one of them having children; that the kids who formed her new family and called her "Aunt" would be his kids; and that the only heirs to the reins of Blessing would be his heirs.

"Just promise me, Sis," her brother said, "that you'll keep Blessing in the family."

Oh Pat, her heart cried out, *don't leave me.*

CHAPTER THREE

"I'M GLAD YOU'RE going to be staying here with me, Kris."

She glanced over. The bleak expression on her brother's face made her heart sink. She turned back to the road. "Did you seriously think I wouldn't?" She reached across the console for his hand.

He gave it to her, his grip firm and somehow desperate. "No, but—"

"But what?"

"At least you won't have to face this alone." In the pause that followed she could feel his scrutiny. "There's Celia…and Drew. He and I have become very close again, since he's moved to Coyote Springs."

Last year, when Blessing's old legal counsel disbanded following the sudden retirement of their senior member due to illness, Patrick had recommended Pruit and Hadley take over the account. Though a relatively young partnership, they'd already earned a good reputation as corporate attorneys. Krisanne wasn't enthusiastic about their selection, but it would have sounded like sour grapes for her to oppose it, because one of the partners happened to be her former lover.

"Are you going to be able to work with him?" Patrick asked.

"Why shouldn't I? He's just another lawyer."

He squeezed her hand. She looked over and saw a

broad grin. "Just another lawyer? Drew? I don't think so."

Krisanne felt her cheeks flush. No, not just another lawyer. When she thought of Drew Hadley, it wasn't in terms of his profession. She pictured the man. The man she'd loved. The man who'd deceived her.

Patrick's smile faded. "It's time to forgive him, Kris."

Forgive him for saying he loved me and then sleeping with another woman? He'd cheated on her, betrayed her. So why was she the one who felt inadequate, a failure, as if it were her fault he'd strayed? "It was all a long time ago, Pat." And Drew had told her to get on with the rest of her life.

"He's had a rough time of it this last year. Lisa didn't want to leave her friends in Houston to begin with. She relented only when Drew's partner, Warren, convinced her our account was worth the move. They'd only been settled in here about six weeks when she was killed."

Patrick had called her last summer to tell her Lisa had died in a car crash. Krisanne hadn't attended the funeral. Instead, she'd sent flowers and a card, but had abstained from adding any personal message to the printed expression of condolence. In return, she'd received an equally impersonal note of acknowledgment. The truth was, she reflected, they had nothing to say to each other anymore…nothing more than everything.

Emotions, of course, told another story. Seeing Drew this morning, being with him, feeling his fingers on her shoulders… The realization that after all these years, his touch could still threaten her determination to resist him brought angry heat to her face.

"I'm sorry about his wife," she said. "Losing the mother of his child couldn't have been easy."

Patrick crooked an eyebrow at her. "He's going through a lot of guilt."

She didn't want to think about guilt, or the nights she'd lain awake wondering what she'd done, or not done, to lose the man she'd loved.

"You said it was an accident," she reminded him. "What's he got to feel guilty about? Just because he or his partner talked her into coming here—"

"They didn't have a happy marriage, Kris. Whether you realize it or not, he still loves you."

She kept her eyes focused straight ahead, wishing the west Texas landscape were more hilly and contorted, the road less flat and straight. Hills and valleys, twists and potholes would explain the hollow swirling in her stomach. She felt as if she were on a roller coaster: the high was that Drew Hadley might still love her; the low was that her brother was dying.

Patrick studied her but said nothing.

She turned into the parking lot at Blessing and pulled up alongside Patrick's Bronco. Unbuckling his seat belt, he opened the door, then impulsively leaned across the console and planted a kiss on her cheek. "I know you love him, Sis. Wait till you meet his son, Travis. You'll fall in love with him, too."

With that, he climbed out of her Honda, walked around to his vehicle and pulled out of the parking lot before she could completely recover.

AT A QUARTER to seven that evening, Krisanne buckled herself into the passenger seat of the Bronco. She didn't bring up the subject of her brother's driving this time. Eventually, he'd have to give it up, but she was no more eager to take the pleasure away at this point than he was to lose it.

"With you in the hospital this past week, I guess Celia's been kept busy at the plant," she said by way of casual conversation.

He waited until he'd pulled out into the street before he responded, "I wish you and she would get along."

His remark annoyed her. She hadn't been aware of censure in her observation, but he seemed awfully quick to find it. "We get along fine, Pat. We're just not close."

Patrick turned left at the first major intersection onto San Jacinto Boulevard. Since it was Saturday night, downtown traffic was moderately heavy with people going to restaurants and dance halls. There was also a symphony concert this evening at the civic auditorium.

"I've learned a lot working with her over the last five or six years," he commented.

"I'm sure you have. She's a sharp businesswoman," Krisanne conceded.

Patrick shot by one car, slowed behind another, then zipped around it as well. "I'm talking about the woman herself, Kris. She's not the cuddly type, I admit, but she's not as insensitive as you seem to think."

"We lived together in the same house for nearly two years, before I went off to college," she reminded him, "and never clicked. We're on different wavelengths. That's not a judgment, just a statement of fact."

Their father had done his best to fill the void after their mother died, but running a troubled business had left him precious little time. More often than not, affection was expressed with stacks of romance novels and expensive clothes for Krisanne, science fiction books and tools for Patrick's growing fascination with things mechanical.

Two years later, Christopher Blessing married his executive assistant. Celia Maddox was almost fifteen years his junior, and very different in manner and interests from the casual homebody Ann Blessing had been.

Looking back with the wisdom of hindsight, Krisanne understood Celia hadn't been prepared to assume the role of substitute mother, certainly not for a couple of teenagers. It had been a no-win situation.

"Celia's a strong woman, Kris. In a way she's a lot stronger than Mom was. Mom had a secure, comfortable life and lived it well. Celia's had to fight for every minute of satisfaction and happiness she's ever gotten."

Krisanne knew Celia had been an orphan and had spent her formative years bouncing from public institutions to foster homes, and had never had a chance to go to college.

"She inspired you, whether you realize it or not," Patrick continued. "She poked and prodded and helped you find your way into veterinary medicine, then convinced Dad to send you to A&M."

What he said was true, though Krisanne had interpreted it differently. She'd expected to go away to attend vet school, but the way Celia had pushed the issue made her feel she was being banished.

Patrick chuckled. "The two of you are more alike than you realize, Kris." He glanced over at her puzzled expression. "You may not think that's a compliment, but it is. You're both strong, independent women who know what you want and go for it.

"While I was in the hospital," Patrick went on a

minute later, "she came by at least twice a day, every day, and dropped off a flood of sci-fi books and motorcycle magazines. In between visits to me, I found out she was giving the medical staff the third degree, demanding to know every detail of the tests they were running."

He put on the flasher and pulled into the long, narrow drive leading to the clubhouse.

"Thursday afternoon she brought me a dozen bright yellow roses. It's not the sort of thing I'd expect a woman to give a man. Then I remembered they were Mom's favorites."

Krisanne looked curiously over at him, but he kept his attention intently focused on the road ahead.

"That's when I knew the news wouldn't be good," he said softly. "It was her way of preparing me."

Krisanne's throat tightened and her eyes stung with unspent tears and a confusing mix of agonizing emotions: grief for the coming loss of her brother, disappointment at not being by his side during the terrible past week, and a sudden, irrational jealousy of the woman who had been there and who had apparently handled the tragic situation with dignity and a subtle, unexpected compassion.

Patrick turned right into the parking lot at the end of the drive. The Coyote Springs Country Club was located just beyond the city limits on a small flat plain surrounded by gently undulating hills. The city's oldest and most prestigious, eighteen-hole golf course consisted of several hundred acres of picturesque trees, shrubs and man-made ponds. A single, massive mesquite, ancient and gnarled, its light spring foliage swaying gently in the evening breeze, towered high above a natural outcropping of creamy white stone. Expert pruning and plenty of well-water had contributed to the hardwood's exceptional height and majesty.

Krisanne was soaking in the melancholy beauty of the tree, and the lavender and gold sunset behind it, when Patrick broke into her reverie.

"I see Drew's here." He inclined his head to a maroon Mercedes-Benz sedan parked a few spaces to the right.

She stared at the shiny luxury car, then tried to convince herself the faint tremor she felt had nothing to do with the mention of his name or the prospect of having dinner with him. She didn't want to feel anything anymore for Drew Hadley, least of all attraction.

Krisanne and her brother strolled up the walk bordered with Asian jasmine. Patrick held the wood-paneled door open for his sister and she stepped inside. Even if the huge room with its dark timbers and cathedral ceiling had been crowded with people, she would have seen Drew first. He had his back to the entrance, but there was no mistaking his broad shoulders. His wavy hair glittered black in the subdued evening light coming through the tall windows flanking the native stone fireplace.

He spun around at Celia's nod of greeting from her chair facing the door. The tawny blazer he was wearing captured and intensified the golden sparks in his eyes.

Celia rose gracefully and held out her hands to Patrick.

"How are you feeling?" she asked, worry lines etched in the corners of her mouth.

"I'm fine." Patrick bent to kiss her lightly on the cheek, then turned to his friend. "Hello again, Drew."

Stepping forward and clasping Krisanne's hands with surprising strength, Celia said, "I know you must be terribly upset with me for not calling you as soon as we knew Patrick was ill. But, as you might have noticed, your brother can be very persuasive. I'm sorry, Kris; I wish there were something I could do.''

"So do I," Krisanne replied. She was referring to herself not being able to do anything, but the hurt expression that fleetingly shadowed her stepmother's face told her the remark had been received as an indictment against her. She released Krisanne's hands.

"More I could do, I mean," Krisanne tried to explain. But as usual, the harm was done. It seemed their relationship had always been like this, two women trying to be polite and civilized, yet somehow condemned to hurt one another with inevitable, careless ease.

"Drew tells me you're staying on." Celia twirled the diamond-studded wedding band on her left hand, the single inconsistency in her otherwise confident poise. "Pat's very lucky to have you for a sister." She turned to him. "How's your appetite? I've asked the chef to prepare one of your favorites, crown roast of lamb."

Patrick grinned broadly and gallantly offered Celia his arm. "I think I can handle that."

As they moved off, Drew stepped closer to Krisanne. The smile came first, then his outstretched arm. Cautiously, as if the gesture would entrap her, she slipped trembling fingers under his elbow. Even through the fabric of his sleeve, she could feel the solid muscles of his arm. She had no trouble remembering the fevered touches of his hard body against her naked skin, or the fire they kindled. He cupped his hand over her fingers, his warm, protective caress sending unexpected tingling currents through her. She hadn't been prepared for her responses to his physical presence. More unnerving, she couldn't say the sensations weren't welcome.

"Why didn't you tell me you were joining us for dinner?" she asked, amazed she could make the question sound normal. They strolled down the hall toward the formal dining room.

"Because I didn't know," he answered lightly. "Celia called with the invitation about half an hour after I got home. I wasn't sure I could get someone to stay with Travis. I don't like leaving him on such short notice. Fortunately, Mrs. Chambers, his regular sitter, was available."

"How is your son?" Krisanne had had thirteen years of her mother's affection to console her, but at the tender age of five or six to have a mother suddenly snatched away was even more heartbreaking.

"He's fine." The pride in Drew's voice was unmistakable. "I'd like you to meet him."

"Pat says he's quite a kid."

Squeezing her hand, he flashed her a confident smile. "Yep."

The two couples entered the spacious dining room and were shown to Celia's usual table by the picture window. It offered a charming view of the largest of the idyllic man-made lakes on the golf course. Against the evening sky, now mauve and pink, a weeping willow dipped long slender-leafed tendrils into the water's placid surface.

Cocktails were ordered. Only half listening to the small talk that followed, Krisanne looked up from the glass-encased candle in the middle of the table and found herself staring at Drew's full, sensuous lips. He was smiling, his warm hazel eyes fixed on her.

When the lamb arrived, the chef came out wearing

a high, white pleated hat and spotless apron to serve it
personally, while the maître d' poured a robust caber-
net. In spite of her mood, the tangy aroma of the meat
and the piquant fragrance of mint sauce had her mouth
watering.

It wasn't until the meal was over, the dishes cleared,
and everyone had settled contentedly back in their
chairs, that Celia turned to a more serious subject.

"This might be a good time to get some business
details out of the way," she said, blue eyes sweeping
her dinner guests without pausing to make real contact.
"This isn't going to be easy, but I think you'll agree
it's better to discuss these things now, rather than wait
until events make clear thinking more difficult...for all
of us."

Coffee was poured and the waiter had moved discreetly off to the side before she went on. "Pat tells
me he's leaving his share of Blessing to you." Celia's
gaze rested on Krisanne.

Patrick sipped the last drops of the single glass of
red wine he'd allowed himself with the main course.

"That will make you and me equal partners, Kris,"
Celia continued. "I'm sorry if this seems callous, but
I have to ask. Do you intend to take an active role in
the company?"

Krisanne bristled. This was her first night back in
town. She'd just learned her brother was dying, and all
this woman seemed interested in was who was going
to run the business. Krisanne took a deep, slow breath.

"I don't know yet," she responded. "I haven't had
a chance to absorb what's going on, much less think it
through."

"Of course," Celia replied. Krisanne sensed her disappointment, but true to form, the woman allowed no

hint of it to show. "This has been a dreadful home-coming for you." Reaching over, she placed her hand on Krisanne's. "I'm so sorry."

Celia was not the physically demonstrative type. There hadn't been the hugs of endearment Krisanne had experienced with her mother, or the kind of easy-going, casual rapport friends shared. Perhaps that was one reason Krisanne had never warmed to the intelligent and socially accomplished woman. Even now, the sensation of her diamond-ringed fingers on Krisanne's hand was cool and oddly distant. Yet, as she glanced over, her stepmother's clear blue eyes seemed to melt with a sadness approaching pain.

"There are several options available," Drew pointed out. He lounged against the back of the tall chair, his long, blunt-tipped fingers slightly splayed against the edge of the linen-draped table. "Naturally, Kris, you can get actively involved in management and work with Celia in running the company like Patrick. You can retain your half interest and give Celia your proxy, effectively retaining veto power, or you can simply sell out to her, in whole or in part."

Krisanne nodded. He'd recited the list of alternatives in so dispassionate a fashion, she was reminded that he was an attorney. She wondered, too, if he was truly neutral, or if he might have an interest in the outcome. But then, why should he?

"Think about it, Kris," Celia advised. "I'm sure you realize the sooner we resolve this, the better and easier it's going to be for everyone." She turned to Patrick. "How is your research coming?"

He shrugged. "It's progressing."

She looped a perfectly manicured finger into the handle of her coffee cup. "I know you've been concerned about what will become of it.'' Lifting the cup, she asked over its rim, ''Do you think you'll have enough time to complete your analysis?'' Her face froze. ''Forgive me,'' she said sheepishly. ''That was thoughtless.''

It was uncharacteristic of Celia to be tactless and equally untypical for her to betray embarrassment. But she barely managed to put the cup back on the saucer without spilling the hot liquid.

Patrick dismissed it. ''No—it's a valid question. Yes, I'll finish it.''

Celia took a moment to smooth out the white linen napkin in her lap. ''I've been wanting to ask you about your experiments…they…I mean…they couldn't have anything to do with your illness, could they?''

The question was as shocking to Krisanne as a cold hand on the nape of her neck. The thought hadn't occurred to her that her brother's job could in any way be responsible for his condition. It should have. Chemical contamination might explain how a perfectly healthy, clean-living young man could be stricken so suddenly with a fatal disease.

''Nothing at all,'' he assured her with a confident smile. ''I've never taken an experimental drug, and the way we handle all substances in the lab is highly controlled.''

But not foolproof, Krisanne wanted to lash out. She would definitely have to examine her brother's work conditions. Maybe she didn't have his professional qualifications, but her biology and chemistry background should be enough to comprehend the nature of his experiments—and she could ask a lot of questions.

''If you're up to it,'' Celia said to Patrick a moment

later, "I'd like you to help me select a new chief of research."

"Actually, I was planning on turning everything over to Nadeen."

"Nadeen Thomas?" Celia didn't look particularly enthusiastic about the idea. "She's awfully young, Patrick. Do you really think she's capable?"

"She's only a year younger than I am, and she's a damn good biochemist." Patrick chuckled. "Almost as good as I am."

"I love it when you're modest," Krisanne teased.

Her brother winked at her playfully, then continued more seriously, "She's also exceptionally good at documenting and writing up research reports."

"There's more to being a department head than doing experiments and writing reports," Celia pointed out. "I'm not sure she has the experience or assertiveness to make high-level decisions."

Patrick conceded the point. "That's where Kris comes in."

Krisanne started. "Me?"

"Nadeen can handle the actual research. Your role, Sis, will be to present her conclusions to the rest of the staff and to help Celia make corporate decisions."

Astonishment at the magnitude of the responsibility her brother was suggesting had Krisanne shifting nervously in her seat. She looked at the other two people at the table. Celia's expression was curious, but Krisanne couldn't tell if she was for or against the proposal. She thought she detected a hint of encouragement in Drew's quiet smile, but it didn't seem to match the worry lurking behind it.

"Pat, I'm a vet. I don't know anything about running a pharmaceutical company."

"Then you'd better start learning, Sis, because pretty soon you're going to own half of one."

SUNDAY AFTERNOON KRISANNE kept herself outdoors, enjoying one of those spring days when the air is crisp and clear, and little, cotton-white clouds float blithely across a cobalt-blue sky. The March wind, more determined than ever, still harbored a chill, but in those rare moments when it abated, the sun promised a new warmth.

She'd always delighted in this time of year, when ash and redbud trees were starting to bloom; when barn swallows were returning from their long winter's migration to build nests of clay and wattle under the eaves of the garage; and purple martins moved back into their high-rise apartment complex on the long pole in view of the kitchen window.

Their grandmother had planted a rose garden long before she and her brother were born. The garden had become a tradition. Their mother had nurtured the roses and Patrick had made them a point of pride since he'd taken over the house. This would be his last spring. Krisanne wanted the roses to help him hang on to his smile and wit, his strength and gentleness.

She finished clawing up the soil beneath the bushes and added granulated fertilizer. She'd paid little attention to the few cars that rippled along Coyote Avenue—one of the city's last red brick streets—until she heard the muffled purr of an engine halt at the curb. Sudden awareness tingled across her shoulders and up her scalp. She climbed to her feet, stretched her cramped back muscles and turned in time to see the passenger car door open, and a young Brittany spaniel scamper out. A boy bolted after it, but not before the pup began favoring its right front paw.

While the youngster picked up the floppy-eared pet, the car's driver, tall and lean, alighted. He closed both doors and approached her.

"Hi, Kris." It wasn't a boisterous greeting, but quiet, intimate and somehow shy.

She wondered why her face felt suddenly warm. "Hello, Drew."

Tension crackled between them. He said something to the boy who now stood by his side. She looked at the child. His brown hair was lighter than his dad's, curly rather than wavy, and his big, widely spaced intelligent eyes were brown rather than hazel.

"This is my son, Travis." Drew looked proudly at the boy. "Say hello to Dr. Blessing."

"Hello, Dr. Blessing," Travis politely complied.

"Hello, Travis." She looked at the animal cradled in his arms. "My, what a nice puppy. What's his name?"

"Gofer." At the sound of the word, the dog wagged its tail.

Krisanne reached out and stroked the spaniel's neck. "What's wrong with your paw, Gofer?"

Examining it, she found a small thorny bur caught between the toes. A tiny pinpoint of blood resulted when she gently removed it.

"We ought to clean that out," she told father and son. "Let's go in the house, and we'll take care of it right away."

"Dr. Blessing is an animal doctor," Drew explained.

"Can you fix Gofer's paw?" the boy asked.

"You bet. And if it's okay with your dad, you can call me Krisanne instead of Dr. Blessing."

The boy looked up questioningly at his father. Drew rubbed his chin, glancing back and forth between Travis and Krisanne while he considered the suggestion. "You call Mr. Blessing, Uncle Pat. I think you should call his sister, Aunt Kris. Is that all right?" Drew asked her.

"That's fine," she said, the words coming out like coarse gravel. She squeezed her lips together, looked away, cleared her throat, and repeated, "Aunt Kris is fine."

Travis romped across the lawn toward the house, the pup dangling between his arms and belly. Drew walked silently up the path by Krisanne's side. They were close enough to hold hands, but they didn't.

She led them into the hallway. "Smells like oatmeal raisin cookies to me," she commented, as they removed their light jackets and hung them on the coat rack.

Patrick appeared from the kitchen doorway behind the broad staircase. "I should have known I couldn't bake and keep it all to myself," he said with a wide grin. "Hello, Drew. Hi, Trav. It's been a while since you've come to my house."

Patrick reached out and petted the puppy, whose tail was wagging furiously. "And how's Gofer doing?"

"He hurt his paw and…uh, Aunt Kris is going to fix it," Travis told him.

"Well, there's no one better at fixing a puppy's paw than Aunt Kris," Patrick said and winked at her.

Krisanne slipped into the half bath across the hall and brought out a small bottle of peroxide and a couple of cotton balls.

"You hold Gofer and pet him, so he doesn't worry

while I wipe his paw," she instructed Travis. "This won't hurt."

Gofer was more curious about what was going on than upset. When she'd finished swabbing out the web between his toes, Travis put him down. Gofer shook himself, licked his paw and sneezed.

"Now," Patrick said, "let's go see if those cookies are ready." He rested a hand on Travis's shoulder and guided him down the hallway to the kitchen. "You know, I think there must be something magical about oatmeal raisin cookies."

"Magical?" The boy looked up.

"Oh, I'm sure of it." Patrick's eyes twinkled. "You see, whenever I make them, friends show up. Like now. I bet you smelled them all the way from your house."

Drew grinned. "They do smell awfully good."

The timer by the gas range dinged, as they walked in. Patrick picked up a pot holder, shooed everyone back with an elaborate flourish and carefully opened the oven door. A hot blast of sweet cinnamon spice filled the room. Patrick used a spatula to slip the cookies off the tray onto waxed paper.

"While they're cooling," he said, "why don't you all follow me?"

Drew and Travis looked questioningly at Krisanne. She knew where they were headed, but said nothing, urging them on with only a smile.

Gofer trailed, as Patrick led them to a room opposite the ornately banistered staircase. When they got there, Drew and his son stood in the doorway dumbstruck.

CHAPTER FOUR

"Wow!" TRAVIS EXCLAIMED, his mouth hanging open.

Before them lay boxes, boards and bits of a miniature world. Mountains, tunnels, bridges, houses and trees were scattered all over the floor.

"Where did all this come from?" Drew asked.

"The attic," replied Krisanne. "He's been dragging this stuff out ever since we got home yesterday."

Travis tiptoed closer to the pristine landscape. "Do the trains go?"

"You bet." Patrick removed a blue-and-white striped engineer's cap from a hook on the wall and plopped it on Travis's head. The boy looked solemn as Patrick tucked it behind his ears. "But first we have to get all this set up. It's an awful lot of work for one person. It might take me a long time."

Travis bounced with excitement. "I can help."

Patrick frowned, feigning doubt. "Well...if you're sure you don't mind."

The boy looked up with eager pleading eyes. "I don't mind."

Patrick stepped over to a square sheet of plywood that had a circle of track mounted on it, which he'd been using to test engines. He coupled a green-and-yellow passenger train to a red-and-black locomotive with a long cow catcher, then pressed a button on the transformer. Car lights flickered on. He pressed another button and a tinny train whistle blew. Gofer let out a howl and ran from the room, making everybody chuckle.

"A-l-l a-b-o-a-r-d," Patrick called out and turned a knob. The train moved slowly along the track.

"Look, Daddy, there are people in the cars."

"Incredible," Drew exclaimed in fascination. "Did you make all this yourself?"

"Yep."

"All the years I've known you and not once did you mention having model trains."

Patrick winked at his sister. "My little secret."

Krisanne smiled proudly. "He must have made his first car when he was—" she turned to Travis "—about your age."

Patrick inspected the wiring on a railroad crossing gate. "Some little boys never grow up."

Krisanne and Drew exchanged pained glances. Some would not live long enough to grow old.

"Those cookies should be cool by now," she said, afraid to let the moment linger. But as she watched their reluctance to leave the room, she was forced to smile: trains or cookies—tough decision.

Travis bounded ahead of them, then stood rooted in the kitchen doorway. "Gofer," he cried in dismay.

Krisanne ran to catch up. Gofer was stretched out under the table. Cookie pieces littered a chair and the floor around him. He held one mushy tidbit precariously between his front paws; crumbs dotted his whiskers, a raisin his nose. He looked up, apprehensively, yet obviously pleased with himself.

Krisanne burst into laughter. Travis, relieved his dog wasn't in serious trouble, scrunched up his shoulders and giggled. Gofer, thrilled at the attention, wagged his tail furiously and spread chunks of cookie farther across the linoleum.

"I think you better get your dog away from there," Drew told his son, "before he does any more damage." He turned to his host. "Sorry, Pat."

Patrick waved it off. "No harm done, though you might find a sick puppy on your hands later."

"Bad dog," Travis scolded his little friend.

"We can't blame Gofer for liking Uncle Pat's home-made cookies," Krisanne admitted with a grin.

Patrick counted those left on the table. "Actually, we only lost three."

Krisanne filled tall glasses with milk while Patrick gathered the remaining treats onto a plate.

"Can I see the trains again?" Travis mumbled through cookie crumbs.

Drew shook his head. "Don't talk with your mouth full, Son."

Patrick grinned. "Come on, kiddo, and bring a cookie with you."

Krisanne picked up Gofer, and they paraded back to the train room. This time Patrick let Travis throw the switches.

"Where do you get the patience to do all this?" Drew asked.

Patrick stood behind Travis, his face aglow in the joy of his make-believe world. "Hobbies teach patience," he said, "because you're doing what you love."

A whistle blew, the road crossing gate came down, tiny red warning lights flashed.

Suddenly Patrick clutched at the boy's shoulders.

Travis jerked around, looking up in panic at his friend. "Did I do something wrong?"

Patrick swayed back. Drew barely had time to grab him before he collapsed.

"Pat!" Krisanne cried out in alarm.

Drew scooped up Patrick's sagging body.

"Bring him across the hall," Krisanne instructed, decisiveness not quite masking her alarm.

Drew followed her to the large, high-ceilinged living room and eased Patrick onto the sofa in front of the white marble fireplace.

Krisanne knelt at her brother's side and opened the collar of his knit shirt. "Pat?" she whispered.

He sighed. "I just need to rest for a minute."

"You've overdone it," Drew said. "We shouldn't have imposed on you like this."

Patrick moved his head from side to side. "Don't go. I'll be fine. It'll pass."

Travis stood back, his eyes big with fear. "Are you sick?"

Drew and Krisanne exchanged worried glances, unsure how to respond.

"Yes, Trav," Patrick acknowledged quietly. "I am."

"Very sick?"

"Yes, I'm...very sick."

Travis peered straight at him, his voice thin and tremulous. "Are you going to die?"

Krisanne was stunned by the boldness of the question. Drew made a noise, intent on diverting his son's attention. Patrick silenced him with a glance, then answered the boy's question forthrightly. "Yes, Trav, I'm going to die."

"My mommy died," the child muttered with a low-ered head.

Patrick reached for the boy's hand. "I know. I'm sorry."

"She's in heaven with the angels now."

"I'm sure she is."

Travis raised his head, his brown eyes brimming. "When you see my mommy in heaven," he said in the softest voice, "will you tell her I miss her?"

Patrick pulled the boy into a warm embrace. "Yes, Trav," he soothed, "I'll tell her."

A minute later Gofer bounced onto the couch and broke the tension by snuggling in between Patrick and Travis, alternately licking one face then the other.

"Yuck. Doggie kisses," Travis exclaimed when the little pink tongue swiped across his lips. He lifted the front of his shirt and used the inside of the collar to dry his mouth and chin.

Drew smiled. "Gofer's been in the house a long time, Son, and after eating those cookies, maybe you ought to take him outside."

"Okay, Daddy." The boy jumped to his feet, ran to the door and called his wiggly tailed pet.

"Take him out back," Krisanne told him, "and be sure the gate is closed."

They heard the kitchen door slam a moment later.

"Is he going to be all right?" she asked.

"He'll be fine," Patrick assured her, before Drew even had a chance to respond. "You've got a wonder-ful kid there, my friend." He hoisted himself into a sitting position. The pallor of a few minutes earlier was already receding.

"We really should be going," Drew announced. "I think I know why you didn't tell me about the trains.

Had I known, I would have pestered you to see them, and then you'd never have been able to get me to leave."

Patrick chuckled. "See you at the lab tomorrow?"

"The lab?" Krisanne asked. "Are you going in to clear out your desk? I can do it for you. I'm sure Nadeen will help. Just tell me what you need."

Patrick gave her a sharp look. "I'm going to work. I do research, remember? And don't look at me that way, Kris."

"What way?"

"Like I'm lying here with crossed arms and a lily on my chest."

She winced and for a split second, actually thought she caught a glimpse of his face against white satin lining. Involuntarily, she shuddered. "I...that's not what—"

Travis came bounding into the room, Gofer right behind him.

"Can we play with the trains some more?"

"I don't think we have time," his father told him. "Uncle Pat needs to rest."

"I'm fine," Patrick contradicted him. "Come on, kid."

"Are you sure?" Drew asked.

"Yep. Go help Kris." Patrick stood up and adjusted his rumpled clothes. "Trav and I have a train schedule to meet. Don't we?"

The boy looked up, face beaming. "Yeah."

Drew and Krisanne followed them out into the hallway and watched them enter the train room. Patrick turned around. "Why don't you make Drew some Earl Grey tea?"

Biting her lip against the casual dismissal, she turned toward the kitchen.

"You seem to have some influence on him," Krisanne said, once she and Drew were out of earshot. "Tell him he doesn't have to work so hard."

"A man's work is important to him, Kris."

Frustrated, she placed the kettle on one of the front burners of the range and lit the gas under it. "He reminds me so much of Dad. He loved his work, too."

Drew went to the overhead cabinet on the right side of the sink where he obviously thought cups would be kept. He found dishes instead. "I'm sorry I didn't make it to his funeral. He was a good man. I liked him."

And he liked you, she almost told him.

"I wasn't here for you then," Drew said. "But I'm here now."

Her fingers trembled, as she removed two of her grandmother's large floral-patterned teacups and saucers from the china cabinet. Mugs never did for Earl Grey. "Dad was always so busy. There was never time to just sit and talk, much less do things together. It was always 'I haven't got time right now, but one of these days...' Then he had his heart attack and it was too late."

How could she possibly be sure her father had understood her feelings for him? How could she trust Drew to stay by her side?

"He loved you and you loved him," he said. "That's all any of us can ever ask for."

Was he talking about her and her father, or about himself and his deceased wife? From Patrick's comments, Krisanne suspected theirs hadn't been an altogether happy marriage. Did that mean he hadn't loved her? If so, it would only make Lisa's death more difficult to deal with emotionally. She knew firsthand how complex the grieving process could be—the bitterness, guilt and anger it stirred. Had Drew forgiven Lisa for dying so abruptly, for denying him the chance to resolve their differences, to say goodbye? Had he forgiven himself for not telling her, or not telling her often enough, that he loved her?

"Let Patrick do what he wants for as long as he can," Drew said, as they faced each other across the room. "When his strength runs out, he'll be able to look back with a sense of accomplishment. Besides, he needs this time to come to terms with what lies before him."

"Death." Her throat tightened, lethargy stole into her limbs and tears crept dangerously close to the surface.

"We all die, Kris. That's not the point. It's what we do with our lives that matters."

"You're a philosopher, too."

He leaned against the counter, arms folded across his chest, long legs scissored at the ankles. "Father, lawyer and philosopher all rolled into one."

"In that order?" she asked, noting he'd put father before lawyer, unlike her own father who always seemed to put his job first.

He flashed her a quirky grin. "In that order."

His eyes met hers and for a breathless moment the two of them were locked in a tunnel that threatened to swallow her. The peeping whistle of a model train down the hall broke the spell. She placed the sugar bowl on the table.

"Patrick's dying," she said, her voice fluttering. "Do you really think he should continue to work?

What could be so important that he can't back away from it?''

Drew pushed his fingers through his hair. ''Has he told you about Troimaline?''

''Troimaline?'' She shook her head and turned off the gas under the bubbling kettle. ''What about it?''

''It's a new designer drug that Blessing bought an option on last year. Something of a miracle, too, if you listen to all the hype.'' Drew was momentarily mesmerized by the grace of her movements, as she poured boiling water into the teapot, swirled it around and dumped it into the sink. ''It's not yet approved by the FDA, so it's not available in this country, but it's been used overseas for some time. Pat's been running tests and lab experiments on it for almost a year. It's potential is tremendous.''

Krisanne measured out tea leaves and added them to the warmed pot, then refilled it again with steaming water, releasing the flowery essence of bergamot. ''What does it do?''

''In small doses, it's a pseudobarbiturate, acting like a tranquilizer and antidepressant. It's nonaddictive, and safe enough to be taken with alcohol. In larger doses, especially in combination with certain other compounds, it's a mind-altering substance. Its chief potential is in behavior control.''

She twisted around. ''Mind altering? Behavior control? Sounds sinister.''

''Not necessarily.'' He went to the refrigerator, found a lemon in the crisper and proceeded to cut it into wedges, while she took the pot to the table. ''It seems to have a calming effect on people who are prone to overly aggressive, even violent, behavior and keeps them on an even keel. Troimaline's been used quite successfully, for example, in several, high-security foreign prisons where violence is a way of life.''

''Sounds great. Unless the prisoners end up channeling their viciousness into more clever and subtle forms of antisocial behavior.''

Drew scooped the lemon pieces onto a plate and deposited it on the table. ''From all accounts, they act rationally and within a normal range of emotions. It's not an intelligence pill, Kris. They don't get any smarter from using the drug.''

''Too bad.'' She sat down on the chair he'd pulled out for her and looked up, a tiny smile on her lips. ''Right now I think I could use something that would make me smarter.''

And I could use better self-control, Drew almost said, as the heat of her back warmed his hand. He quickly withdrew his touch. She'd cut her hair since their college days; it was shorter now, sassy. More practical, no doubt, for a busy vet handling animals all day. But he missed the long golden tresses, and the promise of their silken strands slipping through his fingers.

Krisanne squeezed lemon into her cup. ''So what's the problem?''

''For one thing,'' Drew took the seat across from her, ''the drug must be taken for the rest of one's life.''

''That's true of insulin and lots of other drugs, too.'' She tipped a scant spoonful of sugar into her cup and pushed the bowl toward him. ''Okay, it's not a cure. So what?'' She studied him. ''What's the real problem, Drew?''

Mechanically, he fixed his tea. ''Pat's conclusions are preliminary, but some of the demographics bother him. He's been tracking reported areas of Troimaline use against mortality and other medical records.'' He sipped his brew and returned the cup to the saucer. ''There seems to be an increased incidence of birth defects in the geographical areas where it's been used.''

''He thinks Troimaline's responsible? My God!''

''He's not sure,'' Drew hastened to add. ''There haven't been any scientifically adequate studies performed.''

''Is that why he insists on going back to work?''

Drew nodded. ''He's got a year's research data built up. The only thing left is the final analysis, but it'll probably take several more months... If he's not feeling well...it could take someone else even longer.''

Her heart sank. ''You said the FDA hasn't approved it.''

''And they won't if they suspect there are serious side effects associated with it.''

''So why is Blessing even considering it? Without FDA approval we can't market it.''

''Not in this country,'' Drew pointed out, ''but you can manufacture it for overseas markets.''

Krisanne fumbled the spoon she'd been toying with, making it clatter against the china. ''Are you saying Blessing wants to sell a product overseas, even though they know it might be dangerous?''

Drew reached forward and covered her shaking hand. ''We don't know if any of Pat's suspicions are correct, Kris. He admits himself he could be misreading the data. There are a lot of variables. It's too early to draw any firm conclusions.'' He brushed his fingertips across her knuckles. ''What we do know is that Blessing has the opportunity to get into a very lucrative market with a product that has tremendous potential for doing good.''

"Or evil." She pulled her hand away.

Annoyance deepened his tone. "That's what Pat's trying to find out."

"What's Celia's position on all this?"

Drew inched his cup back from the edge of the table. "The building program she inaugurated after your father died was necessary, but it's eaten up most of the company's reserves. Blessing needs to turn substantial profits in the next few years if it's going to get ahead of its debt."

"So she's in favor of marketing it overseas."

Drew shook his head in frustration. "Not if Pat can prove it's dangerous. Celia wants concrete evidence one way or the other." He saw the look of disapproval on her face. "That's not an unreasonable request, Kris. She doesn't want to pass up a golden business opportunity and a real breakthrough in drug therapy without exploring all the possibilities. Even if Pat's hunch is correct, it doesn't mean a safe use for Troimaline can't be found, or that a slight change in the pharmacology of the substance won't make it safe."

"What's your role in all this?" she asked.

To his relief, it was a question, not a challenge.

"What lawyers do, an exhaustive legal evaluation of Blessing's liabilities if you choose to move ahead with manufacture and marketing." He held out his hand palm up and flipped it over. "It's going to be a tough decision either way. Blessing's future may hinge on it. That's why Pat's so intent on continuing his research for as long as he can." He watched her tug nervous fingers through her hair. "He needs your support, Kris."

"Yes," she said softly. "I can see that now." She stood up and removed her empty cup to the sink. "Okay," she said with a deep sigh. "Pat works as long as…he wants to."

Drew rose and placed his cup on the counter beside hers. "Something else is bothering you." He turned to face her. "What is it?"

She ran hot water into the sink and added dish detergent. Its mild perfume scent rose on the wispy vapor, clean and familiar. "I've got to go back to Austin tomorrow. I barely brought enough clothes to get me through the weekend, and I need to talk to Dr. Lesko, close the apartment, transfer my mail—"

"Pat'll be all right for a few days."

She slammed off the faucet, making the old plumbing shudder. "What about his driving? What happened today…suppose it happens while he's behind the wheel. It's not just his safety I'm concerned about. He could injure, even kill, other people."

"We'll carpool. Blessing and Law Tower are only a couple of miles apart, a five minute detour. I can pick him up and drop him off on my way to and from work. I'll talk to him. I'm sure he'll agree."

He leaned a hip against the counter, watching her as she stared out the window. There was no mistaking the worry knitting her brow. Her lower lip was caught between her teeth, making her look so fragile.

At last she sighed. "Thank you."

He raised a hand to her shoulder. It was stiff with tension. He turned her to face him and was relieved when she didn't resist. "I told you I'm here for you, Kris," he said softly.

She nodded, but avoided his eyes. He touched the tip of his finger to her chin and raised it up. She was

fighting valiantly against the tears he could see pooling
in her cornflower-blue eyes. Impulsively he pulled her
to his chest in a comforting embrace. She wrapped her
arms around him, while he rested his cheek against the
top of her head.

"Together we'll get though this," he whispered and
planted a kiss on her temple.

"I can't imagine going on without him," she murmured. "It's so unfair—"

"Shhh." He rocked her in his arms, inhaling the
flowery scent of her silky hair, feeling the trembling
gradually subside. He couldn't have said when their
hold on each other slipped from comfort to passion.
But when awareness came, he knew it was mutual.
Like a long, stored away reflex action, he tilted his
head to one side and lowered his mouth, seeking hers.

She raised her chin, felt his breath on her lips and
closed her eyes. Sensations, old and familiar, washed
through her, intoxicating, stimulating. As the kiss deepened, her pulse doubled its beat. Seven years faded
away, shattering any illusion that she was in control of
her body or her soul. She was melting into him when
panic struck.

Abruptly she pulled away and spun out of his grasp.

"Kris—" His plea was a ragged whisper.

"No," she murmured, her voice shaky, her insides
tumbling. "Don't say anything."

*Don't tell me you love me. Don't tell me you care.
I couldn't take it—losing you again.*

She spun back to the sink, spread her hands to lean
into the edge of the counter. She bowed her head, took
a slow shuddering breath and felt him take a step toward her.

"Just go," she muttered. "Please, Drew. Just go. I'm not going to get caught up with you again."

WHEN HE WENT to the train room to pick up Travis and take him home, Drew used the opportunity to talk to Patrick about carpooling. Their brief discussion gave Krisanne enough time to get her emotions under control.

She wondered if she hadn't overreacted, if she wasn't allowing herself to be driven by fear. She'd loved him once and he'd spurned her. Just because he'd caught her at a vulnerable moment didn't mean she was going to succumb to his charm again. A little kiss didn't mean anything. He was right about one thing, though; for Patrick's sake she had to forget their past. Drew was her brother's best friend. She'd respect him for his generosity, accept his help graciously, and maybe, just maybe in the end, they could become friends, too. But she wouldn't allow herself to be hurt by him, not ever again.

Krisanne walked Drew and his son to his car, gave Travis a gentle hug and invited him to come back soon.

"Thank you for allowing us to visit," Drew said. The comment was polite, casual and appropriate, but she didn't miss the brooding darkness in his eyes. "I'm sorry if I was—"

"Thanks for coming." She quickly coaxed Travis into the passenger seat and helped him buckle up. By the time she closed the door, Drew had rounded the front of the Mercedes-Benz and slipped into the driver's seat.

"See you in the morning, Kris." He waved as he pulled away from the curb.

MONDAY MORNING KRISANNE was standing at the open back door, drying her hands on a dish towel, when Drew pulled into the driveway and parked in front of the detached garage. She discovered—or was it rediscovered—something fundamentally satisfying in watching him maneuver his tall, athletic frame from behind the wheel, stand erect with a slight muscle-stretching shrug and saunter toward her.

She greeted him with a cup of freshly brewed, black coffee.

"I'm going to need your help," she said, after he stepped inside and took the first tentative sip of the steaming hot beverage.

He raised an inquiring eyebrow. "Problem?"

"Pat's backing out on his promise to carpool with you. He insists he's perfectly capable of driving by himself."

Drew gave her an appraising look. "But I suppose you have a plan." It was a statement, not a question. She found his confidence in her both reassuring and in light of yesterday's kiss, decidedly unsettling.

"Nothing very imaginative, I'm afraid. My car's air-conditioning is on the fritz, so I called a garage and asked them to pick it up."

"And you want to take Pat's Bronco while your car's in the shop," he concluded.

They both turned at the sound of Patrick's feet skipping down the stairs. He strode into the kitchen looking as fit and lively as ever.

"Good morning," he said, as he marched to the coffeepot.

"There's orange juice in the fridge," Krisanne told him, after he filled one of the mugs sitting on the counter. "How about some bacon and eggs?"

"Can't," he said. "Got to watch my cholesterol."

She bit her lip. Cholesterol was the last thing he should be worrying about—the last thing. The words echoed in her head.

Patrick came over and lifted her chin. "Hey, Sis. Relax. That was a joke. You know I don't like to eat anything heavy first thing in the morning. Just coffee and toast for now, and a handful of vitamin tablets with juice. I'll have breakfast at the plant later this morning. They've got a creamed beef on biscuits guaranteed to clog your arteries."

He pecked an affectionate kiss on the tip of her nose, retrieved a glass from the drainboard and went over to the refrigerator.

"Krisanne tells me you're reneging on your promise to carpool with me," Drew said to his friend's back.

She watched her brother's shoulders stiffen. As far as she knew, the two men had never had a cross word between them, but the challenge in Drew's words had the potential to change that.

"I've got a bunch of things to do," Patrick said without turning around, an edge in his voice. The note of anger and pride had Krisanne's palms growing damp. She didn't want to see these friends argue, not now when time was running out, and they might not get the chance to reestablish the bond they'd shared. "I'm quite capable of taking care of myself."

"You weren't yesterday," Drew reminded him in an even but uncompromising tone.

Patrick spun around and faced not Drew but Krisanne. The dark shadow of accusation in his glare tempted her to turn away. She wanted to recoil from the pain she saw there, the forlorn despair she would sacrifice anything in the world to have the power to banish.

"Besides," she tried to ease the tension, "there's another little problem. My car needs some work, so I'll have to borrow yours to go to Austin."

Patrick returned silently to the task of pouring himself a glass of orange juice. "What's wrong with the Honda?" he asked over his shoulder. "It ran all right the other day."

She explained about her air-conditioning compressor going out a week or so earlier.

He put the pitcher back in the refrigerator. Glass in hand, he swung around, his eyes hooded with suspicion. "How come you didn't say anything about this the other day?"

"The weather's been so cool," she explained, "I've been putting off getting it fixed. But it's supposed to get up into the nineties over the next few days."

Her brother leaned against the counter beside the refrigerator and stared at her, then peered at Drew. No one moved. The grating tchek-tchek of a mockingbird stabbed the silence. Krisanne had the urge to go to him, soothe away the tension in his rigid back, assure him— of what? What hope could she offer? He wasn't going to get any better. Everything he gave up from now on would be forever. Was love enough in the face of death?

"Go ahead and take the Bronco, Sis," Patrick said dismissively, then lowered his tone in defeat. "I'll ride with Drew."

An hour later, she was on the road, her mind mulling over her options. Truth to tell, there weren't many. Her plans for opening her own veterinary practice obviously had to be put on hold. Should she resign from Lesko's clinic or ask for a leave of absence?

For the first time, she admitted to herself that she wished Drew were sitting next to her. He had a way of seeping into her psyche, making her feel whole, confident. He enthalled her and scared her at the same time.

The anxiety brought her back to the reason she'd come home. It didn't seem likely Patrick had more than five or six months to live. Six months—such a short time to say goodbye forever. It would be autumn then, the leaves of the trees starting to fade, only to fall lifeless to the ground. Nothing but bare, wind-tossed branches would be left to weather the long, icy loneliness of winter.

She drove on, through Eden and Brady, past the shores of Inks Lake and along the outskirts of Llano. Arriving in Austin a little before noon, she went directly to the clinic. Mondays were always hectic, a catch-up day for all the accidents and ailments accumulated over the weekend. This Monday was no exception. She hadn't planned on working at all, but unable to ignore the frantic pace, quickly found herself in the thick of things. Around one-thirty, the last pet left, a Siamese brought in for shots.

Dr. Lesko asked the receptionist to call out for sandwiches, while he and Krisanne moved to the holding area in back of the reception and examining rooms. He checked several surgical cases but gave her his undivided attention when she told him the reason for her unexpected trip home Saturday and lateness in coming in this morning.

"I was hoping you'd let me take a leave of absence,

perhaps hire a temporary, part-time assistant while I'm away.''

''What about starting your own clinic? Have you given up the notion?''

A pail of cold water thrown in her face couldn't have shocked her more. She looked at the old man, thick white hair a little out of place, bony hands gently stroking a small rat terrier with a broken leg. A knowing smile curled the doctor's lips.

''They all come and stay a while,'' he said. ''The good ones, like you, move on to pursue their own ambitions.''

''I'm sorry,'' she said. But for what? Was what she had planned so dishonorable that she had to be ashamed of it?

''No need to be. I did the same thing forty years ago.'' He locked the terrier's cage door, made a mark on the chart hanging beside it, and turned to her. ''Don't worry about your job. You'll have a place here if you want it.''

She left, grateful for the old man's generosity, but with a gnawing feeling of disloyalty.

CHAPTER FIVE

DREW WASN'T SURPRISED by the call Tuesday morning from Celia's office. He'd more than half expected it and had a pretty good idea what she wanted.

"Morning, Celia," he said when he was shown into the huge office forty-five minutes later.

"Good morning, Drew. Coffee?"

"Thanks."

She moved out from behind her oversized, brass-trimmed mahogany desk to the cluster of more informal furniture arranged in the daylight-filled corner by the window. Celia took her usual chair facing the side lawn while Drew sat at the end of the couch nearest her. Coffee service waited on a tray on the low table between them. She poured.

"I think you know how important it is that we settle the matter of Patrick and Krisanne's half interest in Blessing," she said, passing Drew his cup. "Patrick and I have worked very well together."

They both sipped coffee. Neither of them took cream or sugar.

"To be very honest with you, Drew, I'm not sure Krisanne and I can share the same kind of relationship. After all, Patrick has spent his entire career here at Blessing."

"Circumstances change," Drew reminded her. "Up until now Krisanne's felt no need to be involved."

Celia ran a hand along the sides of her cup. "That's true, and with Patrick's passing she might get interested in the business. But frankly, I don't expect her to. She has her own profession, her own career and interests."

"Is there anything I can do?" Drew asked.

"Maybe. I understand from Pat that Kris wants to open her own vet clinic, but that she needs capital to do it. I can't afford to buy her half of the company, and frankly I don't want to. The business belongs to her family. What I don't know is how much cash she needs, and if she'd be willing to sell me a portion of her interest in Blessing—enough to give me control. Naturally, once we start paying dividends again— which I hope will be soon—she'll have the income from whatever percentage of the company she retains."

Drew pondered what she was implying. "You realize that technically I work for Pat and Kris as well as you," he pointed out. "It would be a conflict of interest for me to represent one partner against the others."

Celia shook her head ever so slightly. "I'm not suggesting you act as a secret agent, Drew. The truth is Krisanne and I tend to hold each other at arm's length. I'm not blaming her. If anyone's at fault, it's me. Krisanne's a very caring, generous person. She wouldn't be putting her career on hold to be with her brother if she weren't." Celia closed her eyes briefly. "Normally I would ask Pat to handle something like this, especially since it's a family matter. But under the circumstances…" She let the words trail off.

Drew sat for a minute contemplating the woman sitting ramrod straight a few feet away. Despite her delicate features, her pale, almost translucent skin, her quiet femininity, he'd always thought of Celia in terms of strength. Now, as she twisted the wedding ring she still wore, he was aware of an insecurity that surprised him.

"When Kris gets back from Austin we'll probably see each other every day. Maybe if I brought up the subject informally..." he said. "Let me try."

Celia rose. "Thank you, Drew. I know I'm putting you in a delicate situation, but I think she'll be more comfortable talking to you than to me. I know you'll be sensitive in approaching Kris with this. She's very vulnerable right now."

WARREN PRUIT, SENIOR partner of Pruit and Hadley, lounged serenely in the leather upholstered chair in Drew's office later that afternoon. One razor-sharp pant leg was crossed over the ankle of the other. The two men were discussing the legal implications of Troimaline.

"It's worth a small fortune," Pruit said, "if they act fast. Overseas manufacturers don't have the production capacity or distribution network Blessing has, and once we get FDA approval, we've got a corner on the domestic market."

"It seems to me the product's on the edge," Drew argued.

"It can be on the edge all it wants," Pruit reminded him, "as long as it doesn't go over it. This may be close, but it's nevertheless within the bounds."

Drew tugged on his right earlobe. "Pat has concerns about side effects, including possible birth defects."

Elbows resting on the arms of his chair, Warren steepled his fingertips and touched them to his chin. "Patrick Blessing is a good scientist and a nice guy, but hardly a businessman. Celia's the one who recognized the potential of Troimaline and negotiated a three-year option for its manufacture. She's the person you have to convince.''

''We're talking about a drug that's still experimental.''

''Come on, counselor,'' Warren said quietly—he never raised his voice in the courtroom and rarely in private conversation. Drew had seen his well-disciplined calmness infuriate the opposition, provoking overblown rhetoric, which made them all the more vulnerable to Pruit's scathing attacks. ''You know the rules as well as I do. We put a clear disclaimer on the label that there may be side effects and we list them, all of them, including the possibility of birth defects.''

Drew shook his head. ''People don't pay attention to those warnings.''

''It's our responsibility to write them, my friend, not read them to the consumer. All the information is in plain sight.''

''And by including major side effects with minor ones, you minimize them both,'' Drew objected.

Warren spread his hands in a familiar gesture of exasperation. His voice, however, retained its cool, slightly patronizing tone. ''If you're going to deny people every drug that might do harm or that they might abuse, you'll have to take away the good ones, too. Aspirin thins the blood, which helps it prevent heart attacks and strokes, but too much will keep blood from clotting. Are you going to take it off the shelves and deny its beneficial effects to thousands, millions of people, because someone might bleed to death from a paper cut?'' He shook his head. ''It's up to the consumer to use the product wisely, and it's our job to defend our client against people who don't. That's what we get paid for—that's how we earn our living.''

Drew had never had any illusions that his old law school buddy was an altruist. Warren was a scrapper who enjoyed a good fight and the renown that came from winning. For him, the practice of law was sort of a high-stakes poker game where bluff was every bit as important as playing by the rules. Matching wits with another attorney in the courtroom was a challenge he relished.

In a way it made him the perfect complement to Drew's more restrained style. Drew was good at his work, because doing his best was important to him, but he'd never felt driven by the practice of law. Lisa had complained more than once that he lacked real ambition—the kind that would make them rich and famous. His only defense had been mockery. He didn't need any, he'd quipped—his partner had enough for both of them. Drew was the one who kept things organized, performed the meticulous research civil law demanded. He wrote the learned briefs that Warren capitalized on in his own flamboyant way. The fact that Warren was the one who got to wine and dine their clients didn't bother Drew in the least, either. He'd given up the partying life a long time ago.

Before Drew could contend his point further, his intercom buzzed and his secretary told him he had a call from Dr. Blessing.

He felt a subtle quickening of his pulse. "Excuse me a minute, Warren. This might be important." He pushed the button on the flashing, in-coming phone line. "Kris? Is everything all right?"

"Yes, fine. How's Pat?"

Pruit rose from his chair and left the room with a wave and a smile, closing the door discreetly behind him.

"He's fine, too, Kris. He worked Trav and me to death—uh, unmercifully last night setting up his trains."

"Thanks for being there," she said.

Drew must have caught the plaintive note in her voice, because he didn't respond immediately. "We called out for two different kinds of pizza. I didn't know pizza was one of his favorite food groups." He chuckled.

"I didn't, either," she said, trying to match his light-heartedness. "Sounds like Pat and Trav are having a good time."

"They get along so well, Kris…" He left the phrase hanging. "Pat may be playacting about pizza, but there's no doubt he and Trav thrive on each other."

"Are you sure you want them spending so much time together? It's going to be awfully hard on a six-year-old who has already lost his mother."

There was a long pause. "They need each other, Kris." *Like I need you.* "How is everything at your end?"

"It's going to take me another day here—"

"Is there a problem?" *Besides not wanting me to kiss you.* He understood her wariness. He also knew he didn't deserve her. But for a moment, for a wonderfully magical moment, she'd kissed him back.

"I'll tell you about it when I get there," she said, then laughed. She was doing the same thing he'd done to her—introducing a subject then dropping it.

"What's so funny?" he asked, clearly baffled, which only made her laugh harder. It would serve him right if she left him hanging. But as her grandmother used to say, two wrongs didn't make a right. Besides, at the moment she could use some sympathy, a shoulder to lean on.

"Life's funny sometimes," she said. "No, there's no problem. Everything's just taking longer than I expected. I still have to arrange for someone to watch my apartment, get newspapers canceled, that sort of thing."

"Is there anything I can help you with? Security agreements, other legal matters?"

"Thanks, but everything is pretty standard."

"Just so you know I'm here, Kris. I want to help."

"I know," she said softly. And she did know. Had they been together instead of joined by a telephone connection, she might have placed her hand on his to confirm her understanding and appreciation. Even now, she could almost feel the grain of Drew's skin against her palm.

"Don't worry about Pat," he said. "He'll be fine."

KRISANNE SET HERSELF a manic pace that evening, partly because she had so much to do in a short period of time; partly because by keeping busy she hoped to avoid thinking about the reason for doing what she was doing. Good plan—reality didn't quite measure up.

Everywhere she looked, there were reminders of her brother. On her way to the bedroom, she passed by the huge Ansel Adams hanging on the wall behind the couch—a surprise birthday present he'd strapped on the roof of his Bronco and personally delivered two years ago.

When she packed her jewelry, she found the turquoise and silver squash blossom necklace he'd picked up for her one summer when he was hiking in the Sangre de Cristo Mountains near Santa Fe, New Mexico.

She was gathering up her toiletries, when she remembered the silk dressing gown hanging on the back of the bathroom door. Patrick had saved up especially for it and given it to her the Christmas after their mother died. It was frayed and threadbare now, and she rarely wore it, but she couldn't quite bring herself to throw it away. Taking it off the hook, she held the delicate fabric to her cheek. There weren't going to be any more Christmases or surprise visits. No more birthdays together or Sunday evening telephone conversations that lasted until midnight.

This would be her last trip home to be with him. Her last chance to say thank you for being her champion and her anchor. Her last chance to tell him she loved him.

Drew was going to be there, too. Patrick's best friend. The man she'd loved once and thought she always would.

If only she could forget his kiss and the disappointment she'd seen in his eyes when she pulled away from him. He'd made a terrible mistake seven years ago. Until she'd seen him again, been with him, felt his arms around her, she'd thought she'd been the only victim of his infidelity. But she knew now he'd suffered, too. The longing she'd sensed in the way he held her, the tremor beneath the strength of his embrace, the desperation in the way his mouth molded itself to hers, had nothing to do with the loss of a wife. But they had everything to do with grief for love lost, for the love they had shared. *Well, the past couldn't be undone and, like it or not, we have to live with the consequences of our actions.*

Krisanne carted frozen foods and canned goods next door. Nelly greeted her with a bear hug and immediately dragged her over to the doll carriage where Davy was curled up in a contented little ball, sound asleep.

"Dr. Lesko checked the stitches," Nelly explained. "I told him you put them in and I helped. He says I must have done a pretty good job, because Davy's going to be 'fit as a fiddle.'"

Krisanne smiled, recognizing one of the old man's favorite expressions.

By Wednesday morning, she'd sorted out a ton of "stuff" to go to the Salvation Army, packed several boxes of clothes and a small veterinary library to take with her, paid bills and filled out a stack of change of address cards. Over it all loomed the specter of Coyote Springs and the people waiting for her there—a dying brother, a lively young boy and the man she once loved. She'd seen the kind of father he was. That alone ought to earn him forgiveness for past transgressions. But was forgiveness enough? What about forgetting?

By the time Krisanne called Drew at his office to tell him she was leaving Austin, she felt more at loose ends than ever.

"We'll be at your house," Drew told her. "Trav and Pat have decided we ought to have spaghetti and meatballs tonight."

"Spaghetti, huh? Night before last it was pizza. Sounds like the three of you are on an Italian food kick."

Drew's laugh was an affectionate rumble over the phone line. "All kids love pasta," he reminded her. "Us big kids, too."

A shaft of loneliness sliced through her, as keen-edged as regret. She shook it off. "I don't expect to get back until after seven. Go on without me. I can reheat something for myself when I get in."

"We'll wait for you."

"Isn't that a little late for Travis?"

"I understand milk and cookies served at strategic times are great at putting off hunger pangs."

"You mean spoiling appetites. Drew, that's not—"

"Hey, waiting an extra hour for your company is worth the price. Besides, I have a feeling it's going to be like pulling shark's teeth getting those two guys out of the train room, even for spaghetti and my super-duper special meatballs."

Super-duper special meatballs? Drew's? This could be interesting. "Well…when you put it that way."

"I do."

"I'll get there as soon as I can."

"We'll leave the light on for you…and Kris, drive safely."

KRISANNE WAS ABOUT to pull into the driveway several hours later, but at the last moment saw Drew's Mercedes-Benz in front of the garage. Parking in the street was more convenient anyway, she decided. The Bronco was crammed to overflowing. The front door of the house gave direct access to the stairs and would make unloading easier than going through the kitchen and down the hall.

Trudging wearily up the gray concrete path, she climbed the wooden porch steps and opened the glass-paneled front door. The rich aroma of spaghetti sauce revived her instantly and made her empty stomach grumble. She was about to call out when she heard childish laughter. Moving quietly down the hall, she stopped outside the train room and was instantly transported to a perfect world of make-believe. Mountains harbored tunnels, bridges spanned rivers, trees shaded parks, houses clustered in villages, and rail lines tied them all together. A freight train loaded with coal and cordwood waited on a siding outside a Victorian station. Lilliputian people were captured in midmotion strolling along immaculate streets. A schoolboy in knickers and a young girl in a ruffled hoopskirt stood at a railroad crossing, their arms upraised to a passing train.

Patrick and Travis were sprawled on their backs, their legs sticking out from under the trestle table. They jabbered away, their silliness feeding off each other. Apparently they were looking for a broken connection to one of the signals or houses on the broad tapestried landscape overhead. Krisanne leaned against the doorframe listening to them, enjoying their uninhibited laughing and giggling. Two little kids, she mused.

She crouched down and peeked under the platform. "Do you guys have any idea what you're doing under there?"

Patrick raised his head and peered between uplifted arms. "Hi, Sis. Finally home, huh?" He continued to tinker with tiny wires. "How was your trip?"

"Long."

"It's almost finished, Aunt Kris," Travis told her enthusiastically.

She jiggled his ankle. "Well, then I guess you better get back to work."

The sound of them, totally absorbed once again in their search, renewed her feeling of being an outsider. Biting her lip, she moved on to the kitchen.

Drew was at the stove stirring the contents of a big iron pot. He was wearing jeans—old jeans, comfortable jeans. Jeans that were molded to his narrow hips and long legs. Jeans faded in all the right places. She lin-

gered in the doorway appraising the taper of his back
and had the maddening urge to run her hands along his
bare arms and greet him with a soft, gentle kiss the
way she used to when they were in college.

Gofer, sleeping innocently under the table, perked
up and scampered to greet her. Krisanne bent to scratch
the pup behind the ears, but he insisted on licking her
hand.

"Some watchdog you are," she chided the happy
creature.

Drew spun around, almost dropping a wooden spoon
into the bubbling sauce. His eyes were wide, his full
lips slightly parted in surprise. The startled expression
lasted only a brief second, however, before his eager
gaze raked over her. His glow of unqualified pleasure
in seeing her sent a tingling ripple of delight through
her.

"Welcome home," he said, a smile in his voice.

"It's good to be home."

"What are you grinning at?" he asked. "Have I got
tomato sauce on my shirt?"

"No, but if you don't put that spoon down, you're
going to have it on your shoes."

He slid his hand under the spoon just as a big glob
of sauce spilled off it. "Ouch! That's hot." He plunged
the spoon back into the pot and bolted to the sink.

"What's so funny?" he asked over his shoulder, as
he ran cold water across his palm.

"Nothing really." How could she explain the little
surge of excitement that finding him in this domestic
setting gave her? "I was just thinking...I haven't lived
in this house for nearly ten years. But in my mind, it's
always home."

His features softened. "It is a nice word—home."

He dried his hand on a towel. "I didn't hear you drive up or come in."

"I'm parked in front."

He must have heard the weariness in her voice. "Rough day?"

The natural thing would have been for him to come over, wrap his arms around her and offer her a tender, soothing kiss. For a moment she expected him to do exactly that, but then he returned to the stove and his boiling cauldron of spice-laden tomato sauce.

"Let's just say long." She leaned against the counter by the old built-in icebox that was used now only for dry storage. She should be pleased at Drew's keeping his distance. After all, she'd put up the barrier and he was honoring her by respecting it.

"Would you like to tell me about it?"

She sighed. "Maybe later."

Something about the set of his shoulders told her he, too, was holding himself back, that the slightest encouragement from her would have him opening his arms to her. For a breathless moment awareness gave her a feeling of power, of being in control, but it also brought the disquiet of knowing that wielding it harbored the capacity to hurt, as well as to heal. "We better get dinner on the table."

He gave her a cursory nod and turned back to the work counter. "They've got the trains almost finished. Quite a setup." He removed a loaf of French bread from a long white paper bag. "Patrick would have made a great dad. He's got a natural rapport with kids."

Krisanne wished they could go back to talking about trains and a world in which people didn't die.

"He always planned on having a big family." She

selected garlic powder from the spice rack near the stove and twisted off the cap so violently some of it spilled onto the counter. "At least he's got the consolation of knowing he's not leaving a fatherless brood behind."

Drew ceased his stirring and looked at her. "That's no consolation," he said softly.

She couldn't ignore the sadness in the comment. Looking over at him, she noted the slump of his broad shoulders, the distant look in his eyes, and knew they weren't talking only about what Patrick would lose. The backdrop of childish laughter was an eloquent reminder of what they, too, had lost.

"No, it isn't," she agreed unevenly.

A barrage of emotions raced across Drew's sculptured profile. Krisanne raised a hand to his shoulder and tugged him around to face her. His melancholy eyes grieved with her, as she wrapped her arms around him.

"Hold me, Drew. Tight."

It was to console her, he told himself, to support her against the tragedy of death looming ahead that he took her into his arms. But as the warm fullness of her breasts pressed against his chest, his body responded. From the myriad of disquieting sensations the soft touch of her skin provoked, he knew having her in his arms wasn't purely for her benefit.

She tightened her hold and snuggled almost childlike against him. Instinctively, he adjusted his body to fit hers and lowered his head into the silky softness of her golden hair. Smelling the feminine scents of shampoo and bath oils, he breathed in her fragrance like a drowning man gasping for air. He leaned back a little, his gaze drifted down at the same moment she glanced up at him.

It took the merest instant for realization to pass between them. She tilted her head at precisely the right angle. He lowered his mouth to meet hers. Their lips barely touched at first, as if each were waiting for the other to give permission to go further. The contact deepened and the tip of his tongue ventured forward, an exploratory wandering across her pliant lips. In acquiescence, she parted them.

Krisanne's whole body sang and she floated weightless, out of control, through a long dizzying tumult of sensations. Her heart ached with pleasure, while her reason, delirious and confused, rebelled. She couldn't allow herself to take this intoxicating journey, no matter how much joy the adventure promised.

Abruptly she wrenched her mouth from his, then nearly wept at the emptiness the separation left. Until he'd held her in his arms, she'd been able to deny her need for him. But now, pressing her cheek to his hard chest, feeling its heavy thudding, she knew she had been fooling herself.

Drew closed his eyes, experienced unimaginable rapture and knew the meaning of pure torment. Humbling need swept over him like a grass fire consuming raw, open prairie. His hammering pulse slowed into a painful dirge and he released her.

Pushing herself away from him, Krisanne refused to make eye contact. She couldn't allow herself to delve into his wounded, pleading eyes, knowing what she'd see was a reflection of her own lonely frustration.

"We can't, Drew," she whimpered raggedly, wrapping her arms around her midsection. She moved to the open back door, trembling inside, as she surveyed the fertile pageant of spring, knowing she was insane to want what she wanted, to feel what she was feeling.

"Can't what?" he demanded, more harshly than he intended.

She turned to him, her expression haunted, tears glistening. "Not now." She looked toward the hallway, to the sound of a little boy playing with an adult man who seemed to have reverted back to his own childhood—a dying man.

Realization of what she meant flooded over Drew like a violent summer rain, dousing the flames, cooling his temper. He exhaled a breath he didn't realize he'd been holding.

"At another time, under different circumstances," she said. "But not now. Not with Pat—I...I can't—"

"That's nonsense," he objected, then gentled his tone as renewed hope filled him. She wasn't rejecting him, not entirely at least. "What we feel for each other isn't bound by time or circumstance."

She shook her head. "Isn't it? How can we be sure of what we feel right now, Drew? How can I? Maybe it's just desperation groping in the face of death for assurance we're still alive."

He moved toward her, inhaled the delicate rose petal scent he remembered so well, and lifted her chin with the side of his finger. "Or maybe it's love."

Her eyes softened, then closed at the same time her jaw tightened. He understood the ache, the fear, the longing.

A light, running footfall echoed down the hallway. A moment later Patrick swooped into the kitchen, pouncing just inside the doorway, his feet spread, knees bent, shoulders arched, in the classic stance of the challenger.

"Have you seen Trav?" he asked, slightly out of breath. "We're playing hide-and-seek and I'm it."

Krisanne stared at him, and for a blinding moment her brother really was a boy again—and she a little girl. The smells filling the kitchen were from their mother's homemade lasagna baking in the oven. The copper-clad pots and pans hanging on the walls gleamed brightly once more. Her father was in the front room, puffing contentedly on an aromatic pipe while he read the Sunday paper.

"Did he come in here?" Patrick asked anxiously, then suddenly smiled, as if he'd just remembered he was a grown man, a serious scientist. "We..." he began, his voice deeper in pitch this time, shattering the illusion of a time long ago when the security of family seemed endless and unconditional. "You see, Trav and I are conducting a scientific experiment using ESP to find missing persons."

"Well, then it wouldn't be fair to tell if he was here," Krisanne sang in a mocking lilt, playing to his childish escapade.

Patrick grinned back, then paused in his game long enough to study his sister and best friend. "No garlic bread?"

Drew snorted, the tension imploding. "We were just getting it ready." He winked at Krisanne and motioned with his hand to the breadboard he'd set out, before she'd asked to be held—before he'd kissed her and she'd kissed him back.

Patrick—the man, not the boy—peered at his sister and his friend, as if he could see the marks of their hands on each other's backs. He gave his friend an approving wink, then darted back out of the room on his own search.

Krisanne bit her lip as her brother retreated. An unexpected tear slithered down her cheek. He was putting on a good act, but she hadn't missed the forlorn sadness and the fear in his eyes, as he'd looked across the kitchen at her and Drew. Had he, too, experienced a flashback to simpler times? Did he wake in the middle of the night and mourn the family he would never have? Had he dreamed of growing old in this house, surrounded by children and grandchildren? Did memories rip through him like shooting stars, bright and magical and oh, so fleeting?

Drew was right. If the attraction they felt for each other was real, it wasn't bounded by the here and now. She wanted love and intimacy and family. More than that, she needed them with a desperation she'd never known before. So why was she behaving as if she were afraid of them, of him?

"For now," she said, "maybe it would be best if we were just—"

"Friends?" Drew finished for her, making the word sound cold, detached, heartless.

CHAPTER SIX

KRISANNE WATCHED DREW turn away and resume his task of cutting bread. She sighed and filled a large, dark blue porcelain enamel pot with water. While it came to a boil for the pasta, she removed a cookie sheet from the cabinet by the stove, buttered the bread slices and positioned them in neat rows on its shiny surface. He sprinkled them with garlic powder. She topped them off with a delicate dusting of paprika. Neither of them said a word during the entire process.

Pasta boiled. Garlic bread toasted. Sauce simmered.

Drew helped her pull out the leaves of the old wooden table. To add a homey touch, she chose blue-and-white checkered place mats from the sideboard in the dining room.

At last, it was time for the two gamesters to join them. Father and son sat opposite each other, brother and sister the same. Gofer settled contentedly in the corner, gnawing on a chew bone.

"Travis, would you like to lead the prayer?" Krisanne asked.

"Let Uncle Pat," the boy suggested.

Patrick smiled and reached out to join hands. Krisanne held Travis's small soft fingers in one hand and Drew's large, tough hand with the other. They all bowed their heads.

"Thank you, Lord, for the food on our table and the friends by our sides."

"Amen," they all chorused.

Drew used tongs to serve the spaghetti from a blue crockery bowl in the center of the table, then topped the pasta with rich marinara sauce.

"How many super-duper meatballs do you want, Son?"

"Seven," came the instant reply.

Drew made a wry face. "Why don't we start you off with three?" He arranged three half-dollar-sized meatballs in the middle of the steaming mound.

"How about you, Uncle Pat?"

"Seven," Patrick snapped and winked at Travis. The boy covered his mouth with his hand and tittered.

"I think you can have five."

Drew gave Krisanne and himself five as well.

"What do you think?" Drew asked, after everyone had had a chance to sample his culinary masterpiece.

"They're delicious." Krisanne was impressed by their savory flavor. "Can I ask the secret?"

Drew grinned proudly. "Poultry stuffing. A couple of years ago when I was making them, the bread I'd planned to use for filler was moldy, so I had to make do with what was on hand."

He used to cook when Lisa was alive. Was that a common occurrence, Krisanne wondered. Or did he prepare only favorite specialties like meatballs and spaghetti?

"Here's to making the best of what we have available," Patrick said, raising his glass of milk in a toast.

Like time? Krisanne and Drew looked at each other across the table, plastered tight-lipped smiles on their faces and lifted their glasses of iced tea. Afterward, she had to force pasta past the lump in her throat. Only the slurping sound of Travis sucking spaghetti strings into his mouth brought a genuine smile to her lips.

He polished off his last meatball. "Dad, this place's cool for playing hide-and-seek."

"Or hiding from wicked housekeepers," Patrick added.

Travis's eyes grew wide. "Wicked housekeepers?"

"Uh-oh, I think I hear a story coming on," Drew commented in an undertone.

"You tell it," Patrick urged his sister.

"Not me." She laughed. "You started this."

His mouth curving up in a mischievous grin, Patrick turned to Travis. "She was an ugly old crone with deep dark eyes and a great big wart right here." He pinched the tip of Travis's nose, making him wince and squirm in his chair. "It had three curly, black hairs sticking out. She had crooked, yellow teeth and long, sharp fingernails. When she spoke—" Patrick deepened his baritone for emphasis "—she sounded like a bullfrog gargling. It used to make the dishes rattle and the cat run for cover."

"Thanks a lot, pal," Drew muttered sarcastically. "Heaven help me if I ever decide to hire a housekeeper."

Patrick grinned. "Naturally, we stayed away from her whenever we could. Bet you can't guess where we hid."

The boy's eyes were as big as his dinner plate. "Where?"

"The dumbwaiter," Patrick whispered.

"What's a dumbwaiter?" Travis asked breathlessly.

Drew and Krisanne exchanged amused glances.

"Come on. I'll show you."

Glorying in his Pied Piper role, Patrick led them over to the wall beside the old icebox and pointed to a wood-paneled door at waist height. It measured about two feet by three feet. Above the plain brass latch was a key-operated, dead bolt.

"Behind this," Patrick confided to the boy, "is a little elevator that goes up and down by pulling on a rope."

"Can I see it?"

"Well…" Patrick stroked his chin. "I guess it would be all right." He patted his pockets. "Have you got the key?"

The youngster shook his head. "I don't have it." He poked his hands into his pants pockets to prove it and his face lit up. He pulled out a paper tag with a key attached to it by a string.

"I figured you had it," Patrick said casually. He took the key and winked at Krisanne.

Putting on a great show of grunting and groaning, he twisted the key in the lock. At last, it clicked and Patrick's face beamed. But then suddenly, he stopped.

"I wonder if anyone's inside," he said in a melo-dramatic hush, sending shivers down Krisanne's spine, though she knew nothing was there. The dumbwaiter hadn't been used in years.

She watched Travis closely. His mouth was a round O, his eyes glued to the door. It made a creaking sound as Patrick inched it from its jamb. Then, all at once, he sprang it open with a quick jerk. Krisanne and Drew involuntarily flinched and joined the child in gasping.

"Well, look at that," Patrick exclaimed. "Ivor." He reached into the compartment and removed a brown-and-cream teddy bear. "So that's where you've been hiding all this time."

Krisanne recognized her brother's favorite stuffed animal. It must have been stored in the attic more than twenty years earlier. She sniffed the faint odor of camphor and noticed that the tin-lined dumbwaiter was spotlessly clean. When had her brother found time to stage this scene for a little boy he'd never see grow up? Without even realizing it, she slipped her hand into Drew's. The gentle squeeze he returned conveyed better than words how deeply affected he was, too.

"Would you like to hold him?" Patrick asked. "In fact, why don't you keep him. I don't think I'll be needing him anymore."

Drew cleared his throat. "What do you say, Son?"

"Thank you, Uncle Pat."

"You're welcome."

Drew rested his hand on his friend's shoulder and squeezed. "Thanks."

Patrick reached up and covered Drew's hand. "My pleasure." He made the briefest eye contact and blinked away quickly. "Why don't we make one last run with the trains," he invited Travis, "while Aunt Kris and your dad wash up?"

There was no argument from the boy.

Krisanne and Drew continued to hold hands as they watched them march down the hall to the train room. There was a tenderness in the way Drew's fingers gently stroked the back of her hand.

"Now," he said, guiding her around the table to face the sink, "you wash and I'll dry, while you tell me about this sinister housekeeper."

Krisanne wanted to follow his lead, to treat the events of the last few minutes as the ordinary generosity of an adult for a child—but nothing about it was ordinary. The man was dying and in his act of giving,

Krisanne recognized a quiet acceptance that his life was indeed drawing to a close.

"Kris?" Drew stepped behind her and placed his hands on the delicate curves between her neck and shoulders and began a gentle massage. This time she didn't pull away but leaned into his strong, soothing pressure. If only life were so simple, she thought. Rub the right spot and the pain goes away.

"Tell me about the wicked housekeeper," he whispered in her ear. She rotated her head, forcing the taut muscles of her neck against his big hands, sampling their power to melt the tension.

"There really was a housekeeper, and we used to hide from her in the dumbwaiter. But it wasn't because she was the ogre Pat painted her to be. Actually, Pat and I liked Mrs. Haggerty. She was a widow who had a dozen grandchildren. With that much practice, she was pretty good at keeping us in line. Her fangs and warts couldn't have been too ugly, either. She left us when she remarried and moved with her new husband somewhere back east—Virginia, I think."

Breaking away from Drew's touch, Krisanne moved over to the sink and filled it with hot water and dish detergent. Drew started gathering dirty plates.

"We loved to play games on her," Krisanne went on. "It took her a while to figure out we were using the dumbwaiter to disappear from one place and mysteriously reappear in another. When she finally did, I think she was sort of proud of our ingenuity, but, of course, she couldn't allow it to go on. She told Dad and suggested he put locks on the doors. He freaked out." She lowered a stack of dishes into the foam-filled sink. "I don't think I ever saw him so upset. He was shaking so much he scared me."

Drew retrieved a washcloth from the hot soapy water and wiped down the table and counters. "You have to admit it was a pretty dangerous thing to do."

"It turned out there was more to it than that. When Dad was a kid, he and a friend from next door were playing in the dumbwaiter, and Dad got stuck between floors. His playmate panicked and ran away. It was over an hour before one of the servants found Dad and got him out of there."

"It must have been terrifying for him."

"He never forgot it. He was always uncomfortable in confined spaces after that, especially elevators." She rinsed a plate and set it on edge in the drainboard. "Did you know Celia's claustrophobic?"

He raised a dark brow. "Really?"

"She disguises it pretty well, but Dad recognized the symptoms. I guess his awareness was what helped bring them together. She was brought up in an orphanage, in a big old house very much like this. It seems one of the favorite ways of disciplining little girls was to lock them in a dark closet for hours on end."

Drew picked up a washed bowl and started rubbing it viciously with a towel. He'd experienced a much different brand of abuse as a child. Krisanne was certain the memory of his parents' lack of affection helped make him the caring, involved father he was.

"God, that's terrible." He placed the dried china bowl on the counter with what seemed uncommon gentleness.

"She's been afraid of closed places ever since. Right after Dad died, she moved from here to the lodge at the River Shore Club where the suites are open and airy."

"It explains her office," Drew noted. "Big and spacious, with her desk facing the windows rather than in front of them. Tough lady. It's a long way from an orphanage to CEO." He reached for another plate and started drying it. "Speaking of strong women and long journeys, how was your trip to Austin?"

She chuckled. "You make it sound as if I trekked it in a covered wagon." She liked the twinkle in the smile he returned. It felt good to share humor with him. It seemed like years since she'd laughed. She told him about Dr. Lesko's willingness to keep her job for her.

Drew looked at her with a curious frown. "You don't sound very enthusiastic about going back."

"He's got a good reputation and a great location, but his practice is too limited. I want to do more than neuter family pets and give them shots."

"Like what?"

"Like opening my own place and expanding my practice to include larger animals."

"Ah." He smiled. "You mean horses?"

She grinned back at him. "Remember the first time I took you riding? You looked like a wooden soldier— all stiff arms and legs." Her smile deepened, as she recalled the image. "You bounced so much in the saddle, I was worried you were going to do permanent damage to your vocal cords."

He laughed. "Not nearly as worried as I was. As it turned out, every other muscle in my body ached so bad the next day, I wasn't sure I'd ever walk again."

Teaching him hadn't been nearly as much of a challenge, as it had been fun. With his athletic ability, it hadn't taken him long to find his seat. Even now, contemplation of his narrow hips rocking in the saddle was enough to quicken the rhythm of her heartbeat.

"Do you still keep a horse?" he asked.

"After Honey Babe died I didn't have the time it would take to train a new horse, not the way I'd want to."

"You never did do things halfway. You must miss it."

"Hmm," she murmured in agreement. She didn't mention that after he left her, trail riding had lost some of its allure.

"So tell me these plans of yours for your very own vet clinic."

Was he mocking her? She looked over at him. His wide-open expression suggested the question was sincere. But was it just idle curiosity, she wondered, or genuine interest?

"I'll still handle small animals and household pets, of course. It's a good steady income. But I'd like to get involved in equine medicine, especially embryo transplants."

He raised his dark eyebrows. "That's pretty specialized." He added another dish to the stack of those to be washed. "Would you open your clinic here in Coyote Springs or in Austin?"

"Actually, I was thinking of Dallas."

Drew sponged sticky finger marks from Travis's chair. "I suppose opportunities would be better there. But tell me, what would you do if some crusty old rancher calls the clinic for a vet to come out and then, when you show up, decides he doesn't want a woman handling his horses?"

She chuckled. "I'd tell him he's going to pay for the call anyway, so it's up to him if he wants to get service for it." She raised a soapy hand and used her wrist to brush away the hair from her eyes. "But that's why I'd like to go to Dallas. Embryo transplants are expensive, too expensive for ordinary ranch horses. Ranchers might use them to improve their cattle stock, but the real market is in very good competition mares.''

He picked up a dish from the drainboard and started to dry it. ''And I imagine the class of people who are progressive enough to deal with that kind of advanced technology are sophisticated enough to get beyond sexist attitudes.''

''Usually.'' She didn't point out that there were still too many men who saw professional women as hobbyists or dilettantes.

''What do you think this clinic of yours is going to cost?''

''In Dallas? Assuming I can get the real estate at a reasonable price, probably half a million dollars to start. I'll need the usual equipment, but I'll also have to build stalls for horses and other livestock...then there's the special lab equipment, additional training, technical staff—''

''You've been thinking about this a long time, haven't you?''

''More like dreaming about it.''

''And now your dream can come true.''

She rinsed off the large bowl they'd used to serve the meatballs. ''If you remember when you called me in Austin, I told you I was planning to come here the following weekend. I wanted to talk to Patrick about—''

Travis came running into the room. ''Daddy! Come see what Uncle Pat and me are doing.''

''Uncle Pat and I,'' Drew corrected him.

''Yeah, come look at what we're doing.''

He dragged his father by the hand to the workbench in the corner of the train room. Wheels, tubes of glue, bottles of paint, and a variety of small brushes and tools were strewn all over it. "We're making a new train. See. A caboose."

Drew cast a bemused grin at Krisanne.

She returned the smile. "A caboose, huh?"

"Yeah, and it's going to be red."

"It's one I started years ago and didn't get around to finishing," Patrick told him. He was sitting at the table experimentally fitting two small pieces of wood together.

"Must be a lot of work," Drew commented to his friend.

"That's all right, Daddy. We don't mind," Travis said, sounding very grown-up. "Uncle Pat's going to show me how to do it. He says it will teach me patents."

"Patience."

"Yeah. We're going to do it together every day after school."

"How long is this project going to take?" Drew asked.

"Maybe a week," Patrick told them. "If he doesn't lose interest."

"He won't." Unable to suppress a note of pride, Drew put a hand on his son's curly head. "When Trav decides to do something, he does it all the way."

"Good," Patrick said. "Perseverance and 'patents' will take him anywhere he wants to go in life."

Drew smiled. "Are you sure you want to do this?"

"Yep."

"Daddy," Travis said, tugging on his father's shirt sleeve, "Uncle Pat wants to know if we can go on a picnic with him and Aunt Kris on Easter Sunday. Can we? Daddy? P-l-e-a-s-e."

"Bluebonnets should be in full bloom over the next couple of weeks," Patrick offered. "I thought we might make a day of it. I'd like to see them."

One last time. The unspoken words ripped through Krisanne. How many things would he get to do one last time? She watched Drew's hand flex momentarily and knew he was thinking the same thought.

"Sounds like a great idea," he said cheerfully. "I know the perfect spot, too, a special place over behind the twin mesas."

"Good," Krisanne chimed in, trying to match his enthusiasm. The boy's face glowed in anticipation, but the sad smile on her brother's lips told her that for him their forced cheerfulness was transparent. She didn't dare look in his eyes. "I'll fix a picnic lunch and we can make a day of it. Hey, Trav, do you like fried chicken?"

"Colonel Sanders?" he asked eagerly.

"Oh, even better than the Colonel's," Patrick assured him. "And no one can make potato salad as good as Aunt Kris."

"Can we take Gofer?"

"Absolutely," Patrick said, after getting a quick nod of approval from Drew. "A picnic wouldn't be a picnic without a puppy and ants. Who's going to bring the ants?"

"I don't want ants," Travis objected, screwing up his eager face. "They're itchy."

"No ants, huh?" Patrick paused dramatically to consider. "Oh well, I guess we'll just have to leave them behind." He winked at Krisanne and Drew standing next to each other. "But knowing how much ants love picnics, I have a feeling they'll show up anyway."

So plans were made. All I have to do now, Krisanne

told herself later, is make the best fried chicken and potato salad the world has ever tasted.

UNPACKING AND OTHER chores kept Krisanne away from Blessing Pharmaceuticals until after lunch the next day. By the time she entered the outer room of Patrick's research department, two burly workmen were maneuvering a long plaid couch through the far doorway into Patrick's private office. She followed them in and found Celia and Nadeen standing side by side behind his cluttered desk. Celia was rolling the sapphire-and-diamond ring on her right hand, while giving detailed instructions to the movers as to where they were to place the new piece of furniture.

Krisanne motioned toward the couch. "What's this for?"

"Pat had a fainting spell yesterday afternoon," Nadeen explained somberly.

A wave of panic swept Krisanne. "Another fainting spell?" Two in less than a week. Three in two weeks, if she counted the one that had originally sent him to the hospital. It definitely wasn't a good sign. He was pushing himself too hard, or the disease was progressing faster than expected—or both.

"It wasn't serious," Nadeen insisted. She raked her blunt-nailed fingers through short, caramel-colored hair. "It only lasted a few seconds. More like dizziness."

The workmen left.

"Nadeen, if there's ever another incident like this, I'd like you to personally notify me immediately," Celia said politely, but with that confident authority that marked her as an executive. "Please don't let me hear about it the next day from someone else."

"Yes, Mrs. Blessing," Nadeen responded unhappily.

Celia addressed Krisanne. "Come see me before you leave."

The CEO left the office quietly, and Krisanne wondered if it was the windowless room that had her so on edge or if there was something else. She turned to Nadeen. "What's going on?"

The woman Patrick had nominated as his successor looked at her with an expression that said, "Don't you start on me, too." Nadeen took a deep breath. "I told you. Pat had a dizzy spell yesterday afternoon. I wanted to call the nurse on duty, and started to, but he stopped me. Swore it was nothing to worry about." Nadeen toyed with the top button of her smock. "He didn't pass out or anything. Said he skipped lunch and insisted it was nothing more than a mild case of low blood sugar. He drank a Coke and continued to work until Drew came by to pick him up an hour later."

Krisanne could imagine Patrick trying to convince her there was no point in telling anyone about the momentary weakness; that he didn't want people fussing. The bit about hypoglycemia might even be true, too, especially if he wasn't eating right. Undoubtedly he'd promised to be more careful in the future.

"If you didn't tell anyone, how did Celia know about it?"

"Before they left, Mr. Hadley probably overheard Pat telling me to keep quiet about it. He's the only one who could've blabbed to her this morning."

Anger simmered in Krisanne's belly. She could understand her brother's silence. He wouldn't want to remind her—or himself—that he was getting weaker. But what was Drew's excuse? Did he really think he was helping her by shutting her out?

"Where's Pat now?"

"Over in production checking on a new compound. He's going to be really mad at me when he sees that couch."

Krisanne looked at the green, yellow, black and red stripes of the new piece of furniture and almost laughed. She had no idea how Celia had managed it on such short notice, but the sofa was upholstered in Ross plaid. Their mother had been a Ross.

She put her hand on Nadeen's forearm and squeezed gently. "He may sputter a bit, but he won't be mad, at least, not at you."

Nadeen bit her lip. "He doesn't like to think about it," she mumbled, fighting tears.

"I know." *None of us does.* Krisanne waited for her to grab a tissue from the box on the credenza behind the desk. "I was wondering if you could do me a favor."

Nadeen's eyes narrowed. "What kind of favor?"

"I know Pat's doing research on Troimaline and is concerned about some of its possible side effects."

Nadeen took a last dab at her nose, nodded and tossed the crumpled tissue into the wastebasket.

"I was hoping you could bring me up to date on your progress."

The woman hesitated a moment, then squared her shoulders and invited Krisanne to follow her. They went back through the outer office. Nadeen removed a key card from her pocket and opened the door to the laboratory proper.

"You need to sign the log." Nadeen handed her a clipboard. Krisanne used the pen dangling from a chain to fill out the required information.

The windowless room reminded her of one of her

vet school labs with its long, hard rubber-topped work-tables, test tubes, glass beakers and Bunsen burners.

Nadeen walked resolutely to a bank of computers, seated herself at the largest of them and waved her guest to a nearby stool. She poked on a keyboard, entering her last name and first initial, then a password.

She was no longer the uncertain, teary-eyed woman of a few minutes earlier. In her place, Krisanne observed the mature professional about whom Patrick had boasted. For the next hour the scientist called up screen after screen of statistical data, and peppered her explanations of them with jargon Krisanne had to struggle to dredge up from her college days—means, mode, standard deviations, coefficients of probability.

"So you can't say with any degree of certainty," Krisanne concluded, "whether Troimaline is responsible for abnormal births or higher mortality rates."

"Not yet. You must understand much of the data has been corrupted by too many unscientifically collected statistics, and undocumented or unaccounted-for variables. If there is a correlation between the incidences of miscarriages, fetal malformations, birth defects, morbidity and the use of Troimaline, we haven't been able to isolate it yet. Anecdotally, there would appear to be a relationship, but we're no closer to determining if it's real, significant, directly associated, or even mitigable."

"Do you have a plan of action for collecting clean data?"

Nadeen nodded. "Pat implemented one as soon as he started his research last year. But it's going to take more—"

"Time."

Nadeen nodded again and broke eye contact.

Time Patrick didn't have.

"I won't pretend to understand all the details you've thrown at me," Krisanne acknowledged grimly, "but I do recognize what their ramifications could be. Has Celia been kept informed of your progress?"

Nadeen exited the computer report they'd been viewing. "Pat presents the status of all our research projects at the weekly staff meetings."

Krisanne pictured a dark-paneled boardroom, lights dimmed, as a white-coated scientist presented slides and graphs to department heads. "Does Drew attend those meetings?"

"Of course."

Weekly staff meetings, Krisanne mused. Maybe she should start attending them.

"Can you e-mail these reports to Pat at home, so I can study them there?"

"Sure."

Krisanne left a few minutes later. She'd made a start in sorting through the Troimaline issue, but the tough decisions were still ahead.

She walked down the corridor, her footsteps against the hard, tiled floor echoing the hollow emptiness she felt inside. She assumed the reason her stepmother wanted to see her was to discuss how she was going to handle her stock. She'd been in the CEO's office suite only once before, when the new building was dedicated six months earlier. Sinking into the thick carpet, she took in the highly polished furniture, designer wall coverings, bold sweeping lithographs and subtle watercolors. Impressive for a small family-owned company.

Celia's secretary, Bruce, a young man in his late twenties, rose politely from his desk when she walked in. With his straw blond hair, medium blue eyes, and peach-smooth cheeks, he had the kind of youthful, clean-cut wholesomeness that would probably keep well into old age. He'd been working for Celia for a little over two years, and according to Patrick was damned good at his work—even if he did look like a prep school teenager dressed up for a date.

"Dr. Blessing. It's very nice to see you again." His voice was surprisingly deep and dramatic. "Mrs. Blessing is expecting you."

He led Krisanne through double doors into the bright, sumptuous office of the corporation's CEO. It was in the northwest corner of the sprawling building and, as Drew had pointed out, was laid out differently from the conventional executive suite. Instead of sitting in the right angle between the two picture windows, Celia had arranged her desk in the opposite corner so she faced the broad expanse of glass. It gave her a sense of space and allowed her a panoramic view of the company's meticulously landscaped grounds and the long drive leading up from the main road. It also meant, Krisanne realized, that Celia got to see the profiles of people being shown into her office before they had to turn right to face her.

At the moment, however, Celia wasn't at her desk, but in the light-filled corner of the vast room. Patrick and Drew were with her.

"Come sit down," Celia invited warmly, gesturing to the couch on her left, facing the two men.

Krisanne took her seat, aware of the men watching her. "I've decided to come to your staff meetings," she announced.

Celia raised a delicate eyebrow. "Good. I'll notify the rest of the staff that you'll be attending and have them prepare background briefings for you."

Krisanne looked at Drew sitting quietly a few feet across from her. The firm set of his jaw, the motionless clasping of one hand over the other in his lap, the fine pulsing of a vein near the dark hairline of his temple, told her he was uncomfortable. She wondered why.

"I was just telling Patrick," Celia said, "he's done so much for Blessing and made so many friends here that I...we would like to host an appreciation dinner for him."

Krisanne was aghast. A farewell party for a dying man!

Judging from the telling glance in Patrick's eye, he'd read her expression correctly. "I've agreed to it," he said, with the crooked smile he always got when he was one up on someone, "but with one condition."

"What's that?" Krisanne asked quietly, trying to substitute a curious smile for the agony she felt.

"That it be like Harry Parker's retirement dinner."

"A roast?" she exclaimed. She'd attended the event four years earlier when one of their oldest employees retired after fifty years with Blessing. The man had been a character and the night had been explosive with ribbing and good-natured jibes and digs. But how do you roast a dying man?

"Oh, and one other thing," Patrick stipulated, "no black ties."

He and Celia exchanged a quiet, secretive smile. She suggested a date three weeks away, a Saturday evening, and he agreed. A minute later the meeting broke up.

Feeling completely off balance, Krisanne moved out of the office and stood numbly in the hallway watching Patrick amble back toward his lab. Steeling herself, she turned to Drew.

"I need to talk to you. Is there someplace we can talk privately? It won't take long."

She followed him around the corner to the double doors of the conference room. He opened one and stepped aside to let her precede him. The room was totally different from what she'd expected—until she remembered her stepmother's abhorrence for dark, confined places. The daylight-flooded room was rectangular, floor-to-ceiling windows forming one long wall. The paneling opposite it was honey oak rather than stygian walnut. Even at night, Krisanne surmised, it would feel open and bright. She stood in front of the multimedia screens near the entry and waited for Drew to close the door.

"Why didn't you tell me Pat nearly collapsed yesterday?" she demanded.

His gaze appraised her temperament. "Sorry. I probably should have."

"Haven't you learned yet that pretending things haven't happened doesn't protect you from their consequences?"

She saw him blanch at the thinly disguised reference to seven years before.

"I'm sorry, Kris. I really didn't mean—"

"I don't care what you meant." She could feel tears starting to pool. She didn't know if they were from rage, disappointment, or knowledge that her brother's condition was indeed worsening. Or was it the frustration of being so close to this man, wanting to touch him, aching to be held by him and not allowing herself to? Whichever it was, she wasn't going to cry. The last thing she wanted now was to get weepy in front of Drew Hadley.

"It won't happen again," he said forcefully, then relaxed and stepped toward her.

But instead of accepting the shelter of his arms, she stomped out of his presence in what she liked to think was full control of herself.

CHAPTER SEVEN

DREW WAITED WITH his son in front of the community church on Easter morning for Krisanne and her brother to join them. Would she still be upset with him about not telling her of Patrick's fainting spell? She never used to dwell on things after blowing off steam, but that was seven years ago. A lot had happened since then, things they hadn't yet talked about.

He saw her approach and it took a mere glance for him to know the incident in the conference room was behind them. His heart did a little leap and his blood moved just a bit faster as she came closer.

She looks like spring itself, he thought, watching her pale yellow dress rippling like a sea of buttercups in the fresh breeze.

"Happy Easter," she said, tossing him a grin. Her delicate scent washed over him like tiny droplets of morning's early light, and penetrated straight to his libido. He watched her bend to plant a kiss on Travis's cheek and give him a hug.

"Beautiful day for praising the Lord, don't you think?" Patrick asked. He shot Drew a Cheshire smile.

"Amen, brother. Just plain beautiful," Drew responded, his eyes on Krisanne, as she rested a hand casually on his son's shoulder and guided him toward the open doors of the church. After they disappeared into the cool shade of the small Spanish-style building,

Drew managed to drag his attention back to his friend who was now busy greeting people.

Dressed in a lightweight blue suit and wearing one of his hallmark colorful ties, Patrick looked as hale and vigorous as ever in spite of his weight loss.

Drew observed people's reactions to him. Some greeted him like an old friend and asked him openly how he was feeling, how he was getting along. They were definitely in the minority. A few avoided him altogether. Most of his old acquaintances, however, seemed torn between congeniality and curiosity. They blustered and tried too hard to be upbeat, asking no questions about his condition, pretending everything was absolutely fine. There was distinct silence when someone, either unaware or unthinking, asked him if he was going hiking in the mountains this summer.

"To the top of Olympus," Patrick replied with a wide grin. The smiles around him faded into embarrassment.

After church, Drew took Travis home so they could change clothes for the picnic and pick up Gofer. Drew found himself as anxious as his son to hurry to Blessing House, though for slightly different reasons.

"You don't think they left without us, do you?" the boy worried when, at last, they got into the car.

Smiling, Drew reassured him. "No, I'm sure they didn't."

When they turned down Coyote Avenue, Drew noticed the trees had budded with the light, cheerful green that heralded new life. His heart quickened. Spring juices again?

He pulled into the long driveway that hugged the side of the house and parked in front of the three-car garage. Entering through the kitchen door with barely

a preliminary tap gave him an uncanny sense of be-
longing. He wasn't a guest anymore. The feeling of
being part of a household was uplifting, yet unsettling
at the same time. His own childhood had been dis-
rupted so many times by changes of address—each one
more exclusive than the last—that he'd never thought
of them as other than places where he lived. He looked
at his son and renewed his vow that the boy would
always have a place to call home.

The huge, old-fashioned Blessing kitchen was red-
olent with the mouthwatering smells of fried chicken
and baking biscuits. Patrick stood at the counter by the
refrigerator spooning potato salad into a large wide-
mouthed jar.

"Right on time," he said over his shoulder to the
new arrivals. "You hungry, kiddo?"

"Uh-huh," Travis replied. "Are we going now?"

"As soon as we finish packing," Krisanne assured
him. She moved from the sink to the stove. "Can you
give me a hand here, Drew?"

"You bet."

"There're two small towels on the chair. Line the
inside of the picnic basket with one of them. As soon
as I remove the biscuits, take the bricks out of the oven.
Use pot holders. They're hot. Put them in the basket
on the towel while I finish wrapping the chicken."

Drew set about doing as instructed. "Bricks?"

"A trick my grandmother taught me for keeping
food warm."

"Cool," Travis said.

The three adults chuckled.

"Trav, would you get the pop out of the refrigerator
and help Uncle Pat put ice in the cooler."

"Yes, ma'am."

Ten minutes later they were on their way and in another ten Drew turned his Mercedes onto a private road. It led them between two eroded mesas to a small, sunken valley.

"It floods here with nearly every rain," Drew explained, "but it also makes for wonderful wildflowers."

There weren't just bluebonnets, but reddish brown and yellow Mexican hats, crimson clover, lemon-tipped, red Indian blankets, wild pink and purple verbena, snowy pink primroses, and acres of others, all lending their vibrant colors to the variegated panoply of spring.

Coming here had been the right thing, Krisanne thought. There could be no thought of death in this place where color and movement dominated, where the earth beneath her feet and the endless sky above were eternally alive.

Patrick grabbed the soccer ball from the back of the car and invited Travis to kick it around with him in a grassy field. Gofer bounced playfully through the tall weeds. A jackrabbit popped up. Which of the two animals was more shocked, the dog or the jack, was hard to tell—or Travis for that matter, who stood motionless and openmouthed. Gofer decided it was his job to pursue. Fortunately, Patrick was able to dissuade him with a call. The jack had already disappeared, anyway.

Drew and Krisanne unloaded the car.

They decided to picnic near one of three ancient mesquite trees, its feathery, light green foliage contrasting sharply with its coarse, gnarled, black-brown limbs and trunk. *You can't kill me,* it seemed to brag. *My roots go too deep.*

"A picnic for four, huh?" Drew lugged the wicker

basket and wooden boxes to the site Krisanne had chosen. "The pioneers didn't carry this much in their wagon trains."

Krisanne made a ritual of setting out their meal. Three times she had Drew reposition the colorful, king-sized blanket she'd brought before she was satisfied. No plastic forks or paper plates for this occasion, either. She'd scoured the attic for her grandmother's antique picnic basket with its white-speckled, blue enamel plates and tin utensils. The cloth napkins had to be folded just right as they were set in place.

Drew understood why she was going to so much trouble for a few hours in the sun. This would probably be their last picnic with Patrick, their last opportunity to share the renewal of spring and smell the sweet scents of young flowers. Krisanne wanted the memory of it to be as perfect as possible—so did he.

He reached into a black leather bag and pulled out a camera. "Hey, everybody, picture time."

Patrick, Travis and Gofer wandered back from their soccer game while Drew set up a tripod and mounted his camera. He took another minute to get everyone lined up behind the blanket. Patrick and Travis sat cross-legged in front, the puppy between them. Krisanne knelt behind her brother. Drew set the timer, then ran around to kneel beside her. The camera whirred and clicked. They started to get up, then there was another click.

"Gotcha." Drew gloated, as the timer continued to purr, catching everyone in midmotion. Patrick turned back to the lens and stuck out his tongue. Travis giggled. Krisanne caught the fever and made a funny face. For the next few seconds each of them took turns posing, usually comically, until the remaining exposures were used. Then the four of them fell to the ground, laughing at the deep blue sky.

"You could have warned us," Krisanne scolded between chuckles. God, it felt good to laugh.

"Wouldn't have been any fun," he replied with a wink. The playfulness in his voice and the dimple in his cheek, created by his grin, brought back memories of college days.

At last he packed up his gear, and they sat down to eat. Krisanne was pleased when Travis raved about the chicken. She thought at first his father might have put him up to it, until the boy ate three drumsticks. Patrick ate the fourth, as well as the livers she'd fried especially for him and a heaping mound of potato salad. His appetite's still hearty, she noted. A good sign.

"You set up, so we clean up," Patrick announced, when they finished their leisurely meal and made a considerable dent in the peach cobbler Krisanne was pleased to serve still warm. "You and Drew take a walk while Trav and I clear this stuff."

"Leave it," Krisanne urged. "I'll pack it in a little while."

"Get out of here," her brother ordered. "There's a spot a little past the tree over to the right that I think you'll find pleasant and private."

Drew took Krisanne by the hand and pulled her from their campsite to the tree Patrick had indicated. His hand was warm, firm, insistent, yet she knew she could slip out of its grasp easily. He wouldn't hold her physically against her will, but did he know the kind of emotional hold he still had on her? Did she?

They stood beside each other, fingers interlocked, and looked out across a broad meadow of bluebonnets, their intensity competing with the brilliant azure sky.

She slid her hand from his, took a step to one side, and shook out the plaid blanket she'd dragged along. "Thank you for sharing today with us and for bringing Trav," she told him, all the time avoiding his eyes. "Pat really enjoys his company."

Drew grabbed two corners as she fluttered the blanket in the gentle breeze. "Trav loves being with him."

Together they spread the colorful wool on the gently sloping ground under the thick-trunked mesquite. She settled on one end of it and looked up. From where she sat the filtered shadows made Drew seem dark, imposing and strangely alone.

"You're doing a wonderful job raising him. It can't be easy by yourself."

He turned and smiled wanly, then sat beside her, his long legs outstretched. "He's a good kid. I'm very proud of him."

A good kid who's had his share of sorrow and would experience more with the death of his "uncle." "Are you sure you want him spending so much time with Pat?" She'd asked the question before but felt she had to again.

Drew didn't answer immediately. "I think it's important for both of them to have this time together." He rose, took a few steps, stopped, looked intently down at her for a brief moment, continued his pacing, then came back and squatted before her, elbows on his knees, fingers laced between them. "I know I've lost the right to ask you to love me."

She dropped her gaze, breaking eye contact. He extended an arm and swung around to sit once more beside her. Close enough for them to hold hands. Close enough for her to feel the tension in his body. Close enough to reach out and touch him.

"Why didn't you ever tell me yourself about you and Lisa? Why did you leave it to Pat to explain what had happened?" She hated the anguish creeping into her voice. But the questions had ached so long, she couldn't hold the words back. "Do you have any idea how it feels to get a card in the mail saying the man you love just married another woman?" An old fury she thought she'd put behind her flared up. It took every ounce of control to keep her voice from turning shrill. "No apology, Drew. No explanation. Not even a rationalization."

He raised his head and looked at her, his expression one of bafflement. "I wrote to you. I explained—"

"Explained? If you think a note scribbled on the back of a wedding announcement suggesting I get on with the rest of my life is an—"

"No," he protested. "My letter. The one I wrote you."

"What letter?" Her pulse quickened. "I never received any letter from you. Are you telling me now you wrote me one?"

"I did. I sent you a long—"

"Yeah, sure," she interjected. "And the check is in the mail."

His brows rose. "Kris, I sent you a long letter before the wedding." He remembered much too clearly the agony of having to confess how he'd messed up their lives.

"Well, I never received it." She heard the bewilderment in her own voice—the doubt. Had he really written to her? What had he said? Had he tried to justify what he had done? "All I got was your wedding announcement with a scribbled message on the back telling me to get on with the rest of my life."

He brought up his knees and rested his arms on them. "I wrote you..." he insisted, then shook his head, as if he could tell she didn't believe him. "I waited for you to call...ached for the sound of your voice at the same time I dreaded it."

She lowered her head, afraid he would turn to look at her, ashamed at her own cowardice in never confronting him. She'd picked up the phone half a dozen times and always slammed it down before it rang at the other end. She was the offended, not the offender, she'd reminded herself. She wouldn't crawl. She wouldn't beg for an explanation.

"It took a long time for me to accept that you weren't going to call." He took a deep fortifying breath. "Do you remember when you came down to see me the weekend after the last game?"

Oh, yes, she remembered it—perfectly. It had been the most wonderful lovemaking she'd ever experienced. Time hadn't dimmed the memory of his fingers tracing her every curve and valley, or the feel of his hard body spooned against her. His kisses—sweet and languorous; his hands—gentle, warm and shyly probing—had been devotional in their explorations. Even when intensity inevitably grew to urgency, when she gasped in delirious pleasure at the passions he unleashed, there had been a kind of awe in the way he possessed her. She could still hear the words of love he whispered in her ear, still see the vulnerability in the mysterious recesses of his eyes. No, she hadn't forgotten.

His fingers toyed now with the blades of grass between his feet. "Lisa hadn't come to me yet to announce her pregnancy." He twisted around, forcing himself to look at her. "You and I weren't officially engaged. I rationalized that at least I hadn't broken a marriage vow. The best thing, I decided, was to put it all behind me; but I also promised myself I would never be unfaithful to you again.'' He closed his eyes, opened them, then looked away. ''All I knew was that it made me more desperate to love you.''

Krisanne concentrated on the woolen blanket's intricate weave of colors, the sour taste of betrayal roiling inside her.

How could he be intimate with me after sleeping with her? How could he fall into bed with someone else, then swear he loved me? How could I have been so stupid that I didn't realize he'd been with another woman?

Like the subtle tints and bold shades of the plaid, there were so many emotions entwined within her: anger, pity, disappointment, love, and above all, shame. In some inexplicable way, she'd failed him. Otherwise, why would he have been unfaithful? If only he'd trusted her enough to acknowledge his indiscretion. She would have been upset, but she could have forgiven him—then. Now it was too late.

''Did you love her?'' she had to ask.

He gave her a crooked smile. ''For a while I wanted to—I even tried to—but Lisa wasn't always a lovable person.''

It was ignoble to feel pleased, to enjoy even a spark of satisfaction at another's misfortune. Realization that she was glad he hadn't found happiness with Lisa, simply added to her sense of guilt.

''Was she a good mother?'' It would explain his staying with her through the years.

Drew made a dismissive gesture, a wave of the hand filled with scorn. ''Lisa wasn't into changing diapers or heating formula. I had to hire someone to take care of Trav when he was a baby. Ironically, having a nanny left her more time to come and go as she pleased.''

Krisanne thought about the boy's plea to Patrick to tell his mother he missed her. "He seems to have loved her.''

"Oh, she could be a doting mother when she wanted to be. And I'm glad he remembers her that way. She was good at playing games and tickling a man's ego.''

And crushing it, Krisanne thought. "It sounds like she was incapable of loving anyone but herself.''

"Love was an amusement for her.'' Drew plucked a long blade of grass. "A lark she liked playing with a lot of men.'' He dragged a deep breath between his teeth. "I think she was having an affair when she died.'' The angry declaration tumbled out as if he couldn't hold the words back any longer. "I don't know who it was with. It doesn't matter now. But I suspect she was going to meet him when she raced out of the country club half-drunk that night. She always drove too fast. It was a rainy night. She skidded off the road, smashed into a guard rail and plunged into a ravine. The initial blow probably broke her neck.''

"I'm sorry,'' Krisanne murmured, knowing the words were inadequate.

"A home, a son...weren't enough,'' he said in a voice tinged with sarcasm, the vein in the side of his neck raised and throbbing.

Or a husband, Krisanne added to herself.

She knew now his pain wasn't just grief over his wife's death, or even the circumstances of it. Lisa Hadley had hurt her husband as only a woman can, by saying he was inadequate as a friend, a lover, a man.

Krisanne studied his profile, the anger tightening his features and the set angle of his jaw.

"We had to have a closed casket, so Trav didn't get to say goodbye. Sometimes I'm not sure he understands his mommy isn't coming back."

Krisanne shuddered. The image of the little boy standing in front of his mother's coffin tore at her heart. To have to confront death so young, to be robbed of youthful innocence at such a tender age, was heart-breaking.

"Maybe being with Pat," Drew said, "will help bring his mother's death to closure."

A gray dove fluttered to the ground a few yards away, pecked at the soil and flew off again.

"What about you?" Krisanne asked. "Have you brought Lisa's death to closure?"

Doubt and something resembling despair robbed his eyes of their luster, and for a split second she thought she saw the kind of pain that can reduce a man to tears. Then, abruptly, he looked away. She waited.

"You're lucky," he said, resting his elbows on his knees and touching the tips of his long fingers together to form the outline of a hollow sphere, a world without substance. "You and Pat have time to talk things out, to settle any differences you might have between you. You can say goodbye. Lisa and I...didn't get that chance. It's a terrible thing to admit but...I think I hated her when she died."

Krisanne's hands stopped their nervous dawdling with the pebbles she'd picked up. She recognized the emotion he referred to, having gone through something similar herself, though far less intense, when her father died. She'd felt rage, bitterness, the empty feeling of abandonment and of being robbed—this was the hardest to bear—she'd felt robbed of that last hug, of those final impassioned endearments, of the chance to tell him how much she treasured the times they'd spent together. She never got to say she loved him....

"Forgive her," Krisanne said softly. "Lisa sounds like she was a very unhappy person."

He shifted his gaze away from her toward the stark outcropping of the timeworn mesa. It had once been a mountain. Now it was reduced to an inconspicuous bump on the horizon. Except when seen close up—only then did it take on any significance.

"I don't know if I can." He rose to his feet and slipped his hands into his pockets.

How ironic, Krisanne thought, that Lisa did to him what he'd done to her. But she'd seen how devoted he was to his son, seen his willingness to help a dying friend. The humiliation of being cuckolded had scorched his soul, but his devotion to his son proved the experience hadn't cauterized his heart against affection. She wanted to reassure him, convince him he was far stronger than he gave himself credit for being.

But before she could express these thoughts, they were interrupted by Travis yelling to them, begging them to come quickly. They ran up the small incline.

"What's the matter?" Drew called out anxiously and bolted ahead of Krisanne. He crouched in front of the boy and held him at arm's length. "Are you hurt?"

The boy was crying. "I didn't do anything. Really I didn't. He was running—"

Drew's head jerked up. Patrick lay on the ground a few yards from the blanket. He looked as if he were taking a nap, except the position of one of his arms wasn't natural. He wasn't sleeping. He'd collapsed.

Drew pushed his son to the side and ran to the prostrate form.

"Tell me what happened," he ordered the boy.

Travis's words were halting. "We...we...were playing with the ball. Gofer was running between us... trying to get it. Uncle Pat was laughing 'cause...' cause Gofer kept tripping over his own feet. Then Uncle Pat stopped. He looked at me funny and fell down. All of a sudden."

Drew pressed two fingers to the side of Patrick's neck.

"He was laughing. And running with the ball..." The boy's words were choked with sobs.

Krisanne, distracted by worry, bypassed the six-year-old and fell to her knees next to her brother.

"I think he's all right," Drew assured her. "His pulse seems strong and steady."

She supported Patrick's head while Drew scooped the limp body in his arms and carried him to the colored blanket. Together they laid him down gently, arranging his feet and hands comfortably. Krisanne immediately rechecked his pulse.

"Is he dead? Did I kill him? I didn't mean—"

Krisanne's head shot up. Travis stood back watching, silent tears streaming down his forlorn face. In all their excitement they'd forgotten him. Jumping to her feet, she gathered the boy in her arms, his warm body trembling. "It's not your fault, Trav. You didn't do anything wrong. He's sleeping, that's all," she tried to assure him and herself. "He'll wake up in a few minutes."

"It's my fault," the boy blubbered. "I wanted to play ball and—"

"So did Uncle Pat," she reminded him, gently stroking his back, but the boy would not be comforted.

Drew fell to his knees in front of Krisanne. "Travis,
Son, Uncle Pat is sick. You know that. It's not your
fault. It's nobody's fault."

Krisanne's heart ached. Drew pulled them both into
a tight embrace. Travis's little body continued to quiver
in tearful spasms. She buried her head in Drew's shoulder. The gentle, perfumed breeze of spring swirled
around them as they rocked in each other's arms and
waited for the dying man to open his eyes.

OVER THE COURSE of the next week, Krisanne became
convinced Patrick was in total and complete denial of
his illness—or had miraculously recovered. At work he
was driving Nadeen crazy, demanding more and more
far-flung data, ordering exotic and expensive tests,
writing and rewriting exhaustive reports. Troimaline
was at the head of his priority list, but there were also
half a dozen other projects he didn't seem to be willing
to turn over to his staff.

He was running Krisanne ragged as well. She spent
half her day at Blessing getting tours of facilities, and
detailed briefings on every aspect of the business from
purchase of raw chemicals to packaging of final products. She was beginning to find some of the work at
Blessing fascinating, though not nearly as rewarding as
being a vet. The prospect of having to work actively
with her stepmother, however, while less daunting than
it once had been, still made her uncomfortable.

The other half of Krisanne's day was spent perform-
ing errands, everything from buying a wardrobe appropriate to her new corporate image to chasing around
town for Patrick, posting ads to sell his vintage 1948

Harley-Davidson motorcycle and his record collection. As an antidote to the depression of helping her brother dispose of his prize possessions, she checked the classifieds for suitable locations for an animal clinic and drove by those that looked promising. Sometimes she would sit in her car and stare at vacant lots, only to leave a few minutes later with the weariness of regret.

Evenings were no less hectic. Patrick had her spending a lot of time in the attic looking for papers, while he worked at their grandfather's huge rolltop desk organizing documents.

Through it all, Krisanne kept thinking about Drew's letter, or the letter he said he'd written her. But what would be the point of lying now, after all this time? Still, it seemed strange that the post office had failed to deliver the most important piece of mail in her life.

What had he actually said in it? What was his explanation? That he'd fallen in love with someone else? Would she have reacted differently if she'd received it?

The big question, of course, was how she was going to deal with him now. She couldn't deny that, in spite of the pain he'd caused her, she still felt the old chemistry stirring between them. Maybe under different circumstances she'd be willing to pursue what was obviously mutual attraction, but not now. How could she be sure of anything anymore? Her brother was dying. Her career was in turmoil. She needed to be able to use her head, to think clearly, not fall victim to her heart. He'd told her to get on with the rest of her life, and that was precisely what she would do.

One evening after work, Patrick sold his bike. Krisanne was shocked at the enormous sum the machine brought. She was also amused at the game he made out of the sale. He haggled implacably over the price. Yet she realized it wasn't the money that was important. It was the challenge. He was enjoying himself, joking and rambling on like a man without a care in the world—until the tattooed, beer-gutted biker in black shirt, black jeans, with chains hanging from his studded black belt, roared away from the house.

Patrick lingered in the middle of the driveway for several minutes, looking down the street at the last wispy gray puffs of exhaust dissipating in the cool spring air. His wide shoulders, leaner now, sagged, and he tramped up the driveway, looking frail and dejected. Krisanne realized with a jolt that another milestone had just been passed.

Friday afternoon Drew stopped by with some papers for Patrick to sign, and Krisanne sensed something might be amiss in another quarter.

"Where's Trav?" she asked, when Drew came in the kitchen door. His son hadn't been to the house all week. Soccer practice? But Drew said the Friday evening game had been canceled, and she'd been looking forward to seeing the boy.

"At home."

"Home?" She poured them each a glass of iced tea. "I thought he wanted to work with Pat on another railroad car. Did they change their minds?" When she got no response, she asked a little more anxiously, "What's going on, Drew?"

He stood by the table and took a deep swallow of the cold drink. "He's been having nightmares all week, Kris. He blames himself for what happened to Pat on Sunday."

And you're blaming yourself for not handling the

situation better. "Have you talked to him? Explained?"

He lifted a shoulder and let it fall. "As much as I can. He's not being very communicative."

Eyebrows raised, she asked, "Has he really been playing soccer all week?"

"He's been going to practice, but he's been so listless, the coach hasn't used him much."

Krisanne refilled his glass, aware of a stirring inside her she could only think of as maternal. "Do you think it would help if I talked to him?"

Relief brightened Drew's eyes. "Would you? I know it's not fair for me to put this burden on you, but—"

She smiled, secretly grateful that he wanted her help. "Let me see what I can do."

After signing the papers Drew had brought, Patrick announced he was going upstairs for a nap before dinner. Under other circumstances she would have suspected it was an excuse to leave her and Drew alone—but not now. His manic pace was catching up with him. A few minutes later, she left the house with Drew.

CHAPTER EIGHT

KRISANNE HAD NEVER been to Drew's home and couldn't quite make up her mind what to expect. Since he said his late wife hadn't been a homemaker, Krisanne tended to picture a strictly male domain, missing only centerfolds pinned on closet doors. What she found was quite different.

He lived in Oakdale, a well-established, middle-class community on the west side of the city. Single-storied, white-sided and well-maintained, the house was hardly unique. A towering bald cypress and sprawling live oak shaded the lawn, but left the carpet of grass beneath them spotty and irregular. Coral pink impatiens, newly planted in a small flower bed at the corner of the house added the single splash of color.

"Nice place," she commented as Drew pulled into the driveway and parked a few feet from the closed two-car garage.

"Lisa would have preferred living in Wood Hill Terrace," he commented as he escorted her down a narrow concrete path to the front door. "I told her we'd have to wait until we won the lottery."

Krisanne glanced at him as he got out his house key. Did Lisa not realize that Wood Hill Terrace was the last place Drew would want to live—or did she not care? The exclusive country club estates were too much like the places he'd grown up in—large, luxurious, impersonal mansions designed to impress. They were residences rather than homes. The unpretentious charm of Oakdale with its air of community and family was much closer to Drew's ideal.

He swung the door open and waved her into the small entranceway. "Anybody home?" he called out.

Closing the door, he urged her ahead into the living room. The furniture was of high quality to the point of ostentatiousness, polished woods and fine veneers with not a hint of practical Formica in sight. A few toys and a baseball mitt tossed on the couch were the only evidence that a boy lived here. To the right, she caught a glimpse of the dining room: shiny mahogany table, upholstered chairs and a glass-fronted cabinet filled with sparkling crystal and silver. She looked down at the champagne plush carpet that covered both floors.

"Muddy sneakers and wet puppy paws can be a problem," Drew acknowledged with a smile that could pass as a smirk, clearly reading her mind that the decor was not little-boy-friendly. He winked when he added, "If you let them."

A heavyset woman with severely permed gray hair, wearing a dark-blue and gray printed dress, came through the far doorway. Drew introduced her as Mrs. Chandler.

"Where's Trav?" he asked.

"In his room watching *The Lion King* again. I offered to play catch with him in the backyard, but he said he didn't feel like it."

Drew thanked her and saw her out, then he led Krisanne down the hall to Travis's room. He was about to open the door, when she put her hand on his wrist.

"Give me a few minutes alone with him," she said softly.

Drew nodded and placed a kiss on her forehead. "Thank you for doing this." He met her eyes. "I love you." Then he turned quickly and retreated.

For a moment the floor tilted and the walls swirled. How often in the last seven years had she secretly longed to hear him say he loved her? And now he had...outside a six-year-old's bedroom. Not the most romantic place in the world. But, strangely, the words meant more in this narrow passage than they might have on the vast dance floor of a lush hotel or the sparkling sands of a sun-drenched resort. So much for her resolve not to get involved again.

She pivoted back to the door and tapped on it lightly. Getting no response, she slipped it open a crack.

The boy was stretched out on his stomach across the bed, his head resting on the backs of his hands spread flat beneath his chin. He glanced up, and for a split second she saw the same intensity in his eyes, she'd seen in his father's a moment earlier.

"Hi," he mumbled despondently.

"Hi yourself," Krisanne answered cheerfully. She remained in the doorway surveying the room. Drew obviously indulged his son. Games and toys crowded the shelves lining one wall and overflowed across the floor.

One item was prominent. At the head of the bed, atop the pillow, was Ivor, the teddy bear Patrick had given him.

"Neat room."

"It's all right," he muttered, without taking his eyes off the animated animals on the TV.

"Uncle Pat and I have missed seeing you all week."

No response.

"I hear, though, you've been pretty busy playing soccer."

"Yeah."

Krisanne wondered how many times he'd seen the young lion king in the movie die, like Patrick, before his time. Not exactly the uplifting theme he needed right now. She moved to the bed and sat by his side.

"Since there was no game this evening, I thought you might come over and have dinner with Uncle Pat and me, and then maybe play with the trains."

Travis scrunched his little shoulders in a shrug.

"Uncle Pat misses you."

He made no movement, but she could tell he wasn't really watching the video. He seemed so small and vulnerable. She stroked his warm back. How unfair for someone so young to have to face the mystery of death. First his mother. Now his friend.

Gofer, who had been sleeping in the corner, jumped up on the bed and swiped a wet, pink tongue across his master's face. Krisanne had seen it many times before, the instinct of animals to comfort and soothe other animals and humans in distress. She wished people could still follow those instincts.

She leaned over, put her face close to Travis's and managed to conjure up a comical grimace. "Doggie kisses, huh? Yuck. Right?"

At first Travis refused to smile as he wiped his nose and mouth with the back of his hand. But when the rambunctious pet gave him another slobbery lick, he had no choice. "Oh, yuck." He giggled and rolled over onto his back, pulling the growing pup onto his chest. The dog's tail wagged frantically.

"Gofer sure did enjoy playing ball at the picnic last weekend."

She watched the boy stiffen and wondered if she was going too fast. "You know, that really was a fun time. I'm glad you liked my chicken. Was it as good as Colonel Sanders?"

"It was good."

Not exactly a rousing cheer for Grandma's old recipe, she thought. But it was a start.

"Uncle Pat wants to know when you're going to help him make another car."

Travis petted the dog without answering.

"I hope you're not mad at him for falling asleep in the middle of your game last Sunday?"

"No," Travis sighed, eyes intent on his puppy.

"He didn't mean to spoil your day. He got real tired, that's all. It's hard trying to keep up with a puppy dog."

"I thought he was dead," the boy mumbled shyly.

Should she tell him she'd thought so, too, and that she'd been terrified?

"You know he's sick," she reminded him calmly.

"I don't want him to die."

Her heart melted. "I don't want him to die, either." She extended her arms to him.

Suddenly, the boy bolted to a sitting position and hugged her tightly. The impulsive act made Krisanne realize how much the child needed a mother's affection. He might be his daddy's little man, but he was a small boy, too. She wanted so much for him to trust her. Glancing down at him, she saw his eyes were moist.

"Uncle Pat doesn't want to die, either." She lifted the boy's chin and turned his tearstained face toward her. "There is something you can do for him, though."

The boy raised his head. "What?"

"Be his friend."

"I'm scared," the child cried.

She pulled him to her breast and was rewarded by his burrowing deeper. "I know. Sometimes I get scared, too. But we just have to go on." She brushed a hand over his thick brown hair. "He loves you, you know, and I love you."

"I wish you were my mommy," came a muffled sob.

THE NOTE WAS on her desk when she returned from her tour of the shipping department the following Monday. "Mrs. Blessing would like you to stop by her office at your convenience."

It was silly for Krisanne to experience a slight tightening in her belly, as if she were being summoned to the principal's office. She and Celia were actually getting along quite well, but then they'd never been less than civil with each other. The problem was it never seemed to mature into anything more friendly.

What did her stepmother want to discuss? Troimaline? Patrick? Maybe get a report on Nadeen's suitability to replace him?

Celia's secretary, Bruce, greeted Krisanne with his usual charm, went to the double doors, tapped discreetly and slipped inside. He returned a moment later to say Mrs. Blessing would see her now.

Celia smiled from behind her desk when Krisanne entered, but immediately rose from the soft leather executive chair and suggested they sit by the windows. The sunny corner seemed to be her stepmother's favorite place. Bruce had already positioned himself there.

"May I get you something cold to drink, Dr. Blessing? Juice, soda?"

"Mineral water will be fine."

"You seem to be getting along quite well with Nadeen," Celia observed while they took their seats and waited for Bruce to bring their drinks.

"Pat's right," Krisanne agreed. "She's absolutely thorough and professional. Thank you," she said, looking up as Bruce deposited individual silver trays in front of the two women. Each contained an opened bottle of French mineral water and a small tumbler, already half-filled. Tiny bubbles dotted the inside surface of the crystal.

"Thank you, Bruce," Celia said. "Please hold my calls. And would you bring us some espresso in a few minutes?" She looked at Krisanne, who nodded agreement.

"Yes, Mrs. Blessing." He left the room, quietly closing the doors behind him.

Celia took a sip of her drink and rested the glass on the edge of the upholstered chair with her right hand. The room was quiet for a minute.

"Drew tells me Pat suffered a major collapse when you were out picnicking. I wish you'd told me."

Krisanne bit her lip. Her stepmother was reprimanding her for the same thing she'd accused Drew of doing—keeping her out.

"You're right," she acknowledged. "I should have been the one to tell you. I'm sorry."

Celia glanced down at her lap and smoothed an imaginary wrinkle from her skirt before continuing. "I'm glad you're taking care of Pat at home, Kris. If you hadn't, I would have, but Blessing House is the best place for him now. For you, too, I think. But please don't exclude me.''

"Of course not," Krisanne protested. "He loves you very much."

Celia's smile was sad, her words just above a whisper. "And I love him." She closed her eyes for a moment. "He's not going to be able to work here much longer. When he becomes housebound, I'd like to visit him at home every couple of days or as often as he'll let me."

"You're always welcome," Krisanne began, then caught movement out of the corner of her eye and looked over to the secretary approaching with a tray. He placed the service on the coffee table in front of his boss.

"Thank you, Bruce."

Celia poured the hot liquid from the silver pot. "Have you reached any conclusions about what you want to do with your share of Blessing?" she asked, handing Krisanne a steamy cup.

"I've been thinking about it," Krisanne acknowledged.

"May I offer an observation and then perhaps a suggestion?"

"Of course."

"The pharmaceutical business is in Pat's blood. He's good at this work, because he loves it. Just as you're a successful veterinarian, because you love helping animals. That's a special gift, too, Kris, caring for God's creatures. I wouldn't want to see you give up the vocation you're devoted to and expert at to work here. I have no doubt you could be successful, but I'm not sure you'd be happy." She paused a moment. "Drew identified some options to you when we first discussed this subject. One of them was to sell your and Patrick's share of the company to me, essentially divorcing yourself completely from Blessing Pharmaceuticals.''

Krisanne started to say something, but Celia raised a hand to forestall comment.

"Let me say right now, I don't favor that option, for two reasons. The first is that I certainly don't have the money to give you fair market value for the half interest you will own. The second and more important reason is that I'd hate to see you sell any portion of your stock to a stranger. Blessing should be owned by a Blessing. Someday you'll get married and have kids. It's something to pass on.''

"My children, if I ever have any, won't be Blessings,'' Krisanne pointed out.

"In name, they won't, but in blood they will.''

Krisanne nodded. Children. She'd been thinking a lot about them lately—especially one little boy.

"Another option Drew mentioned was for you to keep your half interest and either take Patrick's place in running the company, or act as a spoiler for decisions I make.'' She paused, a thin smile coming to her lips. "I can't say I'm very enthusiastic about that idea, either.

"Which brings us to the last option,'' Celia continued. "You can sell me a small portion of your stock, thereby giving me operational control, but retain some financial interest, or simply sell me your proxy. Either course seems reasonable to me under the circumstances.''

Krisanne had considered these options herself and come to the same conclusion. "Yes, I think you're probably right.''

"Pat tells me you're ready to open your own animal clinic."

Krisanne nodded, unable to suppress a smile of satisfaction.

"I know he's very pleased and so am I. In Dallas, is that right?"

"Yes."

"And you estimate it's going to take about half a million dollars to get established?"

"About that," Krisanne confirmed and tried to remember if she'd ever discussed an actual dollar figure with her brother.

"Are you sure that'll be enough? If you're going to build stalls and pens for large animals, you really should go first-class from the beginning. It's much lower maintenance and ultimately less expensive. Drew says you want to specialize in equine breeding and embryo transplants. It's an important and growing field and an increasingly lucrative market. I'm sure you'll do very well at it."

"Drew told you?"

Celia looked surprised at the sharpness of the question. "I told him essentially the same thing I just told you and wondered what your plans were—"

"Why didn't you ask me yourself?"

Celia's lips tightened. Clearly she was uncomfortable, though whether it was at the question or the tone, Krisanne wasn't sure. "I was going to, but he offered to find out—"

"He volunteered to do it for you?"

"Kris, I'm sorry if this has upset you. I certainly didn't intend it to—just the opposite. Drew spends quite a lot of time with you. I thought it might be easier and a bit less stressful for you to discuss your plans with him.''

Was this all a game Drew was playing? Blessing wasn't Pruit and Hadley's only client, but it was their biggest. Was he willing to do anything, including use her, to ingratiate himself with the company's CEO?

"Yes, I suppose it was easier," Krisanne conceded and took a sip of her coffee, tightening her grip on the small cup's dainty handle to hold it steady. Just as it had been easy to let him hold her in his arms. "Half a million will be enough to get started. Setting up an embryo transplant lab will come later."

Celia settled back against her chair, her elbows on its upholstered arms. "The time isn't right now, but when it is, let's discuss this further. I'd very much like to help you achieve your goals, if I can."

Krisanne nodded but felt increasingly numb. Trusting Drew with her dream had been a judgment call, and obviously she'd judged wrong. This latest breach of faith shattered any illusions that a new bond of confidence between them was possible.

Shifting slightly in her seat, Celia changed the subject. "As soon as the research analysis is ready, I'd like to have a staff meeting to discuss Troimaline with you, Drew and Patrick, if he's up to it. I'll also ask other department heads to present their input. The decision, of course, will be made by you, Patrick and me. Any problem with that?"

"No. That's fine."

Celia rose from her chair, indicating the meeting was over. "Thanks for stopping by, Kris." She walked Krisanne to the door, then paused. "Pat's dinner is this Saturday evening. Is he going to be up to it?"

Krisanne closed her eyes for a moment. "I hope so."

THE DRIVE TO Law Tower took only a few minutes, enough time for Krisanne to get her temper reasonably settled down. The building itself, a mirrored glass cube off the loop, was the quintessence of modern sophistication, reflecting the world around it but giving nothing away about the life within. Neat, well-tended but minimal landscaping separated the building from the fitted concrete brick walkway bordering the asphalt parking lot.

The inside of the building was hollow. A glass-covered atrium rose the full six stories. The surrounding balconies were edged with flower boxes trailing pothos and English ivy on every other floor. The alternate layers of light and dark green produced a pleasant atmosphere in the bright sunlight spilling in from the blue sky overhead.

Krisanne took the birdcage elevator to the top. Pruit and Hadley occupied fully one half of the floor. The reception area carpets were thick and lush; the solid, tasteful furniture gleamed. The walls, lined with thick volumes, boasted of order and the tradition of the law.

A receptionist walked in from the office on the left, and Krisanne immediately wondered if being young, slim, blond and buxom were qualifications for the job. Surely not. No reputable law firm would be guilty of such sexist hiring practices. Besides, this young woman might be very good at her job.

"May I help you?" the receptionist asked.

"I'm Krisanne Blessing. I'd like to see Mr. Hadley."

"Dr. Blessing!" a man's voice called behind her. She turned and faced Drew's partner. Suntanned, golden-haired and clean-shaven, Warren Pruit had the look and style of success in a beautifully tailored three-

piece, gray pinstripe suit. According to Drew, the
man's self-assured confidence had earned him a better
than average success rate in the courtroom. She wondered if charm and good looks might also be factors—
at least with female jurors. She'd met him briefly at
the opening of the new Blessing building, a ceremony
Drew had not attended, because Travis had been ill
with chicken pox.

"Mr. Pruit." She offered her hand. "How are you?"

His grip was gentle. "Call me Warren. And please
accept my sympathy on your brother's illness. A terrible tragedy. If there's anything I can do to help, you
have only to ask."

"That's very kind of you."

"Krisanne?"

This time the voice came from the other end of the
room. She didn't have to turn to identify its deep resonance. Drew was standing in the doorway to the right.

"I need to talk to you," she said, trying to keep her
tone from sounding strident.

He stepped forward. "Has something happened to
Patrick?"

She glanced at Pruit and the receptionist who'd migrated to one side when Drew entered, their attempts
at poker-faced smiles failing to disguise their curiosity.

"Is there someplace we can talk?" Krisanne asked
Drew.

He raised an eyebrow, then wordlessly motioned her
into his office. The room was large and square. The
windows that swept from wall to wall gave a glorious
view of the small city, as it stretched toward the north-
ern horizon and the twin mesas where they'd picnicked
amidst bluebonnets. He directed her to the chair in

front of his battleship-size desk, but she remained standing, her back straight. He closed the door.

"I trusted you," she said, sounding more hurt than angry, not sure at this point which emotion she felt more deeply.

He stood before her, his face apprehensive, his tone flat. "Would you mind telling me what I'm supposed to have done?"

"You've been spying on me for Celia."

A muscle in his jaw flinched. "Spying?"

Krisanne's hands gripped the back of the leather chair and for a moment her courage flagged. "When you asked how much money I needed to open my vet clinic, it wasn't out of curiosity or concern for me. You were doing Celia's dirty work."

He took a deep breath, his chest expanding. "I resent that."

"She admitted it to me."

He didn't move from his position in the middle of the room. "You told me what it would cost to start the kind of animal hospital you want," he said in a voice deep in resonance and rich in anger. "I didn't have to pry it out of you. You seemed quite willing to volunteer the information."

"Spoken like a true lawyer." She looked him dead in the eye, though her knees were beginning to feel wobbly. "It was a private conversation. I didn't expect it to be relayed to Celia."

"I didn't relay the conversation," he objected. "I told her what you would need to start your own practice."

She thought about the memories they'd recounted, and the feeling of rightness in sharing her dream with him. "I opened my heart to you, Drew. I bared my soul. And you've used it as part of a business deal. You deceived me.''

"Deceived you?'' His hands were tightly clenched. "To what end, Kris? To get you what you wanted?'' His tone turned frigid, though his eyes blazed. "You don't give a damn about Blessing, and you don't give a damn about Celia. Fine. You've got no legal obligation to give a damn about anyone or anything. But how about a moral duty to care about the business your father and grandfather…and your brother devoted their lives to? Then there's the question of loyalty and consideration for the woman your father loved and who's never done anything to harm you.'' He took a deep breath. "You want to think the worst of me? Go ahead, maybe I deserve it. Maybe I've lost any chance of ever earning your respect. But let me set the record straight. I haven't spied on you. I haven't betrayed any confidences. I haven't used you, and I never will.''

His outburst set her back on her heels, but the instinct to fight rather than retreat had her instantly going on the offensive. She paced nervously in front of the broad expanse of window.

"I'm not some generic Blessing that you plug in for a father or a brother,'' she reminded him in measured tones. "I'm Dr. Krisanne Blessing, D.V.M. It took me eight years to earn those letters after my name, and I'm damn proud of them.'' She stopped and faced him.

"No one is going to make this decision for me, Drew. I can negotiate my own arrangements without your interference, thank you very much.'' She stared hard at him—and wondered if her eyes betrayed the same pain and longing she saw in his. "I don't like being pushed, and I don't like being manipulated.''

"I'm not manip—''

"The hell you're not," she flared back.

Spinning around, away from his accusing glare, she took a deep breath. His allegations stung. The suspicion that in some way he might be right hurt even more. Her heart was pounding when she turned again to confront him. "If Celia wanted to know how much capital I'd need to open a vet clinic, she could have asked me herself. I would have told her. Why did she have to go through you? And why did you let yourself be used?"

Walking over to the front of his desk, he leaned woodenly against its edge. His voice was level when he responded, but there was a tightness in it. "Did it ever occur to you, Kris, that maybe Celia is as uncomfortable with you as you seem to be with her? I gather in the past Pat's been the intermediary between the two of you. Under the circumstances, I didn't think it was right to bother him with this, so I offered to help."

Another revelation—Krisanne hadn't consciously realized her brother had been playing mediator, but it didn't take a moment's reflection to acknowledge it was true.

Drew crossed his arms over his chest. "I've got nothing to apologize for, Kris, and neither does Celia. I could have told you I was asking for her, but why should I have to? Why should what you need be a secret? All we're trying to do is help you reach your goal." He straightened, strode to the door and opened it wide. "Now I think you'd better leave before one of us says something we'll both regret." His tone softened slightly. "I'll see you at the dinner Saturday night."

Krisanne stared openmouthed at the man standing, stiff shouldered, a few feet away. She'd accused him of duplicity. He'd counterattacked by calling her selfish and ungrateful. And now he was throwing her out of his office.

Tightening her jaw, her head held high, she crossed the room and walked out the door. But in the elevator going down to the ground floor, she bit her lip.

Was she really perceived as unfeeling and self-centered? She'd dedicated her life to caring for people's animals. She'd come home to be with a dying brother. Hardly the actions of a self-absorbed egotist. Yet there was something in what Drew said that struck a sensitive chord, some element in his charge that cut deeper than the surface of his caustic remarks.

CHAPTER NINE

"DREW SAYS I'VE become self-centered," Krisanne commented late that evening, as she and Patrick quietly worked on a jigsaw puzzle spread across the living room coffee table.

He leaned forward to fit the last piece of the outer edge in place. "You have to love yourself before you can love anyone else, Kris."

It wasn't the response she'd expected or wanted to hear. But then, honesty was one of the reasons she'd always respected her brother and felt she could turn to him for advice and direction.

"So you agree with him? You think I'm selfish, too?"

His head down, he moved several pieces around. "If that's what he said, he's wrong. You're not selfish, but you have become defensive."

"What do you mean?"

He untangled a jumble of pieces and spread them out. "Drew hurt you. He didn't mean to, but he did. You didn't deserve it, but it happened. Now you've got to get past your fear of ever being hurt again."

She wanted to argue with him, tell him he was wrong, that she wasn't afraid, but he was right. Wasn't that exactly what she'd told Drew the first time he tried to kiss her, that she didn't want to get caught up in loving him again?

"Ever since Drew left you," Patrick continued without looking up from the table, "you've been holding yourself back, afraid to make commitments. Do you think it's just bad luck that none of your relationships have lasted?"

She picked up two pieces and experimented with fitting them together, even though it was obvious they didn't match. "Figured I was slumming, huh?"

He gave her a sidelong grin. "You can joke about it all you want, but you know it's true." He turned his attention back to the board, but she knew he wasn't concentrating on it anymore, either. "You've been searching for the special someone you lost. Now you've found him and you have a chance to start all over again. You've both suffered enough for what should never have happened. Learn from it. Grow from the experience." He snapped a piece in place. "Just remember you don't have forever."

Now it was her turn to look over at him. She didn't like the bent the conversation had taken, but she recognized that he had things he wanted to say, thoughts to express that had probably been swirling around in his head for some time.

"I've had a good life, Kris," he said in the same distracted undertone. "Better than a lot of people get to have." He ran his hand across a pile of pieces, spreading them out for better viewing. "More time would have been nice. But there are worse things than dying and worse ways to die."

An ache settled in her chest, an all too familiar tightness in her throat. She stared at the fragmented puzzle and joined her hands in front of her, lest he see them shaking.

"Those months I spent in Bosnia taught me a lot, Kris."

"It must have been rough over there," she commented. He'd spent three months in the Balkan province a couple of years ago when his reserve outfit had called for volunteers to go on a peacekeeping mission to the war-torn region. He'd talked about the country and its people when he came back, but as a tourist would rather than a combatant.

"Staying alive was a daily struggle for those people," he went on. "There were so many refugees—old men, women and children scavenging for basic necessities. Life is so precious, yet it was so tenuous there, and death so undignified."

He moved a small section of the puzzle he'd assembled and fitted it into a corner. She glanced over at him, but there wasn't even the subtlest grin of satisfaction on his face in doing so.

"At least I'll be able to die at home in bed with some dignity." He took a sip of the soft drink he'd been nursing for the past hour. It couldn't have been cold any longer, but he didn't seem to care. "You can't imagine how grateful I am to you for that gift."

He leaned back against a couch cushion. "There are so many things I wish I'd done," he said softly. "Married...had children. When I remember what this house felt like with a family in it...and I look at the relationship Drew has with his son, I know what I've missed. Don't you miss it, too, Sis?"

KRISANNE WASN'T LOOKING forward to the dinner for her brother Saturday evening. It was supposed to be a fond farewell, a celebration of all he'd achieved. Except she didn't feel like celebrating. Patrick was too young, his life too short. Somehow she couldn't get the picture out of her mind of him taking a nosedive into his soup or slithering out of his chair and under the table just as someone was singing his praises. In a movie or on the evening news it might be comical. In real life it would be a nightmare for everyone.

Patrick's stipulation that there be no black ties didn't mean it was going to be a cutoffs and T-shirt affair. Through a side window, Krisanne watched Drew park his Mercedes, get out, and stride up the brick path. He was wearing a white dinner jacket with a paisley cummerbund and matching bow tie.

When she opened the beveled glass front door, he stopped on the top step and gawked. The recriminations of earlier in the week were all but forgotten and her whole body tingled as he surveyed her. He started with her hair, his gaze gradually slipping down to her bare shoulders. Her nipples puckered as he contemplated her breasts, and she felt a pleasant warmth as his eyes skittered across her waist and hips. His exploration made her feel very feminine, appreciated and…desirable. She was glad now she had stopped off at the little boutique downtown and bought the gold-embroidered, white silk evening dress.

"My God," Drew exclaimed in hushed awe, "you're beautiful."

Joy bubbled inside her and escaped as a chuckle. "I'm not quite sure if that's a compliment or an indictment of my usual wardrobe."

She laughed again when he got flustered. "I didn't mean it that way…I mean…"

"Thank you, Drew," she said, delighted by his discomfort. "I think you look very handsome tonight, too."

He tripped on the runner as he entered the hallway. Yes, she decided, it had been worth putting her hair up and taking the extra time to do her makeup.

"Pat'll be down in a minute," she informed him. "But before he gets here, I want to apol—"

They turned at the sound of feet clattering down the stairs.

Ever flamboyant, never conventional, Patrick was wearing dress jeans with his tuxedo jacket, a Ross plaid cummerbund and matching, oversized, drooping bow tie. His trademark high-heeled cowboy boots were hand-tooled, dark green ostrich.

"Ready?" he asked with a self-satisfied and mischievous twinkle in his eyes.

He looks so vibrant, Krisanne thought, so full of life. His cheek bones were a little more prominent, his blue eyes a bit haunting, but they only gave him a forbidding, mysterious look.

Celia had booked the Crystal Ballroom at the Spring Top Hotel, paying a premium because someone else already had it reserved. Krisanne had expected fifty or sixty people, perhaps up to a hundred with husbands and wives. The room had a posted capacity of two hundred and fifty, but she was sure the crowd was bigger than that.

Celia had arranged an open bar, and people were taking liberal advantage of it. Stories, old and new, were being recounted. Jokes, many of which were probably also vintage, were being played out with howls of laughter. Backs were being slapped in the convivial bonhomie that reminded Krisanne more of a wedding or family reunion than a farewell party. There wasn't a hint of sadness in the place.

"Who are all these people?" she asked Drew as

members of the crowd shouted greetings to her brother
and patted rather than slapped him on the back.

"I told you he had a lot of friends."

Celia appeared as if out of nowhere. Dressed regally
in a full-length gown of ecru lace over royal blue satin,
she wore a small, understated tiara of seed pearls in
her elegantly coifed blond hair, and a double strand of
pearls.

"Right on time," Celia said with a majestic sweep
of her hand. She placed herself between her two stepchildren, linked her arms with theirs, and ushered them
through the crowded room.

Krisanne was tempted to ask if the press of people
was bothering her, but the woman showed no sign of
discomfort. Was it iron-willed discipline or the twenty-
foot-high ceilings and bright lights that made the closeness bearable? Whichever it was, Krisanne had to admire her grit.

A waiter appeared with a tray of drinks: white wine
for Krisanne, imported beer for Drew and mineral water for Patrick. Patrick waved and shouted greetings
and comments to a dozen people as they sipped their
cocktails for a few minutes before taking their seats.
Immediately the other guests took theirs. Servers ma-
terialized and began distributing the main course.
Chicken diablo with wild rice. Salads were already on
the tables.

Krisanne sat to the left of her brother facing the room
full of people. Drew was on her other side, and she
had the pleasantly stimulating feeling he was looking
more at her than the other guests.

The service, though not rushed, was efficiently
prompt. They weren't quite finished with their honey

mousse dessert when Drew took the podium set up at the far end of the head table.

"Ladies and gentlemen, may I have your attention, please. We are here tonight to honor a man who's already taken most of the honors..."

"You mean the virgins," someone in the back of the room bellowed.

Someone else called out, "Hey, Pat, have you heard? Too much sex makes you bald?"

Wide-eyed and pretending to be shocked, Patrick ran a hand through his hair, touching the little spot on the back of his head that was beginning to thin.

"Could be, Charlie," he shouted back. "It's all a matter of priorities. You see, the good Lord gives us just so many hormones. Now, if you want to use yours to grow hair, well, you go right ahead."

Everyone laughed. Not at Patrick, but at Charlie, who had his shoulder-length brown hair tied in a pony-tail.

It went on like that for nearly an hour, Patrick giving as good as he got. Finally, Drew announced a short intermission so tables could be cleared, drinks replenished, smokers duck outside for a quick one, and people could visit the rest rooms.

"How are you doing?" Krisanne heard Celia ask Patrick. "If you'd like to take a rest, there's a room with a couch across the hall you—"

Kris half expected her brother to snap at the suggestion. Instead she heard, "No, I'm fine, but thanks for asking."

"Everything is going so well," Krisanne confided to Drew when Patrick wandered a few feet off to talk to some people.

"It should," he replied. "Celia has everything timed

down to the minute, so it won't last too long. She doesn't want him to keel over, either.''

Krisanne ran her tongue across her teeth. "Drew, I owe you an apology for the things I said the other day. I guess I didn't realize how much the stress has been getting to me. I overreacted. I'm sorry."

He brushed his knuckles along her bare arm, their gentle friction reverberating through her like the chords of a bass violin.

"I owe you one, too," he said solemnly, then smiled. "Celia warned me you were vulnerable right now. I should have explained. Instead I was... bumptious."

She put her finger to his lips to silence him and found them soft and tender. "Can we forget about this?"

His eyes darkened as she started to pull her hand away. He grabbed her wrist in a firm grip and brought her still extended finger to his mouth. Slowly, his eyes locked on hers, he kissed its tip. "I'd forgotten how beautiful you are when you're angry."

"Bull—" But she couldn't help laughing.

The balance of the program was much shorter and more serious. The mayor declared that the first of the following month would be Patrick Blessing Day, and the local newspaper editor announced a writing contest for young people, "Why I want to be a Biochemist." The winner would receive a savings bond for college in Patrick's name.

Finally, Celia rose to speak and the hall went expectantly quiet. Krisanne knew from the way her stepmother's hands fluttered on the podium that she was less at ease than she seemed. But there was a rare whimsical sparkle in her eyes, too.

"I've known Patrick Blessing for less than fifteen years. He was a teenager when I married his father. A kid with long hair and a propensity to play the guitar at two o'clock in the morning. I must admit neither trait was particularly endearing at the time."

"That's because you don't appreciate fine strumming," Patrick piped up.

Celia sucked in her cheeks. "No," she drawled, then paused. "It's because I do."

"Ooh," could be heard throughout the room.

"Critics," Patrick exclaimed with a resigned shrug.

"But I also recognized," the hostess continued after everyone had settled down, "an intellect that approached pure genius, and a determination and integrity that made that quality useful and productive. I discovered I had a stepson who was a lover of truth and a champion of right."

"You forgot my sense of humor," Patrick appended.

Celia gave him a withering look. "As much as I try, I can't forget the horny toad in the cornflakes box or the lizard in my bathtub."

After a few more compliments, quips and barbs, Celia moved over to a heavy steel tripod that had been set up during the intermission.

"It is, therefore, with pride and gratitude that I now announce that from this day forward, the pharmaceutical laboratories at Blessing Corporation will have a new name."

She removed the red velvet cloth draped over the exhibit and uncovered a large slab of polished white marble. Affixed to it was a bronze medallion showing a life-sized profile of Patrick. In a strong, clear voice, Celia read the words under it, also in bronze: "The Patrick Blessing Research Center."

The entire banquet hall rose to its collective feet and filled the room with warm, enthusiastic applause.

Only Patrick remained seated through the long ovation, his head bowed. For a chilling moment Krisanne was afraid the excitement was too much for him, and he might be having another spell. But then she saw him bite his lip and knew he was simply overcome with emotion. She also looked over at Celia and was moved by the tears poised on the woman's lashes.

At last, Patrick rose and went to the podium to use the microphone. His eyes, too, were glassy.

"To Celia Maddox Blessing," he said when the room had finally quieted, "I say thank you for giving me the opportunity to expand and explore. To my sister, Krisanne, and my friend, Drew Hadley, thank you for being here for me. And to all of you, I say, thank you for the privilege of getting to meet and know you—and God bless you all."

THE FOLLOWING MONDAY morning, Patrick hardly touched the buttered, whole wheat toast, orange juice or strong black coffee Krisanne had laid out for him. Lethargically he climbed the stairs to finish dressing for work.

Drew accepted the cup Krisanne handed him and sat at the scarred wooden table. She slid onto the seat opposite him, propped her elbows on its edge, and held the cup to her lips with both hands. "Pat napped most of yesterday. I've never seen him so listless. It's as if he's given up."

Drew sipped. "He's been pushing himself pretty hard, Kris. Maybe it's all catching up and he has to recharge his batteries."

"I guess the excitement of the farewell dinner—"
She broke off with a stifled sob.

Drew was instantly out of his chair and around the
table to crouch at her side. He could feel the tension
in her rigid spine, as he stroked her back. He wanted
to say something to reassure her. But what? Words
were inadequate to relieve the pain he saw riffling
through her. Nothing he could say or do would lessen
the agony of watching someone you love die.

"I need to call Dr. Chaffee," she announced.

But putting off what she knew she'd hear, she rinsed
out the juice glasses they'd used, wiped down the coun-
tertop, and added dish detergent to the shopping list
tacked to the corkboard by the refrigerator.

Finally, she went to the wall phone by the back door
and dialed a number from a card wedged behind it.

Drew leaned against the counter beside her, resisting
the urge to reach up and brush back a lock of golden
hair gone astray. She moved the phone to her other ear,
so he could listen in on her conversation. He inclined
toward her, inhaling her scent, his bare arm touching
hers, the plastic instrument forming an obstacle to the
intimacy they needed.

"The disease is running its natural course," Chaffee
reminded her. "Unless your brother's willing to un-
dergo intensive radiation and chemotherapy immediately, there's really nothing left to do. I must be honest
with you, Dr. Blessing. At this stage—"

"I know. It's too late."

"I'm sorry," he said.

She hung up the phone, tears blurring her vision.
Stop crying, she commanded herself, but her emotions
rebelled against following orders. She turned to Drew,
her head down, her shoulders rounded in defeat.

"Why did I do that? Why did I humiliate myself by calling Chaffee and asking stupid questions when I already knew the answers?" He opened his arms and nestled her in an embrace. "The answers aren't going to change," she murmured into his chest. "What did I expect?"

He leaned back, cupped her chin in his hand and raised it, forcing her to meet his gaze. "You wanted him to tell you someone had just found a miracle cure over the weekend." His eyes were deep and sympathetic. "You wanted him to tell you Pat is going to be all right."

"You must think I'm a fool."

His voice was a soothing rumble in her ear, as he slipped his hands around her back and pulled her gently to him. "I think you love your brother very much and would do anything in the world to help him."

She clung to him, resting her cheek against his shoulder; then the tears came. Great scalding streams cascading down her cheeks, seeping into the corners of her mouth. Salty tears. Patrick was leaving her, and there was nothing she could do about it.

A quiet cough had both Krisanne and Drew turning abruptly toward the doorway from the hall. Patrick stood there, his shirt collar open. His flamboyant tie hung slack around his scrawny neck.

"I think it's time to call Hospice," he said.

AT PRECISELY FOUR o'clock, the doorbell rang.

Krisanne answered it to find a woman of perhaps forty-five standing on the front porch. She had a smooth, milk chocolate complexion and quick, brown eyes that seemed to take in the scene at a glance.

"Dr. Blessing? I'm Pamela Rayburn. From Hospice."

She looked as fresh and cool as sparkling spring sunshine in a sleeveless pantsuit that was the color of butter. A beautiful woman, Krisanne realized. Tall and with a regal bearing, she carried herself with a quiet dignity and self-confidence that was appealing and reassuring.

Krisanne showed her into the library where Patrick was busy sorting through papers in the desk. He rose from his chair, shook her hand and thanked her for coming.

"Let's go to the living room," Krisanne suggested.

She had already set out a tray with a pitcher of tea, ice and tall glasses. They sat on opposite couches in front of the cold fireplace and sipped their drinks. Pamela asked a dozen questions about the old house, which Patrick enthusiastically answered. A good technique, Krisanne deduced, for putting everyone at ease.

Ms. Rayburn smiled sympathetically. "Would you mind leaving me alone with your brother for a few minutes?"

"Of course." Krisanne got up and walked to the door. "I'll be out back if you need me."

She went to the low-walled garden that lay in a straight line from the kitchen door, on the west side of the garage. The afternoon sun cloaked her shoulders and neck, as she crossed the back lawn and slipped past the wrought iron gate. The colors that greeted her were dazzling.

She knelt to pull weeds, her thoughts drifting to the woman from Hospice. What would possess a woman to spend her time with dying people? How does she cope with the constant loss of life? One would have to have a special gift to comfort the terminally ill, and the people who survive them.

"What a lovely spot."

Krisanne was startled by the woman's voice overhead. Only then did she notice the cream-colored canvas skimmers in front of her. She'd been so preoccupied with her own reflections, she'd become oblivious to the world around her. She climbed to her feet.

"It's so peaceful." Pamela spread her hands and breathed deeply, as she took in the sight and smell of nature's offerings. Somewhere off in the distance a blackbird cawed.

Forcing herself to laugh, Krisanne noted, "It hasn't always been like this. Pat and I spent hours as kids playing games here and soaking each other with the garden hose. Over there—" she pointed to a vine-covered depression a few yards away "—we used to make mud pies."

"These are beautiful roses." Pamela cupped her fingers around a crimson florabunda and bent to inhale its scent. "I love gardens, but I've never had any luck growing anything. On the other hand, my daughter could make a rock bloom."

Krisanne clapped her hands to shake off the dirt clinging to her gloves and removed them. The two women went over and sat on the angled wooden benches facing the weathered stone birdbath Great Grandpa Blessing had given his wife on their silver wedding anniversary.

"How old is your daughter?" Krisanne asked.

"Penny just turned twelve. She starts junior high next fall, and frankly it terrifies me. She's a good kid and I'm very proud of her, but she's growing up so fast. I'm afraid for her sometimes, because the world out there is scary.''

''Yes, it is,'' Krisanne agreed. *Death is scary. So is love.*

''Your brother's a remarkable young man. He seems to have come to terms with what's happening. What about you? How are you handling it?''

Krisanne looked down at her hands and realized she was wringing them, rolling one inside the other. She stopped. ''Depends on when you ask me. Sometimes I think I actually forget he's dying, then I remember and get angry—at him for giving up, at myself for not being able to do anything. I tried to get him to take therapy, but...''

''It's his decision,'' Pamela reminded her quietly.

''I know.''

''But it's still hard to accept.''

''He's not even thirty years old.'' Krisanne took a deep breath. ''How about another glass of tea? I'm thirsty. Or coffee if you prefer?''

''Tea would be fine.''

Just then, Drew's Mercedes pulled up in front of the detached garage. The sun glinting off the windshield made Krisanne blink, but it was the driver who made her pulse trip.

''I didn't realize it had gotten so late,'' she said, feeling relief at his arrival—as if it changed anything. ''That's Drew Hadley, a friend of ours. He called just before you arrived to say he was running about an hour behind schedule.''

''Patrick mentioned him.''

Krisanne and Pamela stood up. Krisanne's attention was riveted to the man unfolding his long legs from behind the steering wheel. There was a grimness behind the smile he offered the visitor from Hospice, as he opened the ornamental iron gate and approached. Krisanne made the introductions.

"Before we go inside," Pamela said, after shaking his hand, "it might be a good idea if the three of us talked privately."

They stepped back to the benches facing the bird-bath. Drew sat beside Krisanne, folding her hand in his.

"As you know, we don't have a dedicated Hospice facility here in Coyote Springs like they do in some big cities. Most of our clients are cared for at home by relatives or in nursing homes." Pamela paused and looked at each of them in turn, then addressed Krisanne. "Your brother told me how fortunate he feels in having the two of you with him, and that he's very grateful to you for allowing him to stay here in this beautiful old house. It obviously means a great deal to him."

Forlorn sadness washed over Krisanne even as the sweet scent of roses wafted to her on the gentle breeze. She looked up at the stately old residence, a monument to the past. Drew tightened his grip on her hand, drawing her attention back to the present. His closeness and warm caress were reassuring, yet they couldn't relieve the lump forming in her throat.

"Your brother seems to be well organized," Pamela went on, her dark eyes calm, almost restful. "He's already taken care of a lot of details—his will, insurance policies, deeds and titles—but I think you realize he's running out of energy."

"He's a lot weaker than he was even a few days ago," Drew observed. "What happens next?"

"Physically, he'll be able to get around on his own

for a few more weeks," Pamela said. "That's why re-
solving unfinished business is important to him at this
stage. Knowing everything is taken care of will make
it easier for him to let go later, when he begins to lose
his mobility and independence."

Krisanne nodded dully, a sudden chill penetrated to
the bone, making her shiver in the early summer heat.
Only Drew's hand clutching hers felt warm.

"As time goes on, he'll tire more easily, take more
frequent naps. Physical activity will tax him, and he'll
become very focused on a few specific things that he
wants to get done to the exclusion of all others. He'll
need a wheelchair."

"I'll get one sent over tomorrow," Drew said.

"He might resist using it at first," Pamela warned,
"but having it available will make it easier for him
when the time comes. He'll be able to wheel himself
around for a while, but eventually even that will be too
much for him, and he'll have to depend on you for his
mobility. He'll start drowsing off in the chair perhaps,
then spending more time in bed, until finally he won't
be interested in even getting up."

Krisanne's heart ached at the thought of her brother
becoming dependent on her for the most elementary
things. Her big, strong brother reduced to childlike
helplessness.

"What about pain?" she asked.

"Normally there isn't any pain associated with his
form of cancer, just a gradual loss of strength and stam-
ina. Sometimes, however, the breakdown of the immune system leads to other complications that can be
painful. He'll bruise easily, and of course, as his
strength fades, he'll be more prone to fall and hurt
himself. If that happens, Dr. Bicker, our Hospice phy-

sician, will prescribe whatever medication it takes to keep him comfortable. Since his condition is terminal, we don't have to worry about addiction. The doctor can give him whatever is needed in sufficient doses to keep him free of pain.''

Krisanne's fingers tightened in Drew's while Pamela Rayburn talked in an even, conversational way that gave no hint of the devastating emotional content of her words.

''I also understand your brother's bedroom is upstairs,'' she went on. ''If at all possible, I suggest you consider moving him downstairs. That'll make it easier for you to care for him, and he won't feel so isolated.''

''I can move his bed downstairs,'' Drew offered.

Pamela nodded. ''If he's agreeable, I recommend you get a hospital bed. Right now he doesn't need one, but later when he becomes weaker and bedridden, being able to adjust the contour of the bed can help alleviate the discomfort of being confined to it. It'll also make it easier for you to care for him.''

''Kris, I told you I want to be here for you,'' Drew said. ''School will be out for the summer soon. When Pat becomes bedridden, I think Trav and I ought to move in here so I can help you.''

She shook her head. ''I can't ask you to do that, Drew.''

He stroked the back of her hand. ''You're not asking me. I'm the one asking you. I was going to invite Pat to stay with Trav and me until you offered to bring him home here. Please, let me do this, Kris. For Pat…for me…and for you.''

''But…what about Trav? Do you really think it's good for him to be here when Pat is dying?''

Drew turned to Pamela and told her about his wife's

sudden death in a car accident almost a year before, and his concern that his son didn't fully comprehend the nature of his mother's leaving him.

"It's your decision, of course," Pamela said, "but let me point out that children are incredibly resilient. Death is the natural end of life. It's part of the living process. If your son hasn't put closure to his mother's death, this might help him accept the fact that she's gone."

Drew looked intently at Krisanne, his eyes imploring.

"We'll have to ask Pat," she responded.

They returned to the house. Patrick was in the living room going through an old photograph album when they entered.

"Hey, Pat," Drew greeted him. "I've got some more pictures for your collection." He held out the thick manila envelope he'd brought with him from the car. Krisanne hadn't paid any attention to it, thinking it was more paperwork for her brother to sign. But when Patrick opened the flap, he extracted a large, handsomely framed print of the formal picture they'd posed for in the field of bluebonnets.

"I didn't know you were so good with a camera." Patrick smiled, his Adam's apple bobbing before he added, "Thanks."

For the next hour they talked about the arrangements Pamela had recommended. Patrick agreed to getting a hospital bed.

"Where should we put it?" Krisanne asked.

"I think the library," he said. "I can see the rose garden from there, and it's right across the hall from the kitchen, which will make things easier for you."

"Oh, I see. You intend to keep me in the kitchen

baking you brownies,'' she quipped, not very convincingly.

"I hadn't considered it, but it's a good idea.'' He gave her a brief, crooked grin. "The…library, I'll be able to hear Trav playing with the trains when he comes over.''

"Actually,'' Krisanne said, "Drew has suggested that he and Travis move in here to help me take care of you.''

Patrick looked startled, then uncomfortable. He shifted his gaze from Drew to her and back again. "Are you sure?''

"Absolutely. I'll ask Trav, but my guess is his reaction will be 'awesome.'''

Patrick chuckled briefly, then turned serious again. "What about you, Sis?''

"We'll do whatever you want.''

Again he looked from her to Drew, but this time it was with a gleam in his eye, and she knew the decision had been made. "I think it's a great idea.''

"I'll stop by in a few days,'' Pamela glanced at her watch and rose to her feet, "or you can call me anytime.''

"Thanks for coming,'' Patrick said, rising. "When you come back, I'll give you a tour of this old mausoleum.''

"I'm looking forward to it.'' She offered her hand, which he took.

Krisanne and Drew accompanied her to the front door. Pamela picked up the portfolio she'd left on the hall table and removed several pamphlets and a business card. She handed them to Krisanne.

"Pat is my patient,'' she said, "but I'm here for you, too. If you ever have any questions, need help or just want to talk, call me—any time, at work or at home. Even in the middle of the night.''

After the door was closed, Krisanne glanced at the literature in her hand. "About Grief." "About Overcoming Loneliness." "When Your Brother or Sister Has Cancer." "Gone From My Sight—The Dying Experience."

A shudder rippled down her spine. Drew, who had read them over her shoulder, took them from her grasp and placed them on the hall table. They held each other in a tormented embrace, two aching hearts buffeted between the eternities of love and death.

CHAPTER TEN

HOURS LATER, DREW tucked Travis into bed, read him a story, and fetched him the sip of water he always remembered he wanted only after the lights were turned out. From there he migrated into the back bedroom, the one Lisa had used as a dressing room. He wasn't exactly sure why he'd retreated to this no-man's land, except that he had to keep busy, and there was still cleaning out to be done.

He'd grown weary of her antics long before she died, but he hadn't wished her ill. Her sudden death had nevertheless engulfed him in a dingy gray guilt that had surprised him. He'd done his best for her, given her a comfortable life—and a level of freedom few men would tolerate. He'd also been faithful to her in spite of her own infidelity. Yet, when she died, he'd felt not just sorrow, but remorse and shame, because, he confessed to himself, deep down inside he had been untrue to her. He'd given her his mind and his body, but not his heart. That had always belonged to Krisanne.

He looked around the pink-and-white room. Over by the mock French provincial dressing table the champagne carpet was stained from spilled cosmetics. The accordion doors of the walk-in closet gaped open. He'd donated most of Lisa's lavish wardrobe to a local charity a week or two after her death, wondering as he did so what kind of demand there could possibly be in used clothing stores for gold lamé cocktail dresses with matching pumps, silk and satin evening gowns and Donna Karan suits. There had also been enough shoes, loose and in boxes, to make Imelda Marcos smile.

Giving it all away had been easy. The only things left now were her jewelry and more personal items. He was sure there wouldn't be anything he'd want to keep, no mementos to cherish. He had to consider his son, though. Lisa, for all her faults, was the boy's mother. Perhaps he could find one particular item, some trinket he could give the child as a happy reminder of the woman who'd borne him.

Lisa hadn't been a very neat or organized person. In the built-in drawers, he found purses full of worthless receipts, chewing gum wrappers and sticky breath lozenges, half-used compacts and lipsticks. On one of the back shelves of the closet, he discovered a half-full box of condoms. He winced, took a deep breath and threw them into the black plastic garbage bag he'd positioned in the middle of the room.

He sat on the edge of the vanity bench, his back to the smudged mirror, elbows resting on his knees while he examined his cuticles. The sight of the foil wrappers should hurt. He should feel cheated. Strangely, he felt nothing. They'd had sex often enough. She'd given him the release he needed. But they'd never made love, not the way he remembered the intimacy he'd shared with Krisanne. It wasn't the pleasure of sex he'd missed, but its joy and sense of fulfillment. For a while he'd blamed himself for Lisa's straying, convincing himself she was seeking in other men the satisfaction he couldn't give her. With time, however, he'd come to realize that even if he had been the greatest lover in the world, he wouldn't have been enough—not for

Lisa. She'd been looking for something in those men that she needed to find in herself. Sadly she never had. There was something else he'd learned, too. Had Lisa been a faithful wife, she wouldn't have been enough for him, either. Only one person could fill that void. Only one woman could make him feel complete as a man.

Somehow, he had to win her back.

THE FRENETIC GALLOP Patrick had set for himself the first few weeks after Krisanne came back from Austin had gradually given way to a more leisurely trot, and now, as May slipped into June, he seemed to be breaking down into a walk. Drew or Krisanne continued to drive him to Blessing every day, but only for half days. Even then, he was sometimes forced to stop and rest on the new couch in his back office. At home, his naps were becoming more frequent, too, and longer in duration. Yet, while his pace slowed and he became more drawn and haggard looking, his mind retained its sharpness. His quick wit remained intact, as well, although it sometimes took on the quality of black humor that left people torn between laughter and crying.

On Sunday Krisanne invited Celia over for dinner—roast beef and Yorkshire pudding—her first visit to Blessing House since Krisanne had come home.

"I hope he still likes Mrs. Winter's chocolate pralines." Celia stepped into the tree-dappled light of the foyer. The premium confections were world renowned, hand dipped and hand wrapped. Even in Coyote Springs where they were made, they were expensive. "Where is he?"

Krisanne put the two-pound box on the hall table. "In the train room with Drew and Travis."

Celia's finely etched eyebrows went up. "The train room?"

The question surprised Krisanne. "You mean he didn't tell you he's set up his model trains in the old sewing room?"

"I didn't even know he had trains."

Krisanne grinned. "Then you've got a treat coming."

Celia stopped in the doorway of the train room. The Venetian blinds at the other end were closed, leaving the pristine landscape in a kind of watery dusk, brightened only by the hundreds of tiny light bulbs that lined the streets and shined through miniature windows. Krisanne invited Celia to look closer.

Lips pinched, Celia shook her head. "Might spoil the effect."

The intensity of distress beneath the nervous smile made Krisanne instantly aware of the congestion in the semidark room. Drew, standing inside the doorway on the right, slipped over to Celia's side. He reached out, not to shake her hand, but to hold it. Startled but pleased by the gesture, Celia clasped her free hand over his.

"Hello, Drew." There was hushed relief in the salutation and her expression softened. "Patrick, is this another of the many talents you've been hiding?"

He grinned over his shoulder from the control panel. "What do you think of my little kingdom?"

"I wish the real world were as beautiful."

"Hello, Mrs. Blessing," Travis greeted her. He was standing beside Patrick, one hand on a transformer lever. "Uncle Pat lets me run the trains sometimes. He's teaching me how to build them, too. Want to see the caboose I made?"

"It's getting crowded in here," Patrick said a moment before Krisanne was about to make the same observation. "Let's go out into the garden. Trav, why don't you bring the caboose and the new car you're working on for Mrs. Blessing to look at?"

Krisanne trailed along, and was about to offer iced tea when Drew beat her to the punch and went to the kitchen to get it.

They sat in the rose garden and Celia enthused over the railroad cars Travis had been building with Patrick's help, the latest being a tender to be filled with tiny chips of black plastic coal. She admired the details, asked the boy questions about its construction, and in a gesture that seemed forced—yet somehow sincere—patted him on the shoulder after she handed the models back.

When they finally went back inside the house an hour later, Patrick sat at the head of the table in the old, formal dining room, at the place his father and grandfather had once occupied. But it was Drew who played papa, carving the juicy rolled-rib roast into hearty slices. Krisanne watched his big hands wield the cutlery with confident ease and thought of the many times she and her brother had sat in this room with their parents. Sunday had always been a family day.

"Who wants the first cut?" Drew asked, shifting his gaze between Patrick and Travis.

"Me," the youngster cried out brightly.

Patrick smiled and nodded.

"Okay, Son. First cut coming up."

Krisanne served the egg-rich pudding.

"Must be good," Patrick teased, observing her scrape the bottom of the pan.

It was one of their jokes that the best Yorkshire puddings always seemed to stick. The fresh peas, fluffy mashed potatoes and rich brown gravy were passed. Patrick intoned the simple prayer before meals his parents had taught him, and they settled down to the time-honored family tradition of Sunday dinner.

Predictably, Patrick didn't eat much. His appetite over the past few weeks had been diminishing. But knowing she could still coax calories into him with sweets, Krisanne had prepared a special dessert—home-baked apple pie made the way her mother used to, sweetened with brown sugar, a touch of maple syrup, and chock full of pecans and raisins.

Celia had been very quiet during dinner, smiling at Patrick, helping Krisanne set and clear the table. Shortly after dessert and coffee, she left, thanking one and all for a wonderful day.

Krisanne watched with uneasy regret as her stepmother walked stiff-backed down the path to her Cadillac sedan fully aware for the first time of the terrible memories and emotions the old house must have provoked. It had taken all these years of being away and the tragedy of her brother's impending death for Krisanne to appreciate the sacrifice Celia had made by living here, allowing her stepchildren to stay in the place they called home.

A few minutes later, Patrick slowly climbed the stairs to take a nap and Drew rounded up his son. Time to go. The three of them stood in the front hall, in the golden radiance of the day's waning sunlight.

"Say thank you for dinner."

"Thank you, Aunt Kris."

Drew took both her hands in his, clutched them for a lingering moment, his eyes holding hers. He leaned forward and placed his lips on her mouth—not long—

only long enough for her to taste their softness. "I love you," he whispered as their cheeks brushed. Then he pulled away.

She stood on the porch and watched the man and boy leave, and wept at the hollow ache of longing they'd left behind.

Things took a drastic change two days later.

Patrick made no move to dress Tuesday morning. "I don't think I'll go into work today. I still have a few things around here I want to sort through."

Krisanne was skeptical. He'd reviewed every scrap of paper in the house over the last two months, cataloguing, filing and cross-referencing them into neat folders. Getting his affairs in order, Pamela Rayburn had called it. Predictable behavior for a dying person. Krisanne's first inclination was to challenge him, but she resisted. Respect his decisions, Pamela had privately counseled her in one of her twice-weekly visits.

"Okay. I'll drop by Kramer's at noontime and pick up some Kaiser rolls. I thought we could have roast beef sandwiches for lunch from Sunday's leftovers. How's that?"

"Fine." He raised his cup. "Is there any more coffee?"

"Coming," she said as she grabbed the pot from the coffeemaker on the counter behind him. A month ago he would have gotten up and poured it himself.

KRISANNE BROKE AWAY from the lab shortly after eleven o'clock, stopped off at the bakery and drove directly home, expecting to find her brother at his desk shuffling through papers. More than likely, she mused, he'd insist on returning to the lab after lunch.

But he wasn't at the desk, or in the train room or

the garage or the garden. She found him upstairs on
his bed, sound asleep. He'd changed sometime in the
morning from pajamas to sweat pants and T-shirt. The
sight of him, curled on his side in a semifetal position,
the once sinewy muscles of his exposed arm looking
slack and weak, sent icicles shivering down her spine.
Fingers pressed to her mouth, she tiptoed into the room
and viewed the motionless figure.

*He can't be dead. It's too soon. He can't leave me
like this. Pat, please, don't you abandon me, too.*

She stared through watery eyes for an eternal minute
before she saw him take a long, sleepy, sighing breath.

Her heart lurched and her arms felt leaden, as she
covered her face with her hands. It took another minute
for her to collect herself enough to retreat from the
room.

She closed the door quietly behind her and leaned
heavy-limbed against the frame, her throat thick and
hot, her heart pounding painfully in her chest. A wintry
chill stole over her bare arms. She rubbed them, while
images of Sunday's semblance of a family flashed before her. Drew's words echoed like a mantra in her
ears. *I love you.*

She took her time preparing a sandwich, wishing in
vain for the sound of her big brother bouncing down
the stairs to join her. But she knew he wouldn't—not
ever again. Hardly touching her food, she put the remaining crispy rolls in the bread box, returned the meat
to the refrigerator and wiped the counter. The house
was quiet but for the soporific ticking of the grandfather clock in the hallway.

She called Nadeen and told her she wouldn't be
coming back to the lab that afternoon.

"Is everything all right?" Nadeen asked.

"Pat's taking a nap," Krisanne said simply.

"He's still in bed?"

"I better stay here with him in case…" In case what? In case he wakes up and wants a glass of water? "Just—" It annoyed her that she couldn't seem to articulate her thoughts. But she wouldn't allow herself to say "in case he dies."

"Is there anything I can do?" Nadeen asked softly.

"Yes…" Krisanne swallowed hard to clear her throat. "Yes." She tried to put a happy face in her voice. "Call Celia and tell her I won't be coming in. Oh, and e-mail me the latest reports from Europe we got on Troimaline. I can read them here as well as I can at the lab."

There was a moment's pause. "Sure. And, uh, Kris, if there's anything you need—"

"Thanks. I'll keep you posted."

Five minutes later, the phone rang.

"What's going on, Kris? Is he all right?" It was Celia.

"He's sleeping, but I don't want to leave him alone."

"No, of course not. Your place is with Pat. I'm glad you're there for him."

Ten minutes after that, Drew called. Unconsciously, she closed her eyes at the sound of his deep, mellow voice. For a rapturous instant she could feel the warmth of his arms around her, comforting, soothing away the tension, but the moment was all too brief.

"I've called the medical equipment company," he announced, "and asked them to deliver the hospital bed this afternoon between four and five. He shouldn't be climbing the stairs any more. I'll be there beforehand to help you when it shows up. Then I'll go home and pack some things so Trav and I can move in tonight.''

"Drew…" She hesitated. "I'm not sure this is such a good idea. You may be able to ignore the past, but I'm not sure I can. Living with you under the same roof—"

"Kris, this isn't about you and me. It's about Pat. We've already discussed it and he's agreed. Whatever personal feelings we might have for each other aren't important now. No matter how difficult it may be, we have to put them aside…for Pat's sake.''

She should be grateful, not doubtful. "You're right.''

The bed was delivered and installed, as Patrick had asked, in the library next to the train room. It faced the double French doors allowing him a view of the rose garden. Drew also arranged to have a ramp installed into the garden. The wheelchair, till then rarely used, would now be Patrick's chief means of transportation.

KRISANNE NO LONGER left the house but worked at Patrick's computer, sending and receiving e-mail and faxes from Nadeen and department heads. Whether it was getting educated on the Blessing business or taking care of household chores, she always made sure she was within earshot of the library. She spent a few minutes in the garden every morning, cutting a fresh bouquet of roses for the sick room. Their fragrance sweetened the air and inevitably brought a contented smile to Patrick's wan face.

It was the changed routine in the rest of the house that was driving Krisanne to pure distraction. The house was big, but there were only two full bathrooms upstairs, one in the master suite, the second shared by the other four bedrooms.

"I've figured it out," Drew said the afternoon he'd moved in. "You take the master bedroom. That'll give you privacy. I'll take Pat's old room and Trav can use yours."

"What about the other two bedrooms," Krisanne asked with annoyance. She should have realized he'd have everything planned. He'd never been comfortable leaving things to chance, a quality that, no doubt, added to his success as a lawyer. His focus and energy had always made her feel secure and protected before; now it only irritated her.

"I checked them," he responded. "They're used for storage. Clearing them out would take days. Besides your old room and Patrick's are closest to the hall bath."

"It'll take me at least a day to vacuum and dust my parent's bedroom." She grimaced. "But I'll have my clothes moved by the time you pick up Trav. How you rearrange Pat's stuff is up to you."

"I'll take care of it. Oh, and another thing, when do you normally do your laundry?"

She blinked at him. "What?"

"Your laundry. I'll make sure my schedule doesn't interfere with yours. I usually do ours on Mondays and another load for Trav on Thursdays. If that conflicts with yours—"

"That's fine." She looked at him. "Anything else?"

"Food and utility bills. I'll pay half."

Krisanne felt as if she were in the throes of high-level negotiations. Her temper started to fray at his persistence, until her sense of humor finally kicked in. He seemed so intent on making sure his presence in the house didn't disturb her…as if it couldn't. In the end, Drew agreed to let her pay the utilities, but he insisted on buying the groceries, arguing that Travis would eat most of them anyway. They would also take turns fixing dinner and whoever prepared would clean up—again Drew's idea. That way each was responsible for the mess he or she made in the kitchen.

"One other thing," Drew added.

This time Krisanne smiled. "Yes?"

"I'll install a doggie door in the kitchen, if that's all right."

She chuckled and rested a hand on his arm. "I think that's a great idea."

Krisanne had long been aware that houses have spirits, and it didn't take more than one evening for her to realize that the spirit of Blessing House had changed radically. Travis took to the move like a Labrador retriever to water. He never walked up or down the stairs, but ran. Once, she caught him sliding down the banister. She smiled and told him to be careful. His face lit up when he understood she wasn't telling him he couldn't do it. "Yes, ma'am," he said and strode into the train room with a roguish swagger.

They didn't use the kitchen or dining room for their meals, but the walnut writing table in the library, so Patrick could share their mealtimes. His appetite was waning and he was losing weight, but the boy's presence, especially, seemed to lift his spirits.

After dinner, the table was cleared and they used it to play games, Monopoly or Crazy Eights if everyone was available, checkers or Go Fish if the two adults were busy with chores. It amazed Krisanne how easily and quickly they'd slipped into feeling like a regular family.

Patrick taught Travis how to play chess. The two of them schemed for hours over Patrick's polished wood board and carved ivory pieces one rainy Saturday afternoon. Later, Drew drove them all to various river and creek crossings to see how much runoff there was from the storm. Any amount of rain was always greeted as a precious gift in this semidesert land.

Drew installed a set of room monitors between the library, Krisanne's room and his, so one of them could respond to a call from Patrick. Awakened late one night by her brother talking in his sleep, she got up and rushed downstairs, only to find Drew already at his bedside.

"How'd you beat me down here?" she asked, slightly out of breath.

He shot her an easy smile. "I'm a daddy, Kris. I'm used to sleeping with one ear open."

Patrick, still sound asleep, turned on his side and continued his slumber.

KRISANNE KNEW SHE had to somehow acknowledge all her years of insensitivity to Celia, even if she couldn't make amends for them. So one day, when Pamela offered her a couple of hours respite away from Blessing House, she invited her stepmother to lunch at a small restaurant that had a dining balcony overlooking the Coyote River.

"How's Pat today?" was Celia's first question when they met.

"Sleeping when I left," Krisanne told her. "Everyday he seems to sleep more and to have less energy when he's awake."

They both took thick slices of French bread from the

basket on the table, but didn't make immediate moves to butter them.

"He's starting to withdraw," Krisanne continued. "Pamela, the nurse with Hospice, warned me this would happen. I guess I didn't believe her. I didn't want to accept that he'd lose interest in the things that have always meant so much to him."

Celia sat straight in her chair, but her face took on a gentleness. "He still cares about people, Kris, about you, me, Drew, Travis. He cares about us very much, but he's becoming an observer now, no longer a participant. It's time for him to turn inward, to take stock of himself."

The words surprised Krisanne. They were the same things Pamela had said. Apparently Celia had been studying up on the dying process to prepare herself for what was coming. It was thoroughness Krisanne should have expected. Suddenly she envied her stepmother's strength—and realized it was that very strength that had intimidated her for so many years.

They ordered their lunches and were served iced tea. Several more minutes went by as they watched a pair of swans glide majestically along the river's edge.

"I've been doing a lot of thinking lately," Krisanne finally worked up the courage to say. "I've been thinking about Pat, of course, and about Drew." She paused. "And I've been thinking about us...you and me."

Celia said nothing, but her slightly raised brows and her questioning look expressed curiosity and something more—anticipation, perhaps, of what Krisanne was about to say.

"I owe you an apology," Krisanne said. "I've been unfair and unkind to you."

Celia sat calmly, her hands folded on her lap. She

looked at Krisanne—a deep, penetrating look—but one that held no threat. "Do you know why?"

So you're not going to make this easy for me, Krisanne mused. *Well, I can't say you're being unfair.*

"I don't know if I can give you a simple answer."

"There are no simple answers, Kris, and I'd be disappointed in you if you tried to give me one." She sat quietly, waiting.

"I was afraid of you," Krisanne confessed. "I understand that now. And I resented your coming into our lives, trying to take our mother's place, taking Dad's affection."

Celia's nod seemed one of sadness, not satisfaction. "I respected your mother and admired her, but I never had any illusions that I could replace her. It would have been foolish of me to try. As for stealing your father's affection... What your father and I felt for each other was never in competition with his love for you and Patrick. I'm just sorry I wasn't able to share in the wonderful bond he had with you."

Krisanne licked her lips against a persistent dryness. "I didn't give you a chance."

"It wasn't entirely your fault." Ringed fingers tapped nervously on the starched, white tablecloth. "I'm not an easy person to get to know and definitely not easy to live with."

They buttered bread and took small bites. A waiter passed by with a large tray on his shoulder. The aromas of cooked pasta, garlic and Italian spices floated to them on the river's gentle breeze.

"I was never able to have children," Celia said. "I resented it when I found out, but I think I was also secretly relieved. I wasn't cut out to be a mother, not after the childhood I had. They say abused children

have a tendency to become child abusers themselves—
maybe because the only reactions they've learned in
dealing with stress are the wrong ones.''

She jabbed her side plate nervously with her crusty
bread, then used the edge of her forefinger to line up
the crumbs along the rim.

''Your father and I talked about it before we got
married. I told him how I felt, that I didn't think I could
cope properly with being a parent. He thought—and I
let him talk me into it—that because you were older,
more mature, once you got to know me, we wouldn't
have any problems.''

''And I disappointed both of you.''

The subtle creases alongside Celia's mouth deepened, as she shook her head in disagreement.

''The key phrase, Kris, was 'as soon as you got to
know me.' The problem was I didn't really give you a
chance.'' She took a sip of her iced tea. A moment
passed during which Krisanne realized the older
woman was struggling to say things that made her uncomfortable.

''The way I grew up—''

''In an orphanage. It must have been terrible.''

''A few times they sent me to foster families. In
some ways, they were worse. At least in the orphanage
the staff, cold and bureaucratic as they were, acknowledged they were there to help us. In the foster homes
it was just the opposite. They seemed to think that because they had taken me in, I owed them something.
There was always so much hope at the beginning, and
then they would demand things of me that…well,
weren't right.'' She closed her eyes for a moment, as
if trying to shut out memories.

''One of the things I learned fairly young,'' she continued, "was not to let my feelings show. Never show emotion. Don't let them see how much you want the doll or the coloring book. Don't give them the satisfaction of knowing how much it hurts when they won't give it to you, or worse yet, when they take it away."

Krisanne felt outrage at people who would torment an innocent, defenseless young child so cruelly.

Celia brought her iced tea to her lips again, but Krisanne wasn't sure she swallowed any of it.

"If you force yourself to hide your feelings long enough, after a while you find you don't know how to express them. I'm going to tell you something, Kris, not because I'm proud of it, but because I think you need to know it, and you're ready now to understand."

She smoothed out the tablecloth on either side of the place setting. "The only person who's ever been able to make me cry—no, that's not saying it right—the one person who's ever been able to *let* me cry, was your father. He touched feelings in me I'd hidden so deeply, I didn't even know they were there. He's the first person in my entire life I'd ever truly loved."

Krisanne felt her throat tighten and was about to reach over and touch the other woman's hand when the waiter appeared to serve their lunch. She took a deep breath and saw Celia do the same.

When they were alone again, Celia continued, "Your father was a wonderful man, Kris. I had him for only a few years, but they were the best years of my life. It's the memory of what we had together that keeps me going. Because of him, I know there's love in the world. I know because I was lucky enough to share some of it. That was his special gift to me."

This time she did take a bite of her salad, a small wedge of avocado. She seemed to savor it, or was it the memories going through her mind that brought the contented smile to her lips?

"I hope you're lucky enough to find that kind of love, Kris. I thought for a long time…you and Drew…you seemed to have that special relationship." She looked down at her food, then glanced up, her expression almost shy. "You know, for a while, I think I was jealous of you."

Krisanne's eyes widened in astonishment. "Me?"

"When you and Drew were first going together…it didn't seem fair for the two of you to share so quickly, so easily, what it took me so long to find."

Krisanne didn't know what to say.

"He made a mistake," Celia continued. "A terrible mistake, it's true. But now the two of you have a second chance. I hope it works out for you. I can see he loves you very much."

Krisanne stared at her plate, though she didn't really see it. Drew said he loved her and everyone seemed to agree. Yet she continued to hesitate, continued to resist. If only she could accept his love.

"Of course," Celia went on, "that means you're going to have to forgive him. Do you think you can?"

"Forgive him? Yes. He's a good man, a wonderful father."

"And forgetting?"

"Forgetting? Forgetting is the hard part."

"How are the new living arrangements working out?"

"Oh, fine." She grimaced. "He wants to make sure we don't get in each other's way, so he's made up schedules for everything. A time for everything and everything in its time," she mimicked.

Celia chuckled softly. "Sounds like a lawyer."

"The man's obsessive." Krisanne took a swallow of ice water. "When I get back this afternoon we're supposed to plan next week's menu."

"Sounds like you've got everything under control," Celia offered.

"Under his control, you mean. He's driving me crazy."

Celia's smile twinkled. "Give it time, Kris. You'll work it out."

They made an attempt to eat, but after twenty minutes they'd done little more than rearrange the food on their plates. Finally, Krisanne called for the bill.

The two women strolled out to the parking lot. Their cars were next to each other and they stood between them.

"Thank you for this time together, Kris. I know you're going through hell right now. Not just with Patrick, though that's enough in itself, but trying to decide what to do about your involvement in Blessing, your veterinary clinic and, of course, there's Drew and his son."

Krisanne saw and felt affection in the older woman's gaze.

"If I can help you in any way...I'd like to," Celia went on, "but more than anything else, I want to tell you how much I appreciate what you've done today. I know it hasn't been easy reevaluating your relationship with me." She reached out and covered Krisanne's hand. "I know what I went through when your father died, but I can't imagine what it must be like for you now—losing your parents and now your brother. You're so young."

Krisanne shifted their hands so she was holding Celia's.

"I'm sorry I wasn't much help to you when Dad died," she said softly. "But at least now we have each other."

CHAPTER ELEVEN

OVER THE NEXT month, Patrick continued to withdraw. Drew had moved the television from Patrick's upstairs bedroom into the library and for a while, he'd watched sports, classic movies and an occasional talk show. But as June waned and July approached, the TV fell into disuse. Several books were stacked on the bedside tables that Drew had also moved from upstairs, but Krisanne noticed they were rarely opened anymore and even when they were, Patrick's finger might be stuck between the pages for hours on end.

The one thing he did seem to take regular note of was the framed photo of their picnic among the bluebonnets. Drew had given him the rest of the snapshots, too, and at least once a day Krisanne would see her brother shuffling through them, a smile, sometimes humorous, sometimes nostalgic, playing across his lips.

Krisanne had just brought in a tea tray one afternoon when he was studying the pictures. "What did you and Drew talk about at the picnic?" he asked.

She set the tray down, the scent of steeping tea tickling her nose. This wasn't supposed to be a soul-searching discussion, just a quiet afternoon interlude before Drew came home from the office after picking up Travis from day camp.

"We talked about his marriage to Lisa." She handed her brother his mug. "He said he wrote me a letter explaining how he got involved with her in the first place." Even as she stirred her milky drink, she could feel Patrick scrutinizing her, appraising her. She shook her head. "I never got a letter from him—no word, nothing—just a wedding announcement."

Patrick raised his eyebrows while his hands curved around the porcelain mug. The hands of a pianist, she'd often thought. But the long slender fingers were growing bony looking, the joints too big for the sinewy flesh around them.

She shrugged. "But it was all a long time ago. It doesn't matter anymore."

"Obviously it does." He peered at her. "He told me he'd written you, too, and I've never known him to lie. Have you?" When he got no response, he said, "If Drew said he sent you a letter, he did." He craned his neck to put his head at her level. "He married Lisa to save the life of an innocent child."

She looked away, slid off the chair and moved slowly to the French doors and stared out at the rose garden. "He went to bed with another woman and conceived a child at the same time he was telling me he loved me." God, why did it still hurt? Why, after all these years, did it still rip at her insides?

"I guess he didn't tell you the whole story."

There was a challenge in his voice that forced her to spin around to look at him.

"What are you talking about?"

"Kris, Drew didn't have sex with Lisa the night of the football game."

She blinked twice at the statement, trying to make sense of it. "Don't tell me. It was an immaculate conception. Golly, when do they start beatification rites for Saint Lisa Hadley?"

Patrick ignored the sarcasm. "It was late. He'd drunk more than he was used to, and he passed out on her couch."

She looked skeptically at her brother. He'd never lied to her, either. She turned his words over in her head. Drew didn't have sex with Lisa the night he was supposed to have gotten her pregnant. Was it possible for a man to have sex with a woman, yet be so drunk he couldn't remember it?

"He didn't have sex with Lisa that night at her apartment," Patrick repeated. "Not even when he woke up in the morning and found himself buck naked in bed with her and she invited him to."

It doesn't make sense. If he didn't have sex with her, why did he marry her? Why didn't he tell me this at the picnic or afterward? Why did he let me go on thinking he'd been unfaithful? Most of all, why do I so desperately want it to be true?

"Is that what he told you?" she asked defiantly, feeling sick inside.

Patrick smiled and let the question linger for a minute before he answered. "No, Kris. It's what *she* told me."

Her knees suddenly turning to rubber, Krisanne resumed her seat at the side of Patrick's bed and clasped her hands around her mug, but it had lost its warmth.

"She was quite a piece of work, was Lisa," he said. "I stopped by their house in Houston for dinner about eighteen months ago to talk to Drew about his firm putting in a bid to represent us. She made it very clear she didn't want to leave Houston for some dried-up little town in west Texas. Her friends were in Houston, she insisted, and she wasn't going to rot in some one-horse cowboyville."

"I don't think the Chamber of Commerce would like to hear us referred to that way," she commented dryly.

Patrick's lips twitched in the merest hint of a smile. He finished off the last swallow of tea and stared for a moment at the bottom of the empty mug before continuing.

"Drew fixed dinner that evening while Lisa drank martinis or, rather, straight vodka. By the end of the meal she was sloshed and started belittling him. I'd witnessed a few of her tirades before, but that night was the worse I'd ever seen. He tried to divert her, but it only made her more belligerent. That's when she blurted out the story of how she'd brought him to her apartment the night of the party, primed for a good time, and all he did was fall asleep. She'd undressed him, she said, and put him to bed. But when he woke up next to her, instead of doing what any normal, healthy male would do, he jumped up like a scared rabbit, threw on his clothes and ran home. She was taunting, Sis. Making him sound inadequate. It was embarrassing for me, mortifying for him, and Lisa enjoyed every minute of it."

"Why did he put up with her?" Krisanne objected. "He's a lawyer. Why didn't he get a divorce? If she was playing around on him and such a lousy mother, it shouldn't have been difficult for him to get custody of his son."

Patrick gave her a thin smile. "That's the point, Sis. Travis isn't his, and if Drew asked for a divorce, Lisa threatened to demand a paternity test to prove it. Drew would have no legal right to the boy. If he divorced her, he'd lose Travis to a woman who was an unfit mother."

Krisanne was horrified that a woman could be so

vicious that she was willing to use her own child in such a calculating way.

She bit her lip, wishing she could untie the knot of outrage in her stomach. "If only I'd known this seven years ago. At least I could have respected him for standing up for what was right." She looked at her brother, at the eyes encircled with dark shadows but still bright with intelligence and warm compassion. "I would have been angry, too," she admitted, "but at the witch who trapped him. If I'd known…maybe I wouldn't have felt so rejected…or berated myself for not living up to some unknown expectations." She clenched her fist in frustration. "I wouldn't have felt as if I'd failed him, that I wasn't good enough for him."

Patrick extended both hands. She uncurled her fingers and interlaced them with his. "You didn't fail him, Kris, and he wasn't rejecting you or your love."

"How long has he known Trav isn't his?"

"I think he began to suspect it shortly after he was born. By then, of course, it was too late. There was no way in good conscience he could abandon the child."

She hung her head in a nod. But her brother's silence all this time made her feel doubly betrayed. "When did you find out?"

He took a deep breath. "On that visit I told you about, I asked him the same question you just asked— why he didn't divorce her. That's when he told me, and that's why I'm telling you now—because…after watching the two of you pussyfoot around each other this last month, I realized he hadn't told you everything."

Leaning back against the upraised pillows of his bed, Patrick gazed at her. "He's a proud man, Kris, an honorable man who thought he'd failed you. It's hard for a man to admit he's been made such a fool of—especially to the woman he loves.''

She rose once again from her chair and went to peer out into the garden, though she saw nothing beyond a dim hint of her own reflection in the old wavy glass.

"Give him another chance, Kris,'' her brother implored from behind her. "He's never stopped loving you.''

She'd told Drew to forgive Lisa; now it was time for her to absolve him. Could she slip back into his arms and not be tormented by the ghosts of anger and humiliation? Could she simply accept him for what he was—a good man?

Give him another chance. Did she have any choice?

IT WAS DREW'S turn to fix dinner that evening, stir-fried chicken with sesame and broccoli spears, so he also had the dishes to do.

"I'll take care of them,'' he said when Krisanne started clearing the table and putting condiments away.

She ignored him and continued to stack plates on the counter.

"I said—''

"I heard you,'' she replied, refusing to match his abrupt tone.

He stared at her, then turned and began filling the sink with hot water. He added dish detergent, his shoulders set, obviously annoyed by her continued presence.

"What's up?'' he asked, but the subtext was, "I'm trying to stay away from you.''

She almost laughed. The pussyfooting around each other that Patrick had mentioned apparently had him as edgy as it did her. She waited until he'd turned off the faucet.

"Why didn't you tell me Travis isn't your son?"

He stopped in midmotion and turned quickly toward the open doorway into the hall.

"He's in the train room," she assured him. A peeping whistle confirmed it. "Why didn't you tell me?" she repeated.

"He is my son, Kris. I'm the only father he's ever known. The only one he'll ever know." He picked up several pieces of soiled silverware and dropped them in with the china, only then fixing his eyes on hers. "The one thing I'm not sorry for, that I'm not ashamed of, Kris, is Trav. Whether I'm his biological father or not doesn't matter. Whether Lisa lied to me, made a fool of me, used me, isn't important. Trav is my son. I love him. And I will do anything in the world to protect him."

Krisanne placed a hand on his—it was hot and wet—and with the other tugged his shoulder down toward her. She smiled as she leaned forward and planted a kiss on his cheek. "You've been a good father." His features softened, and she could feel long pent-up tension flow out of him.

Exhilaration swept through her. She reached for a dish towel. "Better get busy. The water's getting cold."

THEIR CAREFULLY MEDIATED schedule fell apart after that. Drew's participation in the routine of the house no longer unbalanced her, instead it helped her maintain her equilibrium. Every morning he looked in on Patrick, then came to the kitchen for a cup of coffee. While Travis slurped his cereal, he shared a muffin or a bagel with her, then dropped the boy off at day camp on his way to work.

At noon he'd show up as usual with lunch: sandwiches or salads, Mexican or Chinese takeout, or maybe barbecue. It didn't make much difference. The food was incidental. Five minutes after clearing away greasy wrappers or plastic containers, she couldn't have said what she'd eaten. It was Drew she needed—having him near.

She looked forward to the evenings most of all. After work, Drew picked up his son and brought him ''home'' where Gofer greeted him with a slobbery tongue and wagging tail. The boy would visit Patrick for a few minutes, perhaps show him the railcar he was working on. Patrick asked few questions these days, gave little advice. He'd offer a word or two of encouragement, smile when Gofer jumped from the floor to the chair to the bed and licked his hand, then close his eyes and nod off. Travis would cast a longing, lingering glance behind him, as he returned to the train room alone.

In the relative cool of the evening, Drew did what every homeowner did: mowed the lawn, trimmed shrubs or fixed a leaky faucet. Krisanne would bring him a glass of iced tea or lemonade, and they would sit on the porch steps and watch the setting sun paint the sky with brilliant, fleeting color.

Preparing supper was no longer an exclusive endeavor, but something they now did together. They would bump into each other setting the table or clearing it, plan menus, bicker lightheartedly over how much curry powder to add to the shrimp Creole, and inevitably agree they'd gotten it just right. The casual contact they made as their hands reached simultaneously

for a salt shaker or a pot holder suddenly wasn't ser-
endipitous at all. There was something within both of
them drawing their fingers together. Their smiles might
be breezy and cheerful, but in their glances they spoke
of growing needs and wants and hopes.

While Patrick dozed, they would call Travis from
the train room to dinner in the kitchen.

"What did you do in camp today, Trav?" Drew or
Krisanne would ask the boy. While Travis prattled on
about projects and pranks, the two adults would be
sending silent signals, messages that words could not
convey. Two people in tune. Two people in love.

After dinner, they might return to the library to work
on a jigsaw puzzle or play a board game. There wasn't
much laughing and joking now, but it wasn't a sad
time, either. They were together—as a family.

The spell wasn't broken when it was time for Travis
to go to bed. They both tucked him in. Inevitably he
asked Krisanne to read him a bedtime story. Drew
would sit quietly in the bentwood rocker in the corner
and listen, a contented smile on his face.

Later, when it was time for them to retire to their
separate bedrooms, Krisanne didn't back away from
Drew's good-night kisses, didn't shy away from his
caress, but they parted in the hallway. Drew always left
Travis's and his own door ajar, so he could hear his
son if he called out in the night. Krisanne did the same,
not so much as an invitation—though the temptation
was there—but as a link to the other lives in the house,
lives irretrievably entangled with hers. She dreamed
sometimes that Drew was there by her side, but when
she woke, she was always in bed alone.

IT WAS HARD for her to watch her brother, once so
active, so full of energy, lying for hours, virtually mo-

tionless. His eyes, always a striking blue, might be open, but they were often vacant, no longer focused on the here and now. More and more they were closed, though she wasn't sure if he was really asleep or keeping out the world at large.

His moods softened into passive politeness. Friends dropped by to visit and found themselves talking too much. He listened, mumbled the occasional "uh-huh" or "thanks" but communicated very little himself. One day, when Krisanne mentioned that Nadeen had stopped by to drop off another set of reports for her to review and wanted to come in to say hello, Patrick said he really didn't feel like having company that day.

"Is Uncle Pat mad at me?" Travis asked shyly one afternoon. "Doesn't he like me anymore?"

"Of course Uncle Pat likes you," Krisanne assured him. "What makes you think he's mad at you?"

"I asked him to help me fix the door on a cattle car, but he told me to take it to Daddy. I didn't mean to break it. Really, I didn't. It slipped and I dropped it." Huge tears spilled from the boy's peach-pink cheeks, and he sobbed as he spoke. "I don't want him…to be mad at me…when he dies."

Krisanne tried hard to swallow past the searing knot in her throat. She sat on the edge of the couch and gathered him into her arms. He smelled of playground dirt and bubble gum.

"Uncle Pat's not mad at you, Trav. He's just very tired, that's all. He loves you a whole lot." She grabbed a tissue from the dispenser on the coffee table and dried the boy's tears. "But right now he needs time by himself. He's got a lot of thinking to do."

"You mean because he's dying? I don't want him to die."

Krisanne nodded, not willing to trust her voice, and tightened her hold on the child. She glanced up and saw Drew standing in the doorway. He came over and sat beside her, placing one hand on her knee. With the other he stroked his son's head.

"Remember when we lived in Houston?" he asked his son. "Remember sometimes I'd leave you with the sitter, because I needed to do some thinking?"

Travis bobbed his head.

"Sometimes we need people around us so we won't feel lonely, but there are other times when we want to be by ourselves. When I want to be alone, I can go somewhere where there aren't any people, and you can go to your room."

Travis again nodded, but looked perplexed.

"Well, Patrick needs to get away sometimes, too. But he's too sick now to get up and go for a walk, so he asks us to leave him alone. It's not because he doesn't love us. He just needs to be by himself for a while. Do you understand?"

"I...guess so."

The next day, after Krisanne mentioned to Patrick that Travis was feeling a little rejected, Patrick asked to see him.

"Hey, kiddo, are you still my friend, my buddy?"

"Sure I am." But Travis bowed his head, as if he were afraid he'd done something wrong. Krisanne glanced over at her brother who gave her a reassuring smile.

"Well then," he said to the boy, "I guess you better come over here and give me a big hug."

Krisanne watched Travis approach Patrick's out-

stretched arms skeptically at first, then run impulsively
into the bedridden man's beckoning hands.

"Do you think you can do me a favor?" Patrick
asked when they separated from a tight, rocking embrace.

Travis nodded. "Sure. Whatever you want."

"See that book over there?" Patrick pointed to a
large pasteboard volume on the lower shelf of the
bookcase to the left of the French doors. "That was
my favorite book when I was your age. I'd like you to
have it." He raised a finger. "But first, would you read
it to me?"

Krisanne stepped quietly out of the room to the
words of Dr. Seuss being read by a small boy to a
dying man.

ABRUPTLY, ON THE afternoon of the Fourth of July,
Patrick rebounded from the introspection he'd been so
deeply immersed in and decided he wanted to go out
to the lake that evening to see the annual fireworks.

"Fix some of your fried chicken and potato salad,
Sis," he suggested, "and cornbread. Let's make it a
picnic."

So Krisanne sent Drew out to the supermarket to buy
a couple of chickens while she started on the potato
salad and cornbread. "And see if you can find some
fresh peaches for a cobbler," she instructed him.

Caught up as much as he was in the enthusiasm of
the moment, Drew started for the back door, then
turned to face her. "You know he probably won't eat
any of this, don't you?"

Patrick had on several occasions asked for particular
foods only to lose all appetite for them when they were
served.

She blinked slowly and smiled. "We're playing pre-tend." Raising herself on tiptoe, she brushed her lips tenderly against his. "But the game only works if you really believe."

While Drew was at the store, Krisanne called Celia who agreed to join them and bring a chocolate cake.

Then Krisanne got out the old picnic basket, and her grandmother's enamel and tin service. Travis helped pack soft drinks, lemonade and apple juice in a cooler. They all piled into the Bronco just before sunset, and Drew drove them out to the lake.

It wasn't quite the same as their picnic among blue-bonnets in the spring. The air wasn't cool with the light scent of wildflowers, but hot and heavy with the pun-gent smells of mesquite-smoked meats and popcorn. Patrick didn't stroll jauntily to their campsite. Drew had to lift him from the front seat of the Bronco and put him in his wheelchair.

Since there was little chance of finding an open pic-nic table so late in the evening, Drew had tied a card table and some folding chairs on the roof rack of the vehicle. Celia was waiting for them. She'd staked out a nearly level spot not far from the water's edge. Pat-rick watched Travis feed stale bread to the ducks on the lake while Krisanne and Drew set out their picnic. Krisanne lit a citronella candle to ward off mosquitoes.

Patrick asked for a chicken leg, which he barely nib-bled, but he did take a few bites of potato salad, a small helping of warm cobbler, a tiny piece of chocolate cake, and he sipped lemonade from a plastic glass. He smiled mischievously and held a lighted punk for Travis to ignite his sparklers with—under Drew's care-ful supervision—and laughed at the young boy's spon-taneous antics. And when the sun finally fell behind the horizon and the fireworks started, he "ooh'd" and "aah'd" with Travis over their crackling, booming reports and colorful displays.

For a couple of hours, Patrick was his old self—in spirit, at least—bright and happy in the company of his family. He gave Celia a hug when it was time to pack up and watched her leave in tears.

Later, as the Bronco crawled back home along the crowded country lane—the one day of the year when Coyote Springs had a genuine bumper-to-bumper traffic jam—Krisanne was surprised when she saw he hadn't fallen asleep. Instead, he seemed to be memorizing all the sights and sounds around him, even in the dark. When they reached the house, Drew settled him again into his wheelchair, rolled him into the library and lifted him into his bed.

"Thanks for a great day," Patrick said brightly as he snuggled—chilled by the house's air-conditioning—under the light covers.

The next morning, it was as if the previous day's respite had never happened.

OVER THE NEXT few days, Patrick slept most of the time, smiling serenely when he woke. Asked if he was hungry, he always said no, though once in a while Krisanne could coax him into accepting a little warm broth or tiny sips of chilled juice. Occasionally, he took a few mouthfuls of Jell-O, but nothing more substantial.

Celia stopped by every afternoon. Sometimes she would do little more than sit silently holding Patrick's hand. He never asked about Blessing or Troimaline anymore, and she didn't mention them. If he was asleep when she arrived, she'd sit by his bedside for a few minutes, watching him slumber, then get up without making a sound and leave the room. But Patrick always knew when she'd been there by the lingering scent of her powder and perfume.

Pamela came by every day now to check on her patient. Systemic changes were beginning to show. His blood pressure was dropping, his pulse slowing.

"It's all quite normal," she assured Krisanne and Drew. "Our main concern now is to make sure he's comfortable. Medication isn't necessary. He's in no pain."

CHAPTER TWELVE

It WAS LATE afternoon on the second Friday following the Fourth of July. The room was quiet. Outside the French doors birds twittered against the whisper of stately trees soughing gently in the summer breeze.

Patrick lay in the middle of his hospital bed, his shoulders and knees elevated slightly, his head cushioned by a feather pillow. His complexion, once a playboy tan glowing with sun and sport and good health, was a pasty, sallow gray. The hair that used to be so thick and shiny, lay now in lank tendrils, thin and lackluster. Against the translucent skin of his concave temples, bluish veins throbbed in syncopation with the ticking of the grandfather clock in the hallway. His life's seconds numbering, tick, tock, tick.

Krisanne stood by the side of the bed peering down at the frail body of her brother. She watched the chest that had been so broad and full, so strong and powerful, barely expand in slow, shallow breaths, pause, then sink again as spent air wheezed through his nose. Another precarious pause, and the erratic process would be repeated. With each respiration she wondered if it would be his last.

He'd been awake that morning when Drew left for work. He'd greeted Travis with a slack wave of his hand and a whispered joke about Travis going to miss the train that afternoon. The boy was going on an out-ing with his day camp to an old Texas frontier fort and would then spend the night at a friend's house.

Patrick slept through lunch, and the sense of time running out hung in the room like a raven perched over the doorway—waiting. Drew hesitated about going back to work.

"He could linger for days, Drew. Pamela told us—"

"Call me the moment..."

She kissed him on the cheek. "I will."

"I don't want you to go through this alone. I promised I'd be here for you..."

He hugged her then, a long, hopeless pressing of bodies, seeking from each other's closeness a consolation neither of them could adequately give. *He promised to be here for me,* she reminded herself after he'd gone. *He promised.*

Returning to the library, she reached for Patrick's hand, a hand that once held hers while crossing the street, that had lifted her into a toddler's swing, wielded a mighty baseball bat, chopped cordwood, stroked its way across swimming pools and lakes, powered down mighty ski slopes. Now it was shriveled to a rawboned claw too weak to hold a glass of water. The fingers were cool, the heat beneath the paper-dry skin feeble. Leaning over, she touched her lips to the alabaster skin of his forehead. He slept on.

Tiptoeing out into the hallway, she groped her way to the telephone table and sank into the chair. Blindly she stared out the glass panel of the front door. It was several hours before sunset, yet it felt like the middle of the night. She watched the afternoon breeze rustle the leaves of the ancient pecans. How many human lifetimes had those stout trees witnessed? she wondered—her grandparents', her parents' and now her brother's. Steeling herself, she reached out with trembling fingers, lifted the telephone and poked an automatic dial button.

"I think it's time," she said in little more than a whisper when Drew came on the line.

"Have you called Pamela?"

"No..."

"I'll take care of it," he said quietly.

"I'll call Celia."

"Okay. I'll be there in a few minutes."

She hit another auto dial. Bruce answered, asked no questions and connected her immediately. There was a silent pause when Krisanne told her stepmother she didn't think Patrick had much time left. They'd already discussed Celia's presence at Patrick's deathbed. Krisanne had assumed her stepmother would want to be there with them at the end, but Celia had declined. She would stop by to say farewell, she said, but she wouldn't stay.

Krisanne hung up the phone, sat wilted for a few moments, then sprang up nervously and returned to her brother's bedside. He hadn't moved since she'd left him. The bony hand she'd placed on the soft blue spread had not wandered. He lay motionless, a waxen effigy of a man, but for the subtle rising and falling of his sunken chest. His breathing, not yet labored, was becoming more shallow and irregular and was starting to make softly rhythmic, fluid sounds through his parted lips.

She removed a gauze pad from the box on the side table, wetted it from the carafe next to the lamp and patted his parched mouth. He didn't stir, didn't lick away the excess. She caught the dribbles with a tissue.

How long now? How long before the brother she

loved, the generous companion who had loved her back without condition or recrimination…how long before this kindred spirit departed his wasted flesh? How long before he was gone and she was left with nothing but the memory of a man who had been her best friend all her life?

She didn't hear the car in the driveway, or the back door being opened and shut. She didn't hear the footfalls across the kitchen floor or down the hall. But she knew when Drew was there, by her side. She wasn't startled when his hand rested on her shoulder. How strong it felt. How firm and caring and reassuring. She would grieve, but not alone. She raised her arm across her chest and touched her hand to his. His grip tightened.

A bell sounded somewhere in the background. She hardly heard it. But she knew when the hand slipped out from under her grasp. Coldness filled her where there had been warmth. Time lingered. Slowly she swiveled and looked through brimming eyes at the man returning through the opened doorway. She registered his nod and saw the woman who preceded him.

Celia moved with wooden slowness to the other side of the bed, one hand pressed to her chin and mouth, the other held in a knot at her stomach. She said nothing as she looked at her stepson. A tear trickled down her powdered cheek.

A moment later the front doorbell rang once more and again Drew went to answer it. Pamela came quietly into the room, swept it with keen dark eyes, and nodded to the people standing there. She checked the pulse of the man in the bed, listened to his breathing, and looked at his hands and feet. They were purplish.

Straightening up, she motioned for the others to follow her out of the room.

"I shouldn't leave him," Krisanne protested in a choked voice.

"He'll be all right for a while yet," the nurse assured her. "Let's go to the kitchen. We need to talk."

"Leave me with him for a few minutes," Celia asked fervently, but there was a quiver beneath the strength. "I'll let myself out."

Drew had already resumed his place beside Krisanne. Now he cupped her elbow with a firm hand and led her from the room.

"Sit down," Pamela bade them when they reached the kitchen. She put the kettle on the stove and lighted the gas jet under it.

"How long?" Krisanne asked quietly as she perched on the edge of the chair Drew pulled out for her, then slouched against its ladder back. Her mouth was dry. She should be helping get out the cups and saucers, but she didn't have the energy.

"A few hours," Pamela informed her, apparently without emotion. "He'll be leaving us tonight."

"But..."

Drew resumed his accustomed seat across from the woman he loved. She reached for his hand. How reassuring and comforting it felt. She wanted to crawl into its sturdy palm, be surrounded by its warmth, experience the strength and protectiveness of its life force.

Pamela took the seat between them, her fingers lightly intertwined above the scrubbed surface of the table. "The end will be peaceful. What you've got to do now, Kris, is help him go, give him permission to leave you."

"I can't," she cried.

Pamela's voice was gentle, sympathetic, but inexorable. "He knows he's dying, Kris. What he needs from you now is your support, your approval. Tell him you love him, that you understand it's time for him to go, that it's all right for him to leave you."

It's not all right, she wanted to shout. *I don't understand.*

Releasing her hand, Drew got up from his chair and circled to the other side of the table. He knelt beside her, stretched an arm across her back and shoulders. Soft, dusky light melted in from the window behind him, as he lifted a hand to her tear-swollen face. A shuddering sob escaped her burning throat. It took no coaxing for her to lay her head in the warm crook of his neck.

From down the hall came the quiet click of the front door closing.

Pamela rose and retreated to the far corner of the spacious kitchen. She put on the small light over the sink, then set out the tea service. A few minutes later, its spicy aroma filled the room.

"What happens now?" Drew asked.

Pamela placed the steeping brew on the table. "He may appear to regain consciousness for a moment or two," she said, standing behind her chair, her dark hands resting on its top rung. "He could even start talking to you. What he says, however, may not make much sense. He might confuse you with people who aren't present."

Krisanne raised her head from Drew's shoulder, allowing him to stand up. He held out Pamela's seat, then took his own. Krisanne's hands were shaking as she added milk and sugar to her drink.

"At the Fourth of July celebration," she said trem- ulously, "he was so alive, so alert, so happy to be with people. He ate more that day than I've seen him eat in weeks."

Pamela nodded and stirred her own tea. "It's not unusual. A few days or weeks before the end a dying person will sometimes have a surge of energy, a last taste of the old zest for life." She looked at the two other people at the table. "He didn't deny that he's dying," she assured them. "In a way, he was acknowl- edging it. It was his final farewell to this world."

Krisanne remembered his alertness, even on the trip back in the dark, the way he seemed to be taking in- ventory of the sights and sounds around him.

They sipped tea in silence for several minutes. Then Pamela explained what would likely happen, what they could expect. Leaving the dishes on the table, they re- turned to the library.

Patrick's eyes were open now, their watery twinkle illuminating his angular features. Krisanne and Drew approached the bed while Pamela remained in the background by the bookcases.

"The roses are perfect," Patrick said in a voice so breathless, it forced Krisanne to lean forward to hear him. The compliment made her smile.

His blue eyes sparkled happily. "You did a really good job with them, Mom. Dad says Gram's pleased as punch that you were able to save the Summer Sun- shine."

A tug of panic tightened the knot in Krisanne's stom- ach even as she struggled to keep the smile on her face. She had the light-headed sensation of standing in a wobbly rowboat in the dark with nothing to hold on to, nowhere to turn. Brilliant yellow Summer Sunshine had been their grandmother's favorite hybrid tea rose, and Krisanne had indeed had to give it special TLC these last few months, because it had gotten black spot and chlorosis. But the roses on Patrick's bedside table were lavender Sterling Silvers, and he'd called her Mom and talked as if he'd had a conversation with their father. It sent a cold shiver down her spine to know he'd been talking with the dead. It was even more unnerving to realize she envied him. What did her father say? Did he talk about her? Was he happy?

Pamela had warned this could happen. She'd also advised not to argue or correct. And even if Patrick appeared to be asleep or in a coma, not to say anything they wouldn't want him to hear.

Krisanne took his hands in hers. "I'm glad," she said. "They came through fine."

Patrick beamed, but his expression slipped into vagueness as he closed his eyes and seemed to drift off into a light nap. Over the next hour, sleep deepened and his respiration became more irregular. He took long, deep breaths and bubbled them out slowly through his sagging mouth. Sometimes there would be pauses between breaths and just when Krisanne wondered if it was over, he'd inhale once more.

"I love you, Pat," she said, holding his cool, dry hand. She knew he was comatose now, but Pamela had assured her and Drew that hearing was the last sense to go, that he could probably still hear what was going on around him. She yearned for even the briefest movement, the faintest curl of his lips, the subtlest nod of his head, the feeblest tensing of his fingers in hers— anything that would tell her he knew and understood.

"I love you," she repeated. "I'm so proud of you, of what you've done with your life, of the way you've helped so many people and made them happy—especially me. I'm proud of you now, too, for your courage, your wisdom. I'm going to miss you, Big Brother. I'm going to miss you a lot. But a part of you will always be with me, here in my heart.''

She had to pause to choke down tears and regain possession of her voice. Drew's hand massaged her neck. She rocked her head, savoring his touch. A minute passed before she was able to continue.

''I know you have to leave me now, Pat. I understand it's time. It's all right. You can go in peace. I just want you to remember, I'll always love you.''

Drew moved up beside her and gathered her hand in his, then brought it to his lips and kissed it. Their eyes met and though his were dry, they were filled with such compassion and love that she pressed herself against his chest. He didn't let her go.

''I guess it's time for me to say goodbye, too, Pat,'' he said in a deep inflection that rumbled through her. ''I'm going to miss you, old buddy, but I know it's got to be this way. It's time for you to move on. Everything's going to be fine here.''

The sudden thickness of his voice had Krisanne looking up. His jaw muscles were tense, his lips familiar, tender. His words, when they came, whisper-soft and intimate, were addressed to the man in the bed, but they honed their way deep into her heart.

''I'm making you a promise. I'm going to take good care of your little sister. I'll do my best, whatever it takes, to make sure she's happy. So you don't have to worry about her.'' His eyes never left Krisanne's. ''You can count on me. We're going to be fine.'' He hesitated another moment as he stroked Krisanne's back and felt her cling tighter to his chest. Tears glistened now and he turned his head to the man in the bed. His voice was raspy when he spoke.

"You've been like a brother to me, Pat, the brother I always wanted. I couldn't have asked for better. I love you, my friend."

Krisanne and Drew stood side by side, tears running down their faces, and looked at the dying man. Patrick seemed to stop breathing, but then, unexpectedly, he opened his eyes, stared at the ceiling above him and raised his hands. He spread them as if he were greeting someone. Just as quickly, he dropped his arms and half closed his eyes.

His breathing became labored again, gurgling sounds rumbling from his congested chest. For several minutes, they listened to the death rattle.

Krisanne and Drew clung to each other, tormented by the life-ebbing struggle going on before them, yet unable to look away.

At length, a strange peace came over Patrick. His short, shallow breaths were almost imperceptible now, and there were long intervals of time between them. Finally, he stopped breathing. Krisanne looked back at Pamela, standing at the foot of the bed, but the watchful nurse made no move toward her patient.

Krisanne almost jumped when Patrick took yet another long, sighing breath. Again he lay silent, his eyes half-open. At last he was still.

Pamela moved to the other side of the bed, pressed the tips of her fingers to the carotid artery in his neck, held them there a minute. Then, lifting her hand, she gently closed his eyes and backed away.

"He's gone."

WAKEFULNESS CAME SLOWLY, awareness dawning in hesitant, gradual stages—the thick-muscled arm spread across her midriff; the warmth radiating along her right side; the old, comfortable, woodsy smell of Drew's cheek against hers; and the powerful sense of security at hearing his soft breathing close to her ear.

Then reality kicked in like an angry mule, popping her eyes open. Patrick was dead. The brother she loved, her lifelong friend was gone.

She shifted slightly in the golden light sneaking between the slats of the old wooden blinds. Drew lay on his side next to her, his undershirt twisted across his chest, exposing a crispy mesh of black hair. His legs were pressed to hers, his body heat penetrating through the worn denim of his jeans.

After Pamela had left the night before, he'd led her to the living room, held her against his chest as her body convulsed in hot burning tears. When at last she was reduced to racking, hiccuping sobs, he'd lifted her into his arms, cradled her like a baby and carried her up to her bedroom. He'd waited while she changed into her nightshirt, then lay down beside her. His kisses had been gentle, soothing, innocent. It seemed impossible that she'd slept, but she had. And he was still here, still by her side.

The wan smile he offered as he stirred almost reduced her to tears once more. His eyes gave eloquent, silent testimony to the sadness and joy she was experiencing. So much lost. So much found. How could she ever have doubted his love, his devotion?

He rose on one elbow, touched his lips to her temple. "Why don't you shower and dress. Take your time. I'll put on coffee and make a few telephone calls."

BY THE TIME Drew picked his son up at his friend's house Saturday morning, Patrick's body had been re-

moved to the Smithson Funeral Home; the hospital bed
had been reclaimed by the medical equipment company; the library was, once again, a room occupied
only by books—and the ghost of the man who had died
there.

Drew had also packed up his things and Travis's for
their return to Oakdale. Krisanne wanted to protest, to
invite them to stay, but on what grounds? She'd objected to their moving in in the first place, then insisted
Drew keep his distance—which he'd done with frus-
trating efficiency. Living together now, after Patrick
was gone, was pointless and hardly a good example for
Travis—even if they weren't sharing the same bed.

"Uncle Pat's gone? I won't get to see him again?"
Travis asked in a halting voice when his father brought
him to Blessing House. "I didn't get to say goodbye."

Krisanne knelt and wrapped him in her arms. "You
can see him at the funeral home this afternoon if you
want to."

She and Drew had discussed whether the boy should
view the body. His mother's casket had been closed,
so he hadn't actually seen death. Lisa had been there
one day and gone the next, never to come back. Patrick's coffin would be open. Maybe seeing the man
he'd grown so close to would help Travis deal better
with his friend's death and his mother's, help bring
them both to closure. Krisanne and Drew had mutually
agreed the decision should be left to Travis and respected, whatever it was.

"You can say goodbye to him then," she explained
to the boy. "Would you like to do that?"

Travis nodded.

Celia met them at the funeral home at two o'clock.

Krisanne had called her the night before. "He's gone," she'd said. "It was very peaceful."

Celia had simply replied, "Thank you," and they'd both hung up.

The four of them stood and looked in silence when the attendant opened the door to the chamber in which the body was laid out. Floral wreaths crowded the casket and lined the walls. Their heavy scent was overpowering even though the room was quite large. The pallor was gone from Patrick's cheeks, and there was a hint of a smile on his lips.

"Is he asleep?" Travis asked.

"Yes," Drew said. "But he's not going to wake up."

Krisanne nearly gasped when the boy stepped up to the coffin and placed his hand on Patrick's and patted it. "Thank you for the trains," he said. "I'll take good care of them, I promise. I'm going to miss you, Uncle Pat. Oh, and don't forget to say hello to my mommy for me."

Celia held a small hanky to her nose. Krisanne reached out for Drew's hand and crushed it in her own. He reached across her shoulders and pulled her against him.

Travis turned away from the coffin. "Can we go now?"

SUNDAY MORNING KRISANNE and Drew attended the midmorning service at the community church while Travis attended Sunday school. She didn't hear anything the preacher said. She was aware only of Drew's hand holding hers, of his fingers periodically rubbing the back of her hand and the comfort she felt with him by her side.

He'd promised to make her happy—a foolish promise. No one could ensure another person's happiness. Yet, when she gazed into his eyes, she knew his vow was sincere, his love real.

She looked up at a shaft of sunlight streaming through a stained glass window, watched dust motes dance in its golden light and imagined the twinkle in Patrick's eyes and his quiet nod of approval. She mourned her brother, yet it took only a sidelong glance at the man beside her, and she didn't feel alone.

Afterwards, they picked up Travis and drove back to Blessing House for breakfast. The boy was somber, sullen, sad.

"How about I make some million dollop pancakes?" Drew asked his son.

Krisanne grinned in spite of herself. "Million dollop pancakes?"

"You bet. They're Trav's favorites. Aren't they, Son?"

"I guess so," the boy mumbled without enthusiasm.

Drew didn't seem to be affected by the sulky tone as he threw an amused grin at Krisanne. "They're little bitty pancakes," he explained brightly, "and Trav here can eat a m-i-l-l-i-o-n of them."

Krisanne tried to get in the spirit. "Well, I've got to see this."

Ten minutes later, Drew was in the kitchen, a frilly apron tied around his waist. The smell of bacon frying competed with coffee brewing. Krisanne went into the room where Travis was standing, looking at the model trains. The boy was fascinated by them, just as Patrick had always been; so was she. This room contained a world of little people, places and things that could be rearranged and changed, removed and added to at will—so very different from real life.

Travis stood surrounded by them now, but he was stock-still, except for the tears running down his face. Krisanne thought she understood why. They were the gift of his friend, and his friend was gone. It usually helped to put things into words, especially for young children. She stood beside him, her hand resting on his tense shoulder.

"What's the matter, Trav?"

He looked up at her, his cheeks wet, his pink face so sad she was on the verge of crying herself, but she had to stay strong—for him. The boy looked down again and said in a small voice, "I have to give them back."

"Give them back? Give what back?"

"The trains."

"Why do you say that?" This was not at all what she expected. "Uncle Pat gave them to you. He wanted you to have them."

"But I can't keep them."

"I don't understand, Travis. Why can't you?"

She could barely hear the whispered word, "Because."

Krisanne moved a cattle car a few inches to one side so she could sit on the bench by the control panel, facing the idealized world of her brother's imagination. "Can you tell me why?"

For a moment she was afraid he was going to repeat the indefinite "because." Instead he said, "You have to be good to keep things. I can't keep them."

She was shocked. "You've always been good with your daddy and me, Trav. And you were wonderful to Uncle Pat. You were his very special friend. That's why he gave you his trains—because he loved you so much.''

''But I'm not good,'' the boy suddenly shouted, angry and confused.

She knelt down in front of him and held his small arms. ''Won't you tell me why you think that? Maybe I can help.''

''You can't. I'm not good. That's why everybody leaves me. God knows it and He hates me. That's why He takes people away from me.''

Krisanne wrapped her arms around the boy. ''Oh, Trav, that's not true,'' she protested, and in a ritual that must go back to the dawn of humanity, she rocked the terrified child in her arms. ''God doesn't hate you.''

He clung to her desperately. ''He does,'' he argued feebly. ''He took Mommy away from me, and now he's taken Uncle Pat. God hates me.''

''Who told you that?''

''In Sunday school. The man said God hates bad people and he punishes them. He's punishing me because I'm not good. That's why he took Mommy away and Uncle Pat.''

Krisanne seriously doubted the Sunday school teacher had said it quite that way, but to a confused little boy any discussion of death and judgment could easily be misconstrued.

''The man didn't mean it the way you think, Trav. He meant that we have a choice to be good or bad, and if we want to be bad, God will get angry. Do you want to be bad?''

Travis shook his head violently from side to side as he continued to press himself against her chest. She felt his tears on her blouse.

"Well, then He's not angry with you," she assured him.

"But He took Mommy."

"He didn't take her because He was angry with you, Trav, or even because He was angry with her. He took her because He had other plans for her, just like He has other plans for Uncle Pat. God's going to make them both very happy. You want them to be happy, don't you?"

"Why can't God make them happy here?"

How can I answer his question, Krisanne asked herself, *when I don't know the answer myself?*

"We don't always understand why things happen the way they do, Trav. But God is good, so there must be good reasons for them. That's what we call faith, believing that God has good reasons for letting things happen the way they do."

Do I have faith? she asked herself. *Do I believe any good can come of this pain?*

"Is dying good?" Travis asked in a muffled voice against her chest.

No, it's not, she wanted to scream. She rocked him gently in her embrace, her head raised to the ceiling as if she could find the answer there. "It takes us back to God, and He's good."

Travis lifted his head and looked up at her. "Will I die?"

"Not for a very long time."

He nuzzled against her, and they hugged for a long, long minute.

"So you see—" she cradled his head with her hand "—you don't have to give the trains back." She swallowed tears that scorched her throat. "Uncle Pat wanted you to have them. It was his way of staying with you.''

''It was?'' He looked up, suddenly interested.

''Sure. Whenever you play with them, watch them chug along the tracks, hear the whistle toot and see the little people waving, you can think of Uncle Pat.''

She paused to regain control. ''It'll be him waving to you, and you'll remember the fun he had making them, and how happy it made him to show them to you and give them to you.''

''She's right, you know,'' Drew's deep voice announced from behind them. Krisanne hadn't heard him enter.

Travis stuck his head up. ''Daddy.''

Drew rested one hand on his son's shoulder, the other on Krisanne's. Instinctively, she leaned into its warmth.

''Aunt Kris is right,'' he said gently. ''Those trains are a very special gift just for you. It would make Uncle Pat unhappy if you tried to give them back.''

''Does he have trains in heaven?'' the boy asked.

Drew smiled and Krisanne wondered if Travis could see the sparkle of a tear in the corners of his father's loving eyes.

''If he wants trains in heaven, I'm sure he's got them.''

''Okay then,'' Travis said, as if that settled everything. ''As long as he has his own trains in heaven.''

CHAPTER THIRTEEN

THE MEMORIAL SERVICE for Patrick Blessing was held on Tuesday morning at ten o'clock at the community church. The crowd, too big for the modest chapel, overflowed onto the steps and sidewalk. Krisanne was overwhelmed by the outpouring of sympathy. Blessing was closed for the day, and it appeared that everyone from the plant was in attendance. Members and staff of the country club who'd known Patrick, played golf or tennis with him, or served him a cold one afterwards, came to say goodbye. Community leaders, including the mayor and other city officials, and members of the Chamber of Commerce who'd worked with him on community projects and charity drives, also showed up. There was a host of friends and neighbors, too, people who'd met and liked the boy and man. Even Dr. Lesko and his wife, Elvinia, drove in from Austin to attend the funeral.

Everyone, it seemed, wanted to pat Krisanne's hand, whisper words of condolence, or proffer their sorrow with quivering chin and red-rimmed eyes. Their wishes were so heartfelt and sustaining that Krisanne caught herself turning instinctively to comment to her big brother about how nice everybody was.

Celia, among the last to arrive, took her place in the front pew with Krisanne. Dressed in black and clutching a matching purse, she looked small and vulnerable.

Krisanne wondered what torment the closeness of the crowd was adding to her ordeal, but the stoic woman assured her with watery, downcast eyes that she was fine.

Krisanne's chest swelled with pride when a military guard of honor, resplendent in white gloves and ceremonial uniforms, preceded the flag-draped casket up the church's centre aisle.

Wide-bladed fans, extending from the high, vaulted ceiling on long poles, spread the cool, sweet scent of floral wreaths. Prayers were read by the minister and laity. Hymns of praise and benediction were sung in four-part harmony by a white-robed choir. The organ rumbled and swelled in profound adoration. Age-old words of consolation and inspiration were recited in hushed reverence.

Krisanne sat between Drew and his son, gripping their hands—Travis's hot, sweaty and seeking reassurance; Drew's warm, dry and giving it. They stared straight ahead, but she could feel the electricity flowing from Drew's steadying touch. He'd promised to take care of her. Holding his hand, feeling his shoulder hovering above hers, remembering the sensation of his embrace and the beat of his heart so close to hers, she couldn't—even in the depths of her sorrow—deny the swell of joy his presence inspired within her.

The minister finished a reading from the Bible. The congregation shuffled in the pews, and Drew rose up beside her and walked to the sanctuary. She felt ridiculously abandoned as she watched his broad back move away from her, saw him mount the pulpit. But when he turned to face the assembly, his eyes met hers and she knew he was still beside her, part of her. When he spoke, the deep timbre of his voice charged through her, a magical vibration, soothing, stirring, comforting.

He gave the eulogy—a remembrance, he said, of a life, not a death. Almost immediately he had people in tears, but out of laughter rather than sorrow, as he recounted instances of Patrick's sometimes dry, sometimes quirky sense of humor, his practical jokes, and the antics they'd enjoyed in college. The congregation nodded and smiled when Drew talked about Pat's quiet generosity, his compassion for people, his love of family. Finally, they cried again with tears of sadness, when he bade a poignant farewell to a good man, a good brother, son and friend.

From there, the mile-long funeral cortege wended its dignified way through the town of Patrick's birth to the Coyote Grove Cemetery on the outskirts of the city. The Blessing family plot sat on the gentle slope of a hill overlooking the river. Above it, a stand of ancient elm and pecan trees stood sentinel against a cloudless, azure sky.

When Drew left her to resume his post as a pallbearer, Krisanne grasped Travis's hand in a kind of desperation. She looked wanly at Celia who returned a reassuring smile through glistening tears. Celia took Travis's other hand, and the three of them watched the pallbearers, Drew among them, carry the polished wood casket to a white canopy that had been set up at the burial site, place it on a framework spanning the open grave and cover it once more with the national flag.

It was all somehow unreal as Krisanne watched fluttering handheld fans give way to fluttering hankies when the preacher began to intone the twenty-third Psalm.

"The Lord is my shepherd; I shall not want..."

Seven riflemen, positioned on the side of the hill a hundred feet to the left of the gathered mourners, fired three synchronized volleys in a twenty-one-gun salute. The sharp report rent the air, startling people, sending birds scurrying, and Travis clinging wide-eyed to Krisanne's waist.

A bugler blew the slow, gut-wrenching notes of taps, provoking tearful sobs from grown women and trembling chins from aging men. Celia sniffled audibly.

Six enlisted men and women lifted the flag from the casket under the watchful supervision of the captain of the guard. With precise, unhurried movements they carefully folded it in tricorner fashion. Spent cartridges of the salute were placed within its folds and the blue triangle of cloth, stars uppermost, was presented to Krisanne by the captain "with the thanks of a grateful nation."

Then something unexpected happened.

From behind a mausoleum on the right side of the hill came the droning dirge of a bagpipe. Everyone turned to see a lone piper in the plaid kilt of the Ross clan approach the grave site. He halted at the head of the casket, fell silent for a long, solemn moment, head bowed. Then, taking up his reed once more, he breathed deeply into the tartan-covered instrument, and began to play "Amazing Grace." Pivoting slowly, he marched in measured cadence up the hill, into the shadows of the sprawling trees, the inspirational notes of ancient homage drifting and fading away on the summer air.

The soul of Patrick Blessing had been taken home.

THE SKY WAS intensely blue and cloudless, the air heavy with heat and the summer scent of fresh-mown

grass, when Krisanne returned to Blessing House with
Drew, Travis and Celia. People had been dropping off
food since noon on Saturday: casseroles and roasted
chicken, barbecued beef and cabrito, pans of spicy en-
chiladas and tamales, homemade breads and pies, cakes
and pastries. As was traditional after the interment,
Krisanne had invited everybody back to Blessing
House to partake of the bounty. People gathered in the
house, filled the kitchen and spilled out into the backyard. Next-door neighbors had set up extra card tables
and folding chairs to accommodate the overflow crowd.
Friends and acquaintances, new and old, ate, drank,
talked and laughed.

"Pat would have loved this," Krisanne commented
to Drew as she looked out the kitchen window, surveying the assemblage.

Drew came up behind her, rested his hand on her
shoulder, then began to slowly work his fingers against
the tight cords of her neck. She cocked her head into
his strong-fingered massage. The sensation was delicious. She shut her eyes, holding off the world around
them. The chattering hum of people, the savory smells
of summer foods, the swaying green of sun-sparkled
trees all faded into oblivion as she rested against
Drew's magical touch.

"The piper was perfect," she added.

Krisanne turned and caught the secretly pleased grin
on Drew's face, as he moved over to the kitchen table.
She watched him resume carving a bone-in, baked ham
into paper-thin slices. "Was it your idea?"

His grin broadened into an open smile. "I wish I
could take the credit. Actually, it was Celia's. She arranged it through Dr. Jones."

Krisanne couldn't help smile to herself. Six months earlier she might have called such a gesture theatrical and dismissed it as putting on a show of affection. Now she realized the quiet, arm's-length sentimentality suited her stepmother and was her way of acknowledging and handling a grief that was genuinely heartfelt.

Krisanne went outside and found Celia sitting on one of the benches near the rose garden talking with the conductor of the Civic Symphony. Dr. August Truley-Jones rose to his feet at Krisanne's approach. He was a tall, spare man in his early sixties, with a pink face and wild gray hair. He extended his right hand, clasped hers, then encased it with his left. She'd expected a musician to have delicate, soft hands, but his were huge and remarkably tough-skinned, making her instantly wonder if he was a woodworker.

"Dr. Blessing," he said with old-fashioned formality, "please let me offer my condolences on the loss of your brother. He was a fine young man. His passing is a great tragedy."

"Thank you. Drew told me you arranged for the piper." She could still feel the plaintive chords resonating in her head. "I want to thank both of you. It was very moving and beautiful."

Celia reached over and placed her hand on Krisanne's. "We're going to miss him."

They briefly discussed the current symphony season and Jones cordially invited her to become a patron. Then he kissed the hands of both women, excused himself and wandered off.

"I feel like I'm in a nineteenth-century melodrama," Krisanne said lightly.

Celia smiled as she watched the conductor's quiet

departure. "He is a bit of a throwback, isn't he? Nice though. He meant every word."

There was something wistful in her tone that caught Krisanne's attention. For a split second, Celia looked the very image of the well-disciplined lady of a bygone age. She fit in perfectly with the courtly manners of the symphony conductor. Krisanne recalled that Dr. Jones's wife had died several years ago. Surely Celia and Jones weren't…Krisanne suppressed a grin, unexpectedly pleased.

Krisanne invited Celia to rejoin her on one of the benches facing the birdbath. As they sat, she let her eyes stray to Drew who was standing on the other side of the lawn, talking with some guests. He'd removed his gray suit jacket, loosened his tie and undone the top button of his white shirt.

"You've been lucky to have him," Celia murmured.

Sudden awareness that she'd been staring brought warmth to Krisanne's face. But the sensation of embarrassment quickly faded. "He's been wonderful." She looked at her stepmother. "I was wrong about him, you know. I blamed him completely for what happened without realizing he was a victim, too."

Celia let the moment linger, then said with a compassionate smile, "We keep looking for our knights in shining armor, you and I. But shining armor is a funny thing, Kris, sometimes we get so distracted by its glitter we forget there's a man inside. Seven years ago you saw only the gleam and felt only the glow radiating from Drew. Then he did something stupid—call it foolish gallantry—and in your shock and distress, you forgot about the sterling character of the man inside the ungainly tin suit." Giving her stepdaughter a wide grin,

Celia leaned toward her and reached out to calm Kris-anne's jittery hands.

"People mature and grow," she continued quietly. "You have. As painful as your experiences have been, you've learned from them and become stronger and wiser as a result. But the basic nature of people doesn't change. The goodness that has given you strength over these last few months had always been there. Now you know that the love and honor that first attracted you to Drew never changed, either."

As the subject of their discussion crossed the lawn toward them, the older woman rested back against the hard wooden slats of the bench, her hands again folded in her lap.

"How are you ladies doing?" Drew settled onto the bench catty-corner to them, throwing one arm over its back. The casual pose pulled the shirt tight against the thick muscles of his broad chest. Krisanne had to choose between gawking and looking somewhere else and only thinking about how sexy he was, how much she suddenly wanted him.

She turned to her stepmother and was surprised to see a small grin. *Why did I ever think I could fool her,* Krisanne asked herself. *She knows exactly what I'm feeling.*

"We're doing fine," Celia responded. "I was about to ask Kris what her plans are for the future."

Drew looked at Krisanne. "Have you made up your mind, yet, if you're going to stay on at Blessing?"

The question had been coming for a long time. "I've learned so much working there these last few months, and I gained a new respect for what the company does..." She looked at Celia who sat patiently waiting for the punchline.

"But…" Drew prompted.

"But my heart isn't in the work. I miss my animals and their owners too much."

"So you're going to open your vet clinic after all." Celia smiled and squeezed her hand. "Good. Pat would be pleased."

Drew's gaze was intent. "Still thinking of Dallas? Why don't you start a vet practice here in Coyote Springs? Property values are a lot cheaper, and if you're interested in equine medicine, I bet you'll find plenty of horseflesh around here to keep you challenged."

It was Krisanne's turn to smile. "I've already thought about that. In fact I've even looked at a few properties."

"That's wonderful," Celia exclaimed, and Krisanne knew she meant it.

"In the meantime," Krisanne pointed out, "there's still the issue of Troimaline. It was Pat's last research project. I'd like to be in on the decision."

"Of course," Celia agreed. "I can schedule a meeting on it in a couple of days."

"BEAUTIFUL CEREMONY YESTERDAY," Warren Pruit commented Wednesday morning when Drew arrived at the office.

"I'm going to miss him." Drew accepted a cup of coffee from his secretary and settled in at his desk. He'd wanted to stop over at Blessing House this morning to share breakfast and Krisanne's company the way he had for the last six weeks—hell, he'd like to do it for the rest of his life—but he decided at the last minute that maybe it would be better to give her some time alone. She'd been exhausted physically and emotionally when he and Travis left her the evening before. Let her sleep, he admonished himself, even as he pictured her curled up in her bed, and remembered the scent and feel of her body pressed against his.

The phone rang. Taking a deep breath, he picked it up. His secretary told him Mrs. Blessing was on line one. He pressed the button.

"Good morning, Celia." As usual, the conversation wasn't very long. "I'll be there," Drew concluded a minute later and hung up.

"Problem?" Warren adjusted the length of his French cuffs to precisely half an inch past his jacket sleeves.

"Celia's scheduled a meeting to discuss Troimaline for tomorrow at one."

"I'm sure she'll be going forward with it immediately. The product's pure gold waiting to be mined. The sooner she starts production, the better. Before someone else captures the market."

Drew flipped absently through the letters piled on his blotter. Nothing urgent. "Krisanne's still worried about the possible side effects."

"There's no proof there are any. Celia hasn't voiced any reservations, has she?"

Drew conceded she hadn't, but didn't mention that she usually kept her cards close to the vest.

"It's time for you, my friend, to bring Krisanne around—for her own good, of course. Go with what you know. After all, Blessing's success is money in her pocket."

Drew poured hot coffee into his cooling half cup from an insulated carafe on his desk. Warren was aware of the previous relationship between him and Krisanne. Drew was grateful for his partner's tactfulness in not asking too many personal questions about how they were getting along.

Warren lifted a small piece of lint from his charcoal-gray, pinstripe suit. "Is she still interested in opening her own vet clinic in Dallas?"

"Actually, she's talking now about opening one here in Coyote Springs."

Warren chuckled softly. "Good for you. But wherever she opens it, she won't have time to stay involved with Blessing. All she has to do is sell one percent of her stock to her stepmother and she'll still be able to collect enough in dividends from the other forty-nine to make her rich."

Drew shoved the correspondence aside. "You're assuming Celia's willing to market Troimaline. That's not a foregone conclusion."

"Then you'll have to convince her."

Drew sipped his coffee. The only thing he was interested in right now was convincing Krisanne that he loved her. "I agree that financially it's the smart thing to do, but frankly, the possibility of stillbirths and deformed babies disturbs me, too."

Warren's tone hardened. "Are you suggesting I don't care?" Drew started to object, but Warren ignored him and bulldozed on. "Correct me if I'm wrong, but the last time I checked, there was no incontrovertible evidence that Troimaline was responsible for a single death or birth defect."

"But if there is—"

His partner lifted his hands as if he were appealing to some deity. "We've been over this before, Drew. Troimaline has the potential to do a hell of a lot of good in this world, as well as make Blessing millions of dollars and improve its market share internationally.

We, you and I, also have the opportunity to ride the tide. If we know there's something wrong with the product, then certainly we should oppose it. I don't want to represent a loser any more than you do. But this is a business decision, and it's got to be made based on clear logic, not sentimentality."

"And if we're wrong—"

"If we're wrong," Warren countered before his partner could finish, "it's because we don't have perfect knowledge of the future."

Drew shook his head. "Can we really afford to take that chance?"

"Look," Warren continued patiently, "your friend Pat did outstanding research, but even he wasn't able to make a convincing case against Troimaline, and obviously his assistant hasn't, either. Otherwise you wouldn't be having this meeting tomorrow."

That much was true, unless the meeting was being called to announce a breakthrough—which Drew didn't really believe.

"You have doubts. Okay, I respect that, though I don't share them. So let me make a suggestion." Warren spread his hands for emphasis. "One of the best ways to convince yourself of something is to take the contrary view. Go in there tomorrow and give all the reasons why Troimaline should be marketed. Put the opponents of the product on the defensive. Make them come up with clear, logical arguments against you. They'll come away confident about whatever decision they reach, because it'll be based on sound business practices, not vague feelings and doubts."

Drew gave him a grudging nod of approval. They'd used the technique on each other before, when one of them had concerns about a case. The result was almost always a stronger conviction one way or the other.

ON HIS WAY home, Drew was again tempted to stop over at Krisanne's house, but he had a son waiting for him at home and enough work to do there to keep him busy. If she'd called, if she'd asked him to stop by, he would have changed his plans, but she hadn't.

Give her space, he told himself. Some grieving has to be done in private. But space wasn't what he wanted.

At home after dinner he went to the spare bedroom. A few more odds and ends to go through, another garbage bag to fill and the room would be cleared out for Travis's trains. Drew didn't look forward to dismantling the elaborate world of make-believe that Patrick had created, or trying to set it up again here. Tinkering had never been his thing. Good, hard manual labor was invigorating; fussing with models and miniatures frustrated him.

At the moment, however, he felt annoyance as he sorted through a box of crushed ribbons and wrapping paper. Useless. He could throw them out. Then there was the pile of old beauty magazines in the back of the closet. They could go on the stack of paper for recycling. Satin covered hangers. He'd drop them off at Goodwill.

Travis poked his head into the room. "I want to go to Aunt Kris's and play with the trains."

"Not tonight, Son," Drew answered distractedly.

"Why not?" he asked belligerently.

Drew raised his head and spoke patiently. "Because it's late and it's not polite to barge in on people uninvited. I'll talk to Aunt Kris tomorrow and see if we can go over this weekend."

"But they're my trains. You said so. Why can't I go play with them?"

"Son, I just explained why. Now unless you want to take a time out, I suggest you stop arguing with me."

Grim-faced, the boy stomped out of the room. "I wish we still lived there," he shouted down the hallway. "Then I could play with the trains whenever I wanted." His bedroom door slammed.

Drew hung his head. "I wish we still lived there, too," he mumbled to himself and returned to the task at hand.

A few minutes later he came upon a shoe box at the back of an overhead shelf. More shoes? He groaned. Did all women have a fetish about footwear? He removed the thick rubber band around the cardboard and looked inside. Not shoes this time, but a collector's series of baseball cards. Baseball cards? Lisa?

Then he remembered one of Warren's friends was a minor league player. Souvenirs? Forget it, he admonished himself. Don't even think about the possibilities, the implications. Put a positive spin on it—Lisa had died only a few weeks before Travis's birthday; maybe she'd gotten these as a present for him.

"Hey, Trav," he called and held out the box when his son reappeared in the doorway. "These are for you. Mommy was going to give them to you for your birthday."

Skeptically, Travis accepted the box with both hands, looked inside and wide-eyed, exclaimed, "Oh, wow!" He immediately sat on the carpeted floor and started sorting the cards with growing enthusiasm, admiring each one as he carefully lined it up with the others in a square pattern.

"Daddy, look what I found," Travis said as he began a new row on the floor.

"What is it?" Drew peered down, expecting his son to be holding out a card with a name he couldn't pronounce. Instead, the boy offered an envelope. Drew's breath caught and a charge, closely akin to panic, suddenly surged through him.

The boy shrugged. "It was in the bottom of my box."

Drew took the slightly crumpled envelope from him. He looked at its face, saw the address and felt a cold shiver run through him, followed by a flash of intense anger—the ultimate deceit.

THE MEETING TO discuss Troimaline started promptly at one o'clock Thursday afternoon in Celia's office.

In spite of her newfound respect for her stepmother, Krisanne wasn't at all sure what the CEO's position was on the subject. At first, she'd assumed the head of Blessing would favor overseas marketing of the product purely for its profitability. After all, the company hadn't paid a dividend in years, was in debt because of her lavish expansion, and was in competition domestically with very strong and much larger companies. But Krisanne realized now that it had been presumptuous on her part. Celia hadn't made a single statement to anyone, as far as Krisanne could tell, that she was either for or against selling the controversial drug.

Only four people would sit in on the full discussions: Celia, Krisanne, Drew and the newly appointed head of the Patrick Blessing Research Center, Nadeen Thomas.

"Thank you all for coming," Celia began as she

scanned the familiar faces at the oblong table in the conference room. Krisanne and Nadeen sat on her right, Drew on Celia's left, facing them. "We've got a lot of information to review before we begin discussions, so let's get started." She pressed a buzzer under the lip of the table top with her right hand.

Fritz Hanssen, the head of the accounting department, came first. Tall and spare, with wisps of gray hair spread across a shiny pate, the sixty-year-old CPA greeted Celia by name and the others as a group, then distributed the stack of papers he'd brought with him.

"In the interests of time," he said, remaining standing, "you'll find an executive summary on top with all the backup figures beneath it. The bottom line is that we'll be able to quadruple our current gross revenue within five years and increase our net profit by a minimum of 150 percent during that same time period."

Drew let out a little whistle. Krisanne looked at Celia for her reaction, but the woman in the gray business suit sat passively taking it all in.

"I might point out," Hanssen added, "this is a conservative estimate. We bean counters don't like to be too optimistic."

Everyone gave him a polite smile. Observing the muted reaction, Krisanne realized how tired everyone was. Maybe calling this meeting so soon after Patrick's death had been a mistake.

She flipped through the document in front of her. "I see here that you project an increase in reserves against litigation. Do you feel we risk exceptional liability with this product?"

Drew answered for him. "In the case of a suit against us, we would normally have FDA approval to use as a defense, and they would, by default, constitute codefendants. In this case, we don't have that cushion nor do we need it. Successful foreign claims against us are highly unlikely. This is merely a prudent precaution.''

His guarded, formal tone surprised her, and she wondered if he realized how it put a symbolic distance between himself and the subject at hand.

Kermit Dawkins, head of production, was next. He painted an equally rosy picture. Based on market research already conducted, he recommended discontinuing manufacture of two current products, which were only marginally profitable, for this new one, which promised extraordinary earnings.

''Aren't they essentially loss leaders?'' Krisanne asked after scanning his handouts. ''The kinds of basic commodities that prompt customers to buy more profitable products?''

In the corner of her eye, she caught a subtle shift in the woman sitting beside her. Celia pursed her lips and bobbed her head in a tiny nod of approval. Krisanne felt like she'd just passed a test—in this case, by asking the right question.

''Yes,'' Dawkins acknowledged a little grudgingly, ''but the high profitability of Troimaline will offset any losses.''

Krisanne didn't like the answer or the perception she received that the production chief was more interested in change than good management.

''But if, for some reason, we're forced to halt Troimaline production, we will lose its profitability and the toehold in the market for other products as well. Is that true?''

For a split second, Dawkins's expression narrowed into a scowl, but he quickly recovered. ''Yes, but—''

"Troimaline will be marketed only outside this country for the foreseeable future," she quickly followed up. "Won't such a large commitment to this single product shift our profit base from domestic sales to foreign? And won't that also make us more vulnerable to foreign influences, which are less predictable?"

"It's possible," Dawkins agreed unhappily, unwilling now to meet her penetrating gaze. After a few more questions, he left.

Finally, Nadeen pushed back her chair, rose to her feet, and distributed her sheaf of papers.

Her presentation, meticulous and exhaustive, took nearly an hour. She reviewed all the established applications of Troimaline; showed maps depicting the places where it was in use, gave detailed statistical data, broken down in half a dozen different ways, and identified the holes in her own research. She also proposed alternative explanations and interpretations for some of the discrepancies she'd uncovered.

Celia rewarded her with an approving smile. "Questions?" she asked the others.

Drew tapped a finger on the handouts before him. "I have a few."

CHAPTER FOURTEEN

DREW'S POSTURE DURING the briefings, while not exactly rigid, hadn't been relaxed, either. Krisanne noticed that he seemed impatient at times with the level of detail. She kept waiting for him to make eye contact with her, give her one of his smiles of encouragement, but he didn't. Maybe it was just as well, she thought. This wasn't the time or place for smiles. Not when the way he curled the corners of his mouth could be so distracting.

He glanced at her now, his expression pensive.

"You said your research has been orderly and well documented," he commented, "but that your analysis is not based on scientifically sufficient data."

"Correct. Our samples are not—" Nadeen began.

"Not enough for the FDA to base a decision on. They'd want to conduct their own analysis, is that right?"

Nadeen frowned, a little taken aback by the adversarial tone, but she answered evenly. "Yes."

"Have you passed reports of your research on to them?" he asked.

Krisanne studied him. His dramatics seemed forced. She'd assumed he'd lobby against marketing the controversial drug, if not because of the normal caution of attorneys not to take risks, then on the basis of Patrick's misgivings about the substance.

Krisanne massaged her temples. Was she missing something?

"Not yet," Nadeen answered. "There's no point in forwarding data that could prejudice our case in the future."

Drew rubbed the bridge of his nose. "Very wise."

Sudden awareness of what he was implying slammed into Krisanne like a body blow.

"Are you suggesting we intentionally suppress adverse information in order to market a substance we know is unsafe and potentially harmful?"

"Certainly not," Drew rejoined in a mild tone that nevertheless managed to intimate umbrage at such an accusation. "I just want to make sure I have the facts straight." He folded his lower lip between thumb and forefinger, then looked at Nadeen. "Back to the record of Troimaline use overseas. Is the data you do have significantly out of line with prevailing rates of morbidity or deformity in those countries?"

"In gross terms, no."

Krisanne fidgeted. "Here we've got a bit of a dilemma. Foreign, especially Third World country statistics are sometimes unreliable. Reporting can be erratic and incomplete, and there may be any number of cultural and dietary variables, for example, that make it difficult, or even impossible, to establish a direct link between cause and effect."

Drew nodded impatiently and continued to quiz Nadeen. "So they're within the normal range, not outside one standard deviation," he concluded.

"They're borderline."

"But not over the line," he persisted, an edge in his tone.

Nadeen took a deep breath, her discomfort with the

hostile witness technique beginning to show. "No, not over it."

"Thank you."

Celia had shifted her attention from one speaker to the other during the exchange. Now she asked the group at large, "Are there no reliable statistics at all on which to base a decision?"

Krisanne squirmed. The fact of the matter was that there was no scientifically sound data to prove Troimaline unsafe. All she had was Patrick's suspicions and her own gut feeling that something might be amiss. "It comes down to a perceived doubt and a gamble," she acknowledged and peered at Drew.

"Is there any question," he countered, this time holding her gaze, "about the beneficial effects of Troimaline?"

"No," she conceded. "It's been used extremely effectively in lowering hyperactivity and controlling violent behavior—better than any other compound currently available. The question is not whether it works as advertised, but if there are any side effects we don't know about, long-term or short."

"Controlled future use, of course, can be used to determine that," he countered, his deep voice assuming a slightly reproving tone.

"Of course," she replied, uncomfortable with his attempt at intimidation but unwilling to flinch from it. "That's what research is all about." She turned to Celia. "But it comes with a price. It means we have to assume a higher risk—and liability—for whatever decision we make."

Celia tapped a finger to her lips. "Can we identify specific conditions under which Troimaline should definitely not be taken?"

"It shouldn't be prescribed for women who are pregnant," Krisanne answered, "or who are trying to become pregnant."

"So we market it for use by men only," Drew commented, "and for women who are permanently infertile due to age or other condition."

"I'm not sure that's enough," Krisanne objected. "You heard what Nadeen said. There's some indication of chromosomal damage with prolonged use, which could affect men as well as women. Which means we can safely market it only for use by women past menopause and men who are sterile."

"A pretty narrow market," Celia noted. "I don't think we're going to get the return on investment we heard about earlier."

"Let's not get carried away with what-ifs," Drew cautioned. "You can find instances of almost every drug having some kind of adverse side effects on someone. Is a one-in-a-million possibility worth denying its beneficial effects to the other nine hundred—"

"If you happen to be the one, it sure as hell is," Krisanne shot back, daring him to contradict her.

Drew smiled thinly. "I agree, but I also have to ask the question. If one person in a million is adversely affected by a particular substance, is the flaw in the substance or the person? I think you'll have to agree there's reasonable doubt about the product being to blame. It's more likely the recipient."

"Reasonable doubt?" Krisanne repeated, tight-lipped. "We're not talking about finding a rationalization, an excuse—"

Drew raised his hand to silence her. "If you'll let me finish."

The glare she gave him could have frozen lava pouring from a volcano.

"Given that there is doubt," he continued, "let me turn the question around. Is it reasonable—for that matter, is it moral—to deny to the rest of the population the use of a valuable drug, because one person who is incompatible with it, might be affected?"

She should be arguing with him, Krisanne told herself. She should be pointing out that the greater good shouldn't trample on the individual, that the greater good can only be a collection of individuals.

"Is there a course of action you can recommend?" Celia asked Drew.

With his elbows resting on the table, he clasped his hands in front of him, and said in a tone that sounded both reasonable and convincing, "I suggest a four-pronged approach.

"First, commence the manufacture and distribution of Troimaline in phased increments for overseas markets. This will allow time to evaluate the true scope of the market and readjust the production line without significantly disrupting present sales patterns."

He held up his hand, two fingers prominent. "Second," he emphasized, "clearly identify the full limitations of the product on Troimaline's label. This will absolve us of any liability for its misuse."

He extended another finger. "Third, continue to conduct laboratory research, while at the same time monitoring the use of the product in foreign markets."

Before Krisanne could interrupt, he unfolded his pinkie. "Fourth," he concluded, "after two years of use in foreign markets, apply for FDA approval, providing, of course, there's no conclusive evidence that the product is harmful beyond the limitations already identified.''

Krisanne was appalled. She stared at him dumbfounded and felt her face grow hot with frustration. She looked over at her stepmother for her reaction. Celia had brought her right hand to her cheek, the index finger covering the crease running from nose to the side of her mouth, her thumb positioned delicately beneath her chin. There was something almost cynical in the way she rested back against the chair, elbow propped on the armrest.

The room fell silent.

''Does anyone have any other facts to bring up or discuss?'' she asked, dropping her hand and scanning the faces of the three other people at the table.

''No, ma'am,'' Nadeen replied.

Drew shook his head when Celia looked at him. Krisanne did the same.

''Thank you all for coming,'' Celia concluded and pushed back her chair, a signal for everyone else to rise as well.

Nadeen gathered up her papers and left immediately.

Celia turned to Krisanne. ''Let's sleep on this, Kris. It's a big decision, one with many facets to consider. The reputation and success of Blessing could very well be at stake.''

KRISANNE AND DREW left Celia's office together. Out in the hall, past the huge framed posters celebrating turn of the century Paris art shows, beyond the hearing of Bruce or any of the other staff, he turned to face her.

''How are you doing?'' His voice, now intimate and

solicitous, flowed through her, soothing some of the tension she felt from the session they'd just concluded.

"I...the house is too big and empty, Drew. It's lonely there by myself, without you. I miss Trav running through the rooms and the sound of the trains. I even miss Gofer going flap, flap, flap through the doggie door."

He reached out and stroked her arm. "I've missed you, too. So has Trav. He's been a pill lately. Nothing I fix for him anymore is as good as your cooking. Oh, before I forget, he wants to know if he can come over and play with the trains this weekend."

She smiled. "I'm surprised you have to ask." She raised her hand to his cheek. He clamped his hand around her wrist and brought her palm to his lips and kissed it. They stood still. Their eyes met. He leaned slightly forward. She raised her head. Their lips were within inches when the sound of a door opening down the corridor had them shrugging away from each other.

"Drew, what was going on in there?" she asked as a secretary rushed by them.

"I was taking part in a balanced discussion on the merits of marketing Troimaline." He ran his fingers through his hair. "Surely, you didn't want the decision to be a slam dunk. I know Pat would have wanted debate to consider all the options."

"I didn't hear you discussing options." She didn't like the implied comparison with Patrick, either. It made her feel inadequate; even after all these months, she felt like an impostor when it came to Blessing. "What I heard sounded more like an agenda for a particular course of action. Do you really think Troimaline should be marketed?"

He adjusted his gold tie clasp. "What I think doesn't

matter, Kris. The decision is going to be Celia's and yours. My job is to advise you of the legal implications of whatever course of action you choose.''

''All you recommended was a four-point program for marketing Troimaline.''

He shook his head. ''Kris, I was playing devil's advocate.''

''So you don't really believe we should market it overseas?''

His jaw muscles suddenly flexed. ''After all we've been through together you honestly believe I would play with people's lives?''

Shame brought heat to her face. She bowed her head. ''No, of course not.''

''I said conduct lab research—on guinea pigs or whatever you use. I never said experiment on people.'' His voice was low, intense. ''But if you do market it, we have a moral obligation to monitor its use by humans.''

He did a half pivot and began a slow amble down the corridor toward the main lobby. She stayed by his side.

''Look,'' he continued, sounding very reasonable, ''there are essentially two choices available—market Troimaline or don't market it. If you decide not to go forward with production, end of story. There's nothing more to be said or done, and obviously you don't need legal advice. On the other hand, if you decide to market Troimaline, you'll need a strategy, a plan of action, both from the practical perspective and the law. What I've offered is a way to do it that's lawful and low risk, but it applies only if you decide to go into production. The decision is yours, not mine.''

She heard the door to the executive suite opening behind them and turned.

"Dr. Blessing. I'm glad I caught you." Bruce approached in long, hurried strides. "There's a call for you in the office from a Mrs. Lesko. It sounds urgent."

Krisanne wrinkled her brow questioningly. "Mrs. Lesko?" She followed the secretary to his desk. Bruce backed away, giving her privacy. Drew, however, remained close by.

"Elvinia? This is Krisanne. Is something wrong?... Oh, Vinny, I'm so sorry... Yes, of course." She sank into the secretary's chair, asked questions, scribbled words and numbers on a notepad. "I can be there tomorrow... Are you all right?... Take care of yourself, too... I'll see you then."

She cradled the receiver slowly and looked up at Drew's questioning expression. "That was Dr. Lesko's wife. He's had a heart attack. They don't know yet how serious it is. She wants me to come to Austin and take over the clinic for a while, until he's recovered and can return to work, or until she can convince him to sell."

"Sell?" Drew asked. "I thought you said he wasn't interested in selling."

"He always said he wasn't, but Elvinia seems to think he'll have to now."

Drew searched her face. "So you're going?" But it wasn't really a question. More like a conclusion. He could see it in her eyes, the hunger to get back to her professional career.

"I don't see how I can say no under the circumstances. He's a friend as well as a colleague." She tore the sheet off the pad and folded it. "He knew I was looking at other vet options, yet he gave me a leave of absence. And I know Vinny wouldn't have called me unless she felt desperate, especially since Pat just died." She rose. "I need to talk to Celia."

Bruce stepped out from the tiny kitchenette discretely tucked behind a partition in the corner. "Go right in," he told her, not even trying to disguise the fact that he'd been listening. "Mrs. Blessing has no one with her." He opened the door and ushered them in.

Celia looked up, surprised by their return. Krisanne and Drew took the upholstered guest chairs in front of her desk. Krisanne explained the news about Dr. Lesko.

"I'm so sorry," Celia said. "You've certainly had your share of tragedy." She leaned back, hands gripping the ends of the armrests. "Perhaps we can get this issue of Troimaline resolved before you leave." She picked up her pen and nudged the legal-sized, yellow tablet on the desk in front of her. "I was jotting down some notes on the subject, but I'd like to hear your opinion first."

Krisanne took a deep breath. Her decision, the negative one, would rule. She wondered how her stepmother would react.

"I don't think we should market Troimaline overseas," she declared, "or begin the process for FDA consideration yet. It's too early. I'd like us to pursue laboratory experiments, more aggressively if we can afford to, for at least two more years before we take the next step."

"Very interesting." Celia picked up her notes and handed them across the desk to her stepdaughter. Krisanne saw an enigmatic smile as she picked up the pad. She read the concise one-liners. No production or sales for now. No request for FDA approval. Intensified research for one and a half to two years, then reconsider the product's marketability. Celia was recommending exactly the same approach.

Krisanne looked up, unable to hide the surprise from her voice. "So you agree?"

"Great minds think alike, it seems." A rare humorous grin curled Celia's mouth.

"There's something else," Drew noted to Celia. "Kris thinks she may have an opportunity to buy Dr. Lesko's practice in Austin."

A complex of emotions scattered across Celia's usually placid face. There was interest certainly, and perhaps satisfaction that something positive was coming out of an unpleasant situation. But Krisanne wondered if she wasn't seeing something else, too, disappointment that she wouldn't be staying in Coyote Springs as they'd earlier discussed. It gave Krisanne a strange feeling to realize that her stepmother might actually miss her, and an even stranger one to recognize she would miss her stepmother, as well. But it wasn't as if she were moving to another continent. Austin and Coyote Springs were but a few hours driving time from each other. In the end, however, Celia reserved any personal comment and asked only if there was anything she could do to help.

"You made an offer several months ago of a half million dollars in exchange for controlling interest in Blessing. Is the offer still open?"

With a sinking feeling Drew knew Krisanne was going back to the life she'd created—without him. He tried to ignore the ache he felt in his heart. Patrick, his best friend, was gone. And now Krisanne, the woman he'd always loved, was choosing to leave him. At least, he consoled himself, he had Travis. He still had his son.

"Yes, of course..." The older woman hesitated, her expression clearly troubled now. "I didn't renew the offer because I understood Patrick had asked you to keep your share of Blessing..."

Krisanne's stomach began to tie itself into knots. She could follow her brother's wish for her own independence, it seemed, only at the expense of her promise to him to retain ownership of Blessing.

Celia's steady gaze at her confirmed the quandary. "Have you decided not to keep—"

"Perhaps I can help," Drew interceded. He turned to Krisanne. "You said you needed half a million dollars to open a new clinic in the Dallas area."

She nodded.

"Now, it seems, you'll be able to take over an established practice in Austin. Will you need the same amount of capital investment?"

Krisanne pursed her lips and thought before she responded. "I honestly don't know. Obviously I won't have to build from scratch or buy as much new equipment. But I have no idea what Dr. Lesko will ask for his practice, or how much it'll take to upgrade and expand his facilities. It might be less, but I can't say for sure—not until I've had a chance to discuss it with him and get some estimates on renovations and new construction."

He nodded. "Next question. Do you want to sell your interest in Blessing?"

There had been a time when she would have sold out without a backward glance. But that was when Patrick would have been the buyer, before she'd promised him she'd make sure Blessing stayed in the family. "I was hoping there might be a way I could retain ownership of my half interest but sell my proxy." She looked at Drew. "Is that feasible?"

He looked at Celia.

Celia looked at Krisanne. "You understand you would be giving me complete operational control, that my decisions would govern, even if you disagreed with them?"

"I realize that...and I have no qualms about it. Patrick trusted you implicitly, and so do I."

Drawing in her cheeks and closing her eyes, Celia nodded slowly, then opened them. "Thank you, Kris. That means a lot to me."

The two women held each other's gaze for a moment. Finally they smiled and together turned to Drew.

He cleared his throat. "Are we agreed on the amount—half a million dollars?"

"Can you raise that much?" Krisanne asked.

"I can manage it."

Celia began twisting the wedding ring on her finger, and Krisanne saw a shadow of fear haunt her face.

"You wouldn't have to give up the lodge, would you?"

Celia's hand fluttered.

Krisanne thought of Celia's claustrophobia and understood the extent of the sacrifice she was willing to make, not for power, but out of genuine love. "I can't let you do—"

Drew held up a hand. "Maybe there's an easier solution." He looked at Celia. "Would you be able to handle two hundred and fifty thousand?"

A flicker of hope lightened her troubled expression. "Yes."

"Then I propose an agreement whereby Krisanne yields her proxy to you for a period of five years in

exchange for two cash payments of two hundred and
fifty thousand dollars, each to be paid one year apart.
Will that work?''

Celia looked expectantly at Krisanne. ''Would you
be satisfied with that? Can you set up your practice
under those terms?''

A surge of joy ran through Krisanne. She was close
to her goal of having her own equine vet practice. ''It
sounds like it might be the perfect solution for both of
us.''

Celia sighed and suddenly looked very tired. ''Drew,
would you—''

''I'll get the paperwork started immediately.'' He
turned to Krisanne. ''When are you leaving for Austin?''

''I told Mrs. Lesko I'd be there in the morning, so I
should probably leave tonight.''

This was the career break she'd been looking for. It
would be foolhardy to pass it up.

''And when do you expect to be back?'' he asked,
sounding businesslike, not as if he were desperate to
see her again. ''So I'll know when to have the paperwork ready,'' he added.

''Tomorrow's Friday. Give me at least a week. I'll
have to get the rest of my things and, of course, there's
the house to close up and—shoot, I'm just beginning
to realize how much there is to do.''

''I'll have the agreement ready for signature by noon
a week from Saturday.''

A few minutes later, Krisanne and Drew were again
in the hall outside the executive suite.

''Do you really have to leave this evening? I thought
we might have dinner. Trav is spending the night at a

friend's house…we would have some quiet time together to…talk.''

''I really shouldn't,'' she said too quickly and saw
his features wilt, then his expression neutralized as if
he were trying to tell her it didn't hurt, but she knew
it had. She saw it in the way a corner of his lip
twitched, in the way his gaze slid from hers.

The anticipation of sitting across from him in a restaurant, or more likely at her kitchen or his dining room
table, stirred a hunger that had nothing to do with food.
She could see the same gnawing need reflected in the
way he started to raise his hand to stroke her face, and
for an imaginary instant she could feel the heat of his
caress on her skin. *Yes, touch me.* But the hand fell
short and hung now in a loose fist by his side. She
looked up at him. She'd seen it before, that far-off con-
centration in his eyes as if he were scanning the horizon, trying to see the future.

She raised her hands and studied her fingernails, then
drawled, ''I suppose I could leave early tomorrow
morning.''

His face lit up, the gold flecks in his hazel eyes dancing in a way that made her want to laugh. She was
about to throw her arms around him when an employee
turned the corner and approached them on his way to
the CEO's office. He greeted them, a funny expression
on his face, and passed on.

''Let's get out of here.'' Drew cupped his hand on
her elbow and steered her toward the main entrance.

She chuckled. ''Hey, slow down. I still have to go
back to the office, clear my desk and let Nadeen know
where I'm going and how to reach me. I'm sure you
have things to do, too. Why don't we agree to meet
later—''

"At my house," he prompted. "Say six?"

There was no suppressing the grin she gave him. "Six o'clock at your house." She raised herself up on tiptoe and gave him a modest peck on the cheek, sensing he was barely restraining himself from grabbing her and kissing her much harder. What would she do if he did? She smiled self-consciously. She'd kiss him back.

"Don't be late," he urged her, as she turned down the corridor to the lab.

"I'll be there," she called out.

CHAPTER FIFTEEN

DREW LEFT BLESSING Pharmaceuticals feeling like a teenager about to go on his first "serious" date—nervous, excited, a bit worried and not quite sure how to approach it. Should he take her out to dinner to some fancy restaurant? There weren't many places in Coyote Springs that boasted table linen and soft lights. Besides, she could get that kind of treatment in any one of dozens of restaurants in Austin. Should he pick up a couple of steaks and grill them on the patio while they quenched their thirst on wine, maybe a bottle of champagne?

He struck his forehead with the palm of his hand and laughed at his inspiration. Hamburgers—with chopped onions mixed into the meat. The way they used to fix them. Their link with the past, the good past. The one he was determined to recapture.

He got home after five. Mrs. Chambers had Travis all packed for his night at Jimmy's house. The boy seemed to be coming out of the surly funk he'd been in all week. Maybe it was the prospect of going over to Blessing House on the weekend that had his spirits brightening. Or maybe it was, as Pamela had said, the normal resilience of kids.

Drew watched his son give Gofer a big hug, then he dropped the boy off at his friend's house, thanking

Jimmy's mother for having his son over. Next stop—
the supermarket.

It was ten minutes to six by the time he returned to
the house. Hardly time to change clothes. He hung up
his business suit, tossed his white dress shirt in the
hamper and slipped on tan shorts and a blue T-shirt.
While he changed black socks to white, he thought
about the envelope he'd found. Removing it from his
dresser top drawer, he pondered the crumpled paper,
tapped it on his thumbnail and tried to ignore the hol-
lowness creeping down from his chest to his belly. He
should hate Lisa for this and maybe a part of him did,
but it was only a small part now. The fact was that
Lisa didn't matter anymore. Krisanne had said he
should forgive her. He wasn't sure if what he felt at
this point was forgiveness or pity. Whichever it was, it
left him feeling empty inside.

The front doorbell chimed and his heart jumped. It
was still hammering when he swung the door open.
Krisanne was standing in the shadow of the entrance
alcove. Her hair had grown long in the months since
she'd come back to Coyote Springs. Backlit by the afternoon sun, it framed her face and hung to her shoulders like a silky gold veil. He'd never seen her more
beautiful.

She cradled a cake box with both hands, as if it were
a delicate object needing protection.

"Hi," he said roughly, then cleared his throat.
"You're right on time."

He stepped aside. Her scent as she passed had more
than his nostrils twitching. "I'm running a little late."
He closed the door behind her. "What have you got
there?"

"Chocolate éclairs."

A smile bubbled inside him. Éclairs had been one of their special treats in college. They would sit across from each other, silly grins on their faces, watching the creme filling spurt out one end as they bit the other, then lick chocolate from around their mouths. He watched the sway of her hips as she sauntered to the kitchen and knew he was losing control.

She placed the box on the counter and turned. "What would you like me to do?"

It took monumental will power not to throw his arms around her, pin her to the counter and kiss her sense-less. He pointed to the grocery bag next to the refrig-erator. "I picked up a couple of spuds. Why don't you zap them in the microwave for a few minutes to get them started, while I light the charcoal. We can finish baking them on the grill when the fire's ready...uh, the way we used to."

She grinned and reached for the paper bag. "What else are we having?"

"Uhm... There's salad in the fridge. I bought it pre-made. If you want other veggies there are some in the freezer. Pick out whatever you want."

Amusement percolated inside her. No question what was on his mind. He was as jittery as a randy teenager.

"What?" he asked with a note of panic.

"Potato, vegetable and salad. Nothing else?"

She'd never seen Drew blush, but he came as close, at that point, as she figured he was likely to. She sup-pressed a giggle.

"Oh, yeah, I forgot—hamburgers. We're having hamburgers with onions. Is that all right?"

She was tempted to say, "What, no oysters?" but decided he didn't need oysters.... "Great."

He didn't move.

"Aren't you going to light the fire?"

They both smiled this time. The fire, she thought, was already lit and burning hotly.

He turned, opened the kitchen door to the patio and disappeared through it.

Krisanne found herself humming contentedly as she washed the potatoes, poked them with a fork and placed them on paper towel in the microwave. After setting the power level and punching the start button, she went to the refrigerator. She chuckled when she discovered a jug of their old favorite white wine on the top shelf. It didn't need a corkscrew or fine crystal. Grabbing a pair of juice glasses from the cabinet over the sink, she put them on a tray with the wine and was about to carry it outside when the kitchen door swung open almost knocking it all out of her grasp. But before she could drop it, Drew's hands were over hers steadying her. Or unsteadying her. His firm grip threatened to weaken her knees. She let out a little gasp.

"Sorry," he murmured. "Didn't mean to be so—"

She smiled up at him from lowered brows. "Bumptious?" The dimpled grin he flashed was amused, eager and enough to catch her breath.

"Here, let me take that." His voice was a deep, ragged murmur.

Together, they guided the tray back onto the counter. But he didn't lift his hands from hers or shift his gaze. Leaning slowly forward, he brushed his lips across hers. Theoretically, she could have backed away, could have pulled her fingers out from under his. In reality, she was powerless to resist him. She tilted her head up. His mouth lingered less than an inch from hers. There was nothing tentative in the way his eyes held hers, or the gentle way his hands slipped up her arms, guiding her away from the counter and tugging her close to him.

His mouth ravaged hers, fierce, exploring, demanding. Heat waves spiraled through her with each sweep of his tongue against hers, the frantic caress of his fingers across her back, the nudge of thigh against thigh.

The microwave dinged.

She half expected, half prayed he would ignore it and lead her to his bedroom. But when he broke off the kiss, he gave her a tight squeeze and separated himself from her.

"Let's go outside." His voice was a hoarse rumble, flavored by passion and seasoned with hope. "It's comfortable in the shade." He opened the door and picked up the tray. "I have something I want to show you."

She followed him out onto the flagstone patio. He set the tray on a glass-top round table under a big, tasseled umbrella.

"Pour us some wine," he said over his shoulder and disappeared back into the house through a sliding door at the other end of the patio.

Filling the glasses, she realized she'd forgotten paper napkins. But instead of returning inside to get them, she settled into a cushioned, wrought iron chair. The breeze that shimmied through the young trees in the far corners of the neatly trimmed, green lawn was still warm, though the sun was low enough now to have robbed the day's heat of its sting.

She heard the whoosh of the sliding door opening and closing and turned to watch Drew approach. The angled daylight cast his muscular arms and legs in sensuous relief. She noted he was carrying some kind of paper. He stood over her a moment, a look of regret and disappointment tightening the even planes of his face. Sitting on the edge of the chair opposite her, he placed the envelope face down on the table. His eyes skittered over hers before he took a deep swallow of the wine in front of him—a man fortifying himself.

"You asked me several months ago why I hadn't explained to you personally why I was leaving you. I told you I'd written a long letter explaining everything, but I could tell you didn't believe me."

"Drew, I—"

He made a waving motion with his hand. "I probably wouldn't have believed me, either, Kris. Of all the letters to get lost in the mail...well, it didn't seem very likely, did it?"

She slumped back in her chair, afraid to say the truth, unwilling to lie. She'd managed to convince herself in the time they'd spent together that whether or not he'd sent the letter didn't matter anymore. He was a good father, a good friend. The past was over, behind them, unchangeable and beyond recrimination.

"I've been clearing out the last of Lisa's...stuff...to make way for Trav's trains and I came across a box." He picked up the letter, glanced at the face of it for a split second and placed it in front of her. "In it I found this."

She stared at it. The bold sweep of his handwriting was unmistakable. There had been two postal rate increases since the stamp on it had been affixed. She pictured him licking the stamp, pressing it in place and could almost feel the torment that rippled through him as he did it. Here before her was the long awaited explanation, but she made no move to pick it up.

Drew studied her. "If you remember the apartment house I lived in, you know we threw our mail in a box on a table in the downstairs hallway. I didn't tell Lisa

I was going to write you, but she was smart enough to figure out that I would. It never dawned on me that she might go through the outgoing mail.'' He shrugged fatalistically. ''I should have. It was the type of thing she did, though I didn't come to that realization until much later.''

For a moment Krisanne was tempted to extract the letter to see what he'd said, how he'd explained himself, whether he'd said anything about loving her, but the urge passed as quickly as it came. One look at his face was enough to tell her the words he'd used didn't matter. Right now, at that moment, she knew how he felt—then and now.

She picked up the letter, pushed back her chair and rose to her feet. Carrying the envelope by one corner, she walked over to the grill. The pyramid of coals was lightly dusted with gray ash. Curling the fold of papers slightly, she scraped away the top surface, exposing a smoldering pink glow.

''I needed this once.'' She placed it on the coals.

He jumped lithely to his feet, his features set in stunned disbelief at her action. ''But—''

''I needed it to prove to myself that the flaw wasn't in me. That you hadn't left me, because my love was inadequate. And maybe so I could blame you for events I didn't understand.''

Drew came up behind her, bracketed her shoulders with his hands. She could feel the heat of his body against her back, feel his breath against the top of her head. She leaned back as his arms encircled her and his cheek pressed against her temple.

The brittle paper turned brown in the middle as gray-white smoke spiraled up before orange-yellow flames licked its edges and consumed it in fire. In a matter of seconds it was a black cinder lifted by the heat, scattered by the wind.

She turned to face him. "These last months, Drew, I've seen you for what you are—a loving father, a good friend, an honorable man. I never knew Lisa and I'm glad. I'm sorry she stole so much from us, but that's in the past, too."

It took no coaxing for her to settle into the warmth of his embrace. They held each other tightly as the evening sun cast long shadows, and the errant wind blustered around them. Drew framed her face in his hands, his words a soft murmur. "She can't take anything from us anymore." He pulled her forcefully against his chest. "It's you and me now. Just us."

He dragged his mouth across hers, nuzzled his lips along her cheek, nibbled her earlobe tenderly between his teeth and let his tongue wander down her neck to her collarbone.

"I love you, Kris," he murmured, his words soft, breathless, tattered by longing. "I always have. I always will."

Her arms tightened their grip around him, greedy for the fever of his body, the sweetness of his kiss.

He took her hand and led her back through the sliding doors into the house. A quiver of excitement ran through her, but no resistance, no will or power to turn back. She sensed the room was large and cool and filled with shadows, but there were no ghosts. They were alone. Just the two of them.

They faced each other at the foot of the bed. Drew touched his hand to her cheek. A gentle caress that sent silvery flashes, like enchanted moonbeams, coursing through her. She could hear nothing but the rapid beating of her own pulse; feel nothing but the heat of his hand and the ruthless hammering of her heart.

She closed her eyes in anticipation of his kiss, then shot them open when her knees buckled and her body began to float. He'd scooped her up, cradled her against his hard, pounding chest. She threw her arms around his neck and held him even after he'd deposited her on the bed. At last the kiss came, hot, fierce, bold, intoxicating. A mere prelude to the sensations that were to follow.

"I WISH YOU wouldn't go." Drew scraped the last of the peanut butter onto a graham cracker and offered it to Krisanne. When she shook her head, he devoured it in one bite and stuck the spreading knife back into the empty jar. They'd never gotten to the burgers or the baked potatoes or even the éclairs. Instead, they'd made hot passionate love, then slow sensuous love and slept in each other's arms only to wake and do it all again.

Krisanne slid off her side of the bed, pulled down the tails of the shirt she'd appropriated from his closet after their shower together and bent over to retrieve the tray from the pillow that had served as a table between them. Drew watched the clean, white material balloon away from her naked breasts. He was about to reach out and fondle them when she abruptly stood up, seemingly unaware of his erotic designs.

"You know I have to go," she said matter-of-factly and started toward the open doorway.

Wearing only briefs, he got up and followed her, as barefoot as she, down the hall to the kitchen. He'd hoped that after a night of lovemaking, she'd abandon her trip to Austin.

"Why?"

She placed the tray on the counter by the sink. The coffee she'd started earlier filled the room with its robust fragrance.

"You know why." Her movements were shaky as she filled two mugs with the steaming brew. Watching her, Drew questioned if her annoyance was at him for suggesting she break a commitment or at herself for having made it. "Lesko's been very good to me," she reminded him as she handed over his mug. "I can't leave him in the lurch."

Maybe he was being paranoid, Drew told himself, but he wondered if there was an allusion to his past in her words. If so, perhaps she hadn't really forgiven him as she'd claimed. Would there always be digs, reminders, accusations. The idea depressed him at the same time the sight of her, half-naked in his kitchen, stimulated him.

"You said you've been looking at real estate here for a clinic. Are you saying now that you'll buy his practice if he offers it?"

She spun around, nearly spilling her coffee. "Are you suggesting I shouldn't?"

He leaned against the counter, one hand curled around its edge, the other holding the mug in front of him. He recognized the challenge in her question, the self-doubt beneath the anger.

"I can't tell you what you should or shouldn't do, Kris. I don't have the right or the wisdom. All I can say is that I love you and I want to marry you. But it won't work if you're in Austin and I'm here in Coyote Springs."

"So I have to give up my career to marry you."

"Austin isn't the only place where they have animal hospitals and veterinary jobs."

Her mouth quivered. "Job?" she muttered. "Is that all you think this is about, a job?" Her tone hardened, but there was a tremor in it, too. "Coyote Springs isn't the only place where they have law firms and legal jobs, either."

He took a gulp of coffee to soothe his nerves and gain time. All he succeeded in doing was burning his mouth.

"If I were by myself," he said more calmly than he felt, "I would have no qualms about following you, Kris, but I'm not alone. I have Travis. He's lost a mother and a best friend. I won't uproot him again. Don't ask me to choose between the two of you. Travis is my son, my responsibility, and he comes first."

She stared at him for a moment. "Tell him I love him and that I'll see him when I get back." Then she turned away.

IT WAS MIDMORNING when Krisanne arrived in Austin. Her first stop was at the hospital. Dr. Lesko had been moved out of intensive care to a private room on the eighth floor. She expected to find Elvinia with him, but the doctor's wife hadn't arrived yet. Lesko himself was wide awake and alert.

He greeted Krisanne with a smile. "You didn't need to come right away. I told Vinny that, but she can be stubborn." He reached out his hand and grasped hers.

"How are you? What have the doctors reported?"

"It was a very mild attack. More a warning than anything else. They don't seem to think any real damage was done."

"You're lucky then. What you need to do now is heed the warning. Take care of yourself."

He nodded as he released her hand. "You sound like Vinny. But you're right, I suppose it is time I slowed down. She wants to travel."

"Good idea. Go visit those wonderful grandkids of yours."

"Did Vinny tell you she wants me to sell the clinic? I thought I'd want to keep working there until I dropped."

"You have dropped," a woman's voice said behind Krisanne. "Fortunately, it wasn't dead."

"Vinnie!" Dr. Lesko said sharply.

Krisanne turned and peeked around the edge of the wide door.

Elvinia gasped. She was a small, birdlike woman with delicate bones and feathered wrinkles. "Oh, my dear, I'm so sorry. That was thoughtless of me." She came over and took Krisanne's hand and patted it. "Thank you so much for coming under the circumstances."

"It'll be good to get back to vet work. I've missed it. I'm tired of paperwork and staff meetings."

"Your brother's funeral was very moving. I don't think I'll ever hear "Amazing Grace" again without remembering the bagpipe. But I must admit I'm glad that neither of us will be attending another funeral so soon." She walked up to the side of the bed, leaned over and pressed her cheek to her husband's. "How are you feeling this morning?"

"Fit as a fiddle and ready to dance."

The old woman compressed her lips, but there was a sparkle in her eyes, a radiance that belied her seventy-plus years. "Then where shall we dance? The Caribbean or Alaska?"

Lesko looked at Krisanne and winked. "The woman won't give me a moment's rest." He turned back to his wife. "As if I had a choice. I bet you've already decided and bought the tickets."

Elvinia grinned. "Alaska, of course. I can't take a chance on your having another heart attack over a bunch of girls in bikinis in the Caribbean." She turned to Krisanne. "Has he talked to you about the clinic?"

Krisanne hesitated. He'd said his wife wanted him to sell. He hadn't said he did, or that he was offering it to her.

Lesko adjusted the bedspread across his small potbelly. "We were getting to that, dear, when you came barging in." His tone was playful, but there was a mild hint of rebuke, too. Krisanne suspected he probably would have preferred discussing it in private first, but then he shrugged, and addressed Krisanne, "You interested in buying the place?"

"It's a wonderful opportunity," she said diplomatically.

"There's plenty of room to expand. And we have a good client list. As for price... I'm not sure what the market value is right now, but I think we could probably come to some agreement. If you're interested."

"Let me think about it. In the meantime, I can keep the place going for you."

"Fair enough." Lesko rested back against his pillow and turned to his wife. "Alaska, huh? I don't know. I might have a fetish for polar bears or something."

Elvinia snickered softly. "You just leave your fetishes to me, old man."

WARREN PRUIT STOOD stiffly in the doorway of Drew's office, his normally placid face flushed, his right fist clutching a piece of paper. "What the hell is this?" He strode up to the desk and slammed down a copy of the letter Drew had forwarded late yesterday afternoon to Celia.

Drew had expected a reaction from his partner, but not such an emotional one, not from the man whose perpetual imperturbability was legendary.

"Celia and Krisanne decided to hold off on Troimaline. I simply confirmed their decision."

Warren's nostrils flared. "You also endorsed it. You were supposed to convince them to market Troimaline, not kill it."

"I played devil's advocate," Drew responded, strangely calmed by his partner's show of anger. "I even gave them a plan of action for going forward with the project. But it was their decision." He smiled. "And I think they made the right one."

His features bunched, Warren's complexion turned dark. "You damn fool. You just killed the goose that was going to lay us a crate of golden eggs."

Drew leaned back in his chair. "What are you worried about? Even if Blessing doesn't expand right away, it's not as if we weren't growing. We've picked up more new clients here than we had in Houston." Suddenly he leaned forward, his elbows propped in the padded armrests of his chair. He narrowed his eyes. "You were looking forward to lawsuits, weren't you?"

He'd always known his partner enjoyed the challenge of the battle, but what he perceived now was a predatory side of his friend he'd never seen before, or maybe hadn't wanted to see.

"That's how we make our money, counselor." Warren took a step back and moved over to the window, obviously fighting to gain control of himself.

Feeling his own calm beginning to falter, Drew forced himself to lean back in his chair. "Is that all this is about—money?"

Warren spun around to face him. "Isn't that enough?"

Drew shook his head. "No, it's not. We're talking about people's lives and the duty we have to protect them, make them better if we can, not put them at risk." He pressed the palms of his hands against the edge of his desk. "It's called ethics."

Warren waved a hand and made a snorting sound in exasperation.

Drew splayed his fingers, then relaxed them. "I asked myself one question when we were discussing Troimaline—would I want to give it to someone I love. The answer was an unequivocal no."

If a smirk could provoke violence, the one on Warren Pruit's face sufficed. "Lisa was right. You're nothing but a bleeding heart."

Drew straightened up in his chair. "Lisa? What has she got to do with this?"

Warren shook his head, his mouth hooked down in a frown of malice. "Do you think she and I came to these boondocks because we liked the barbecue? You idiot, I came here because of Blessing—and I'm not talking about your darling Krisanne—and Lisa came because I told her to. Blessing Pharmaceuticals was going to be my ticket to the big leagues. Litigation over Troimaline could have gone on for years, gained me an international reputation, and earned enough in legal fees for Pruit and Hadley to move its main offices back to Houston or Dallas or some other civilized place. We could have enjoyed ourselves in luxury.''

Drew's blood pressure rose to dangerous levels, as he stared at the derision on the face of the man he'd taken as a partner and trusted. He knew now who Lisa was going to meet when she died. His lungs burned, and he realized he'd been holding his breath. He exhaled and suddenly, as if the air had been let out of a balloon, the tension dissipating.

He rose slowly from his chair and pushed it back. Looking squarely at the deceiver in front of him, he said with quiet dignity, ''I am hereby giving you the required sixty days notice of the termination of our partnership. You will have it in writing within the hour. Now I would appreciate it if you would leave. I have a lot of work to do.''

CHAPTER SIXTEEN

DR. LESKO HAD hired two part-time assistants to replace Krisanne after she'd returned to Coyote Springs. One of them had since left to join another practice on the other side of town, but Saralyn, fresh out of vet school, had willingly agreed to work full-time until Dr. Lesko returned. As enthusiastic as she was, however, the clinic was too much for one person, especially an inexperienced novice.

So, in addition to her regular workload at the clinic, Krisanne found herself serving as mentor for the young woman. Her days were taken up with other tasks, as well: she inventoried stock, reviewed client accounts receivable, vendor accounts payable and checked tax records. In every spare moment, she investigated other real estate opportunities in the city, studying their relative merits and advantages, and explored construction options and costs with contractors—all in an attempt to get an objective idea of the net worth of the business. She couldn't help but grin one evening as she performed a cash-flow analysis. As much as she disdained paperwork, the last several months at Blessing had given her a business sense she could otherwise not have imagined.

She got home late every night, exhausted by all the running around, overwhelmed by information and the need for decisions. She'd been preparing herself for years for the chance to open her own animal care center, to be her own boss, to be completely in charge. Now the dream was easily within reach. So why did she feel only a dull heaviness?

It wasn't until the second Friday evening that she finally got back to the apartment complex early enough to pay a visit to Nelly next door. The little girl wrapped her arms around Krisanne's waist and hugged her tight. "Davy and I missed you," she said, then added immediately, "We're moving away."

Nelly's mother smiled. "John's been reassigned to a naval base near San Diego." Sharon was six months pregnant and exuded that euphoric glow that Krisanne had seen in so many pregnant women, a proud contentment Krisanne suddenly envied.

"I don't want to go," Nelly shouted defiantly, pulling herself away from Krisanne and running over to the couch to pick up the black-and-white cat, nearly fully grown now. "All my friends are here."

"Moves are always difficult," Sharon explained as she ushered Krisanne in and closed the door behind her. "But you'll like it in California," she told her daughter. "They've got palm trees and beaches—"

"I don't care." Nelly's lower lip quivered. "I want to stay here with my friends."

Had Travis gone through the same kind of anxiety when he had to leave his friends in Houston? Drew said he wouldn't put the boy through that kind of trauma again, not so soon after losing a mother and an "uncle." Had she really expected him to?

"I'm sure you'll make new friends," Krisanne offered.

"I don't want new friends. I like the ones I have."

The little girl looked up at Krisanne. "Can I stay here with you?"

Sharon gasped, then made an apologetic face.

Krisanne shook her head at the girl's mother to forestall comment. "You know," she said to Nelly, "I think you're taking your best friends with you."

The eight-year-old looked at her, puzzled.

"Aren't your parents your best friends? Aren't they the ones who are always here for you, who take care of you, make sure you're safe and that you do the right things? Seems to me you're not going to find any better friends than those."

Nelly sulked, clearly disappointed with Krisanne's response. "It's not the same."

Krisanne sat on the edge of the couch and beckoned Nelly to sit beside her. "We really have two kinds of friends, you know." She draped her arm around the child's shoulders.

The girl looked at her skeptically.

"Those we like," Krisanne went on, "and those we love. It seems to me no matter where you go, you can always find people to like, but the ones you love are very special. Like the little brother or sister you're going to have pretty soon."

"Mommy's going to have a boy." Nelly said in disgust. "I wanted a sister."

"A sister would be nice, but I had a brother, and he became my best friend."

"I'm so sorry..." Sharon muttered.

Krisanne closed her eyes for a moment. "I'm going to miss him. Thank God I had Drew there."

"Drew? Who's he?" Sharon asked as she settled herself slowly into the easy chair by the sofa.

Krisanne paused, picturing him. "He was my

brother's best friend in college. Later, he and I got sort of serious and I thought we...but he married someone else.''

Sharon rested her hands on the growing mound of her belly. ''Nelly, go out to the kitchen and get me a small glass of cranberry juice, please. Would you like some?'' she asked Krisanne who declined.

''Okay,'' Nelly replied. ''Can I have grape juice?''

''Yes, you may, but please drink it in the kitchen.'' Sharon watched her daughter leave the room before turning back to Krisanne. ''He left you? Just like that?''

''Yep. Just like that.'' Krisanne said the words lightly, as if it didn't matter. Perhaps, she realized with sudden insight, because it no longer did. There would always be regret for what had happened, but the pain was gone. ''I didn't see him for seven years.'' Krisanne let out a soft chuckle. ''I read some of the Hospice literature on grieving...and looking back now...I guess I must have gone through all the classic stages of grief after he left. Anger at him for rejecting me. Guilt and the feeling that I must have done something to deserve it. There was never any closure to our breakup...and all these years I kept worrying at it like you do a sore tooth.''

''Yeah,'' Sharon muttered with a shake of her head, ''we always blame ourselves when things go wrong.''

Krisanne nodded. ''I was depressed for a while, too, until I made up my mind that I didn't need him. After all, I wasn't exactly helpless. So I went on to vet school and graduated at the top of my class.''

Sharon punched her fist in the air. ''Good for you.''

Nelly returned, carefully balancing a small plastic glass, which she'd filled too full. Krisanne held her breath. Fortunately, the girl managed to get the berry-red beverage to her mother without spilling any of it on the beige carpet.

"Thank you, honey. Next time don't fill it quite so full, and it'll be easier to carry. But you did very well. Now you better go wash your face. You've got a grape mustache."

Nelly scurried from the room.

"So what happened?" Sharon asked. "Obviously he came back."

"He's a lawyer working for our family business now. He was the one who called me back to Coyote Springs to tell me Patrick was sick."

Sharon emitted a soft tsk. "And he helped you take care of him?"

He did more than that, Krisanne wanted to say. *He held me in his arms, kissed me, made love to me.* She felt a warm stirring as she relived—just for a fleeting moment—the ecstasy of his touch.

"He was always there at my side when I needed him."

Sharon's eyebrows were slightly raised, as if she recognized the sensations her visitor was experiencing.

"Is he still married?"

Krisanne couldn't help but smile at the subtle note of censure in her neighbor's questions. "No," she said, turning serious once more. "His wife died in a car crash last year." Nelly reentered the room carrying Davy. "He's got a son a bit younger than Nelly, and instead of a kitten, Travis has a puppy named Gofer. We all went on picnics together."

"And?" Sharon asked impatiently, her face brightening.

"He's asked me to marry him."

"Does that mean you're going to move away, too?" Nelly asked.

Krisanne smiled, warmed by the rightness of the question. "Yes, I guess it does."

THE FOLLOWING MORNING, Krisanne visited Dr. Lesko, this time at home. He'd been released the day before. Elvinia served sweet herbal tea and no-fat cookies. Krisanne asked her to stay while she explained her recommendations for the clinic and her own plans for the future.

"The new woman you hired, Saralyn, is good. I've been impressed with her knowledge, and I like the way she handles animals and people, but she needs more experience. I suggest you put her on full-time and hire another assistant, as well. That way you can come and go as you please, as soon as she's up to speed."

"Sort of a vet emeritus, huh?" the old man suggested with a note of enthusiasm, allowing Krisanne to breath a sigh of relief.

"Go travel," she urged the septuagenarians and caught Elvinia's smile of approval.

"So you're not interested in taking over the place?" Dr. Lesko asked.

"There was a time when I would have jumped at it," she admitted, "but things have changed."

Elvinia's eyes twinkled. "That nice Mr. Hadley and his son."

At the front door of their house a little while later, Elvinia looked up at Krisanne and patted her hand. "I think you've made the right decision, dear."

Impulsively, Krisanne bent down and kissed the woman on the cheek and received a hug in return. She left feeling a great burden had been lifted from her shoulders.

A POLICE CAR was parked outside Drew's house when Krisanne pulled up in front of it. Immediately she began to imagine all sorts of things gone wrong—an accident involving Drew or Travis or both. Her fingers tightening on the steering wheel, she dropped her head, but only for a second. Clenching her jaw, she straightened up and turned off the engine. She wouldn't allow herself to think the worst. How did she know Drew didn't have friends on the force? Police and lawyers could be friends, couldn't they? The idea brought no comfort.

Slamming the car door harder than she intended, she ran up the walk. Drew's front door was slightly open. She walked in. He was standing over by the fireplace, his back to her, talking to a uniformed policeman who appeared to be scribbling in a little notebook.

"Who else, Mr. Hadley?" she heard the officer ask.

Drew kept rubbing the back of his neck.

"Drew? What's happened?" Fear had her voice trembling.

He spun around in a startled, jerky motion. Relief seemed to wash over him when his eyes met hers, but it was quickly followed by agitation. He rushed up to her, his too-short embrace anxious rather than reassuring.

"Trav is missing."

Krisanne's heart stopped. "What do you mean, missing?"

"He's disappeared. Along with his bicycle and Gofer."

"Where did he go?" Silly question. If they knew

that, he wouldn't be missing. "I mean when did you realize he was gone?"

"About two hours ago. I was putting together saw-horses in the back bedroom for his trains and went to his room to see if he wanted to help, but he wasn't there."

The policeman closed his notebook. "Could he have gone over to a friend's house or down to the minimall to check out some of the new video games? Kids do that sometimes."

"You asked me that before. I told you he's never gone anywhere without telling me or Mrs. Chambers first."

In a motion Krisanne recognized as total frustration, Drew ran both hands through his hair. She hoped the policeman was right, that Travis had simply gone out playing with some friend and had forgotten to tell his father. The alternatives were too terrible to even consider.

She reached out and grasped Drew's arm, very much aware of the warmth of his skin and the tightness of the muscles beneath. "Where have you looked?"

"I've called all his friends." Drew squeezed the bridge of his nose, the torment of losing his son gouging deep ridges across his forehead. "He hasn't been over to visit any of them."

"We checked his school," the policeman added. "Kids sometimes mope around the playground when the excitement of summer vacation wears off. He wasn't there, or at the community church. Any other places where he might hang out?"

A sudden thought struck Krisanne. "Have you checked Blessing House?"

Drew's mouth dropped open. "Of course. Why

didn't I think of it? He's been bugging me to let him play with the trains."

He explained to the policeman where they were going, then grabbed Krisanne's elbow so tightly it almost hurt. Together they ran out the door to the Bronco.

"Let me drive," he insisted.

He took a great circle route that bypassed all the traffic lights and downtown congestion. The only problem was that it was a two-lane road. If they ran into an obstacle...

Krisanne's mind was racing. "Has Travis ever done anything like this before?"

Drew maneuvered easily around a slow-moving car. "He's been talking back and not doing his chores lately, but he's never run off."

"Has he been upset about something?"

Drew's fists tightened on the wheel. "You mean other than Pat dying, and you leaving town without saying goodbye to him?"

A slap across the face couldn't have hurt more.

He shot her a contrite glance. "I'm sorry, Kris." He curved his fingers around hers. "That wasn't fair. He's not your responsibility. He's mine."

Strange, she thought, how much his words of reassurance sounded even more like an indictment. The child loved and needed her, and she'd deserted him as surely as Drew had abandoned her before the boy was born.

Drew made a left turn onto a side street and two blocks later turned onto Coyote Avenue. Ahead, on the left, loomed the Blessing family house half-shrouded by stately pecan trees—her home. The place where she'd been loved and nurtured, a place alive with memories of parents and grandparents and a brother. Where she'd first met the man she loved and had learned to love him all over again. Where she'd come to love his son—a boy who was now lost.

Drew pulled up in front of the old residence. Krisanne felt embarrassed when she realized the lawn was freshly cut, the shrubs trimmed. She hadn't thought about having someone look after the place while she was gone, but she knew without asking that this was Drew's handiwork. They both jumped out of the vehicle and ran to the porch.

There was no sign of Travis or his bicycle.

Drew darted down the right side of the building toward the garage. Krisanne ran along the left. She rounded the back of the house as Drew raced to meet her. He shook his head, his face set, anxiety making the vein in his temple pulse.

They moved together toward the foot of the steps.

"Did you check the windows?" he asked.

She nodded. "Including the little ones to the basement. Nothing's open or broken and I didn't see any signs of tampering."

One hand raking again through his hair, he stared at the kitchen door. "Did you put the security panel in the doggie door before you left?" He was already up the three steps to the little covered porch.

She looked up at him. Travis could easily have crawled through the portal. "I...remember thinking about doing it."

He kicked at the rubber flap. She expected his toe to drum against the solid board behind it. Instead the flap swung gently from the top. Drew twisted the doorknob, but it was firmly locked.

She leaped up the steps. "Have you got the car keys? The door key is on the same ring."

They entered the dark kitchen. No oatmeal raisin cookies cooling on a rack. No Gofer munching them under the table. Except for the remote twittering of birds in the tall trees outside, the room was so quiet it echoed—and for a terrible, wonderful moment, Krisanne could almost feel the ghost of her brother hovering in the familiar coziness of the room. Shaking herself from memories all too fresh and fighting a tightening in her throat, she joined Drew in calling out his son's name. "Travis, honey, are you here?"

Intuition told her there wouldn't be a response.

"He's not here," Drew said dully. He led her, nevertheless, to the train room.

The thin patina of ten days' dust was undisturbed. Confidence sagged. They checked anyway through the rest of the house, upstairs and down, calling the boy's name. They were about to give up when a cold shiver careened down Krisanne's spine. She clutched Drew's arm. "The dumbwaiter!"

In near panic, they ran to the kitchen, directly to the small oak door in the wall.

"It's locked," Drew announced, his words marked in equal measures of relief and disappointment.

"Pat kept the key over here." She rushed to the counter drawer by the pantry.

"Kris, there's no way he could crawl in and lock the door after him."

"Unless he brought a friend to show him the trains Pat gave him." She retrieved the key still attached to the tag Patrick had planted in Travis's pocket. Memories of her brother's playfulness threatened to overwhelm her.

"When Dad got stuck in the dumbwaiter, his buddy

ran away." She opened the lock with shaking fingers. "Travis," she called up the long shaft. "Trav, sweetheart," her voice quivered, "are you hiding?" She realized she didn't want to hear an answer, didn't want to think of the little boy trapped in the tin-lined box. Would he be forever afraid of confined spaces? Would he, like her father and Celia, break out in a sweat when an elevator door closed? "If you are, Trav, please let us know. Your daddy and I are worried about you."

She heard nothing. Drew reached from behind her to close the door. "He's not here, Kris."

Hope and despair, panic and desperation had Krisanne's legs going rubbery. Her fingers trembled as she locked the dumbwaiter door. The click of the tumbler echoed through her and conjured up another image—the little boy standing where she was standing; Patrick turning to him with the old teddy bear in his hands, offering it.

Folding herself into Drew's arms, she welcomed his hands stroking her back. She could hear the thudding of his heart and fought a flood of tears, but she couldn't beat back the painful ache in her chest.

Suddenly she shot out of his grasp and dashed to the library. Dappled sunlight played on the floor where Patrick's deathbed had been. In spite of the haunting memory, there was a quiet peacefulness about the room. She could feel her brother's closeness. Strangely there was no sadness.

"They're gone."

Drew was right beside her. "What're gone?"

"The pictures. I put them between Mark Twain and Sherlock Holmes. Somehow it seemed appropriate—"

"I remember. And you didn't move them?"

"There was no reas—" She stopped and stared at him.

"Bluebonnets." They said it together.

The beveled glass rattled when they slammed the front door behind them. Hand in hand they bounded down the porch steps to the waiting Bronco.

Intense hope filled the narrow space between them, while fear wrapped itself around them like a suffocating blanket.

"Please God, let him be all right," she murmured, only half aware she was praying the words out loud.

Krisanne didn't want to think of him hit by a car or truck, his blood oozing out onto the hot, dirty pavement, but the images came to her mind unbidden. Perspiration stung her eyes.

The air-conditioning was turned up to max, yet hot sweat continued to trickle down her back and between her breasts.

"I shouldn't have gone away. I shouldn't have left him."

Drew shot her a quick glance, then turned his attention once again to the road ahead. "There's nothing for you to blame yourself for, Kris."

"I shouldn't have left you," she blurted out.

This time when he looked over at her, she knew he understood. He reached for her hand, and she gave it to him like a drowning person desperate for a life preserver. His touch was solid and absolving, and she knew that whatever the future held, they would meet it together.

"Trav is all right," he murmured. "You'll see."

"Drew, if anything happened to him—"

"We're going to find him, Kris."

His calm insistence didn't fool her. They were both holding their breath, fighting the demons of fear and helplessness.

He pulled his hand from hers when he took the turn-off to the twin mesas. His foot teased the brake as they skidded through the sharp turn onto the caliche road. Over her shoulder, Krisanne saw the trailing cloud of dust billow up, an impenetrable wall, shutting out everything they'd left behind. They bounced over and veered around boulders and potholes, making the Bronco pitch and roll like a storm-tossed dinghy. The tires b-r-r-r'd as they passed over the cattle guard at the open gate.

"Do you really think he's here?"

"He's got to be." White-knuckled, Drew concentrated on the road.

Krisanne's breathing shallowed as they rocked to the edge of the saddle of land between the two mesas. Cold panic had her pulse tripping, her mouth going dry, when she peered down into what had been a beautiful, fertile meadow a few short months before. Now it was parched and brittle, the dominant colors gray and tan. Only the mesquites, like recalcitrant teenagers, defiantly boasted their mantles of green.

Drew pulled up as close as he could to the old tree they'd picnicked under. A blast of hot air assaulted Krisanne as she jumped out of the vehicle. She searched the sun-scorched landscape. "Do you see him?"

Drew's long legs pumped through tall dry grass toward the mesquite. "No." The word was frantic, terror-filled. Travis had to be here.

"His bike!"

Her head shot up and her gaze followed Drew's out-stretched finger. The two-wheeler lay on the ground beside the tree.

"But where's—"

"There!"

Her heart galloped and her scalp tingled. A profound weakness came over her, and she was sure she was going to collapse. Then the adrenaline of optimism and joy jolted her into motion. She ran forward, tripping once, skinning her palm.

The boy lay curled up on the far side of the fat-trunked tree. One arm was stretched across Gofer's back, the other hand clutching the pictures from the library. The dog raised his head and began to wag his tail at Drew's approach.

"Is he all right?" Even having to ask the question frightened her. She was beside Drew now, looking down at the boy, watching his small chest inhale and exhale rhythmically.

Drew knelt and placed his hand on his son's shoulder. The eyelids fluttered. The boy looked up. "Daddy."

She pressed her fingertips to her half-open mouth. Tears slid down her cheeks. How cool they were. How impossibly refreshing.

Sitting up, Travis rubbed the sleep from his eyes. Finally, he saw Krisanne and stopped. "You went away. You didn't even say goodbye. Daddy said you might not be coming back."

She was crouched beside him now and folded him in her arms.

"I said—" Drew started to object, but Krisanne shook her head to ward off his protest.

"But I am back now, Trav."

"Are you going to stay?"

"Would you like me to?"

He pressed himself against her breasts and nodded. "Yeah."

Drew's expression was a confusion of hope and doubt. "What about Lesko's—"

"I turned down his offer."

His eyes widened, sunlight dancing in their hazel recesses. "So you really are staying...here in Coyote Springs?"

"If you'll have me."

He reached his arm around her in response, pressed his lips to her throbbing temple. "What about your clinic?"

She brushed a soft wave of hair away from Travis's brow. "I'll build one here."

Drew's embrace deepened. "Kris...tell me you'll marry me."

The heat that rolled through her had nothing to do with the summer sun. The music in her heart wasn't made by songbirds. She smiled up at him through tears she couldn't hold back.

"I love you, Kris." The soft murmur of his words melted away all doubts, all confusion. This was where she belonged—with this man, with this boy.

She snuggled into his shoulder. "And I love you."

Travis pulled himself away enough to look up into her face. "Are you going to be my new mommy?"

"If you'll let me."

He threw his arms around Krisanne in a bear hug. "Oh, yes."

Gofer wouldn't be left out. With slobbery tongue he licked their faces.

"Yuck," they said together. "Doggie kisses."

She looked down at the boy and saw at his feet the snapshots they had taken at this very spot so long ago. One was turned up and on it was the smiling face of her brother. As tears blurred her vision, she could have sworn she saw him wink.

EPILOGUE

The Following April

"GET A MOVE on, Trav. It's time to go," Drew called from the bottom of the staircase.

"Coming, Dad," the seven-year-old called out. "Gofer, where did you put my hat? Oh, here it is."

A moment later the boy came skipping down the stairs, baseball cap on backwards, soccer ball under one arm and Gofer glued to his side.

"Where's Ivor?"

"Oh, yeah, I forgot." Travis shot back up the stairs, Gofer at his heels, and came flying down again before his father could catch his breath. This time his son was toting the teddy bear his Uncle Pat had given him.

His hand resting comfortably on his son's shoulder, Drew guided Travis to the kitchen. It was filled with the rich aromas of fried chicken, freshly baked biscuits and warm peach cobbler.

Krisanne was screwing the top on a wide-mouthed jar of potato salad. "Let's get the car packed," she said over her shoulder. "Grandma Celia's going to think we got kidnapped, if we don't get a move on."

Travis walked over to the scrubbed wooden table and looked inside the big picnic hamper already lined with a towel. "Can I put the bricks in?"

Krisanne hesitated, then caught the approving look

on Drew's face. She handed the boy a pair of pot-holder mitts. "One at a time," she instructed him. "And use both hands."

Twenty minutes later, they were driving up the ca-liche road between the twin mesas. A dark Cadillac sedan was already parked near the big mesquite.

Celia moved quickly to meet them, Dr. August Tru-ley-Jones a few steps behind her. The four adults greeted each other happily, the women exchanging hugs, the men shaking hands. Travis did both.

Everybody helped unload the Mercedes and carry the food to a pair of tables the older couple had already set up under the tree.

"Smells awfully good," Dr. Jones commented as he sniffed the basket of hot food Drew hoisted on the square portable table. The two women were already setting the larger round table for five. A sixth folding chair was set up slightly back from the others on which Ivor sat.

Krisanne looked out over the field of bluebonnets and felt a quick tightening of her throat.

"They're beautiful, aren't they?" Drew had stepped up quietly beside her and rested his hand on her shoulder. She dipped her head to one side to rub her cheek against his fingers.

"Thank you for suggesting we do this." She would never forget the day her brother died, but the third Sunday of April would be the memorial day she'd keep locked in her heart—their last picnic together. Patrick among the bluebonnets, playing with Travis, romping with Gofer, pushing her after Drew to begin the process of reconciliation. Had he lived a few months longer, he could have been part of their fall wedding, but then, his spirit had been a very real part of it.

"It's ready, Mom," Travis called behind them.

The word, coming so easily from the boy's mouth, warmed her heart. She planted a soft kiss on Drew's hand before they turned together to join the others.

"Wonderful food," Dr. Jones commented for the third time as he accepted a second helping of dessert. "If you ever get tired of tending to animals, perhaps you'd consider catering to men's stomachs." He closed his eyes in approval, as he took another spoonful of cinnamon-dusted cobbler.

Celia watched the symphony conductor and smiled.

"How are you enjoying your new role at Blessing?" he asked Drew. Following the breakup of his law partnership with Warren Pruit, Drew had been hired on at Blessing, managing production and acting as Krisanne's nonvoting representative on the board.

"I feel like I've finally found my niche," Drew admitted. Law had been his father's mandate, not his own.

"And he fits in very well," Celia added. "Speaking of business, how's your clinic coming?"

"I hired another assistant this week," Krisanne responded.

"That's three she's got on the payroll now." Drew's pride in her achievement was unmistakable. Not that he didn't have something to do with it. He was the one who'd found the small feedlot that had been closed for years on the north end of town. The stalls and pens were ideal for holding horses and other large animals. He'd also located the temporary school classroom they'd been able to buy at auction to replace the tumbledown shack at the lot. The modifications they'd made to the building weren't exactly the ideal setup, but it was a good start. As far as Krisanne was concerned, the most satisfying part of it was the sign Drew had given her. The Blessing Animal Care Center. An unusual wedding present, but one that continued to send a ripple of delight through her every time she looked at it.

"This is, I think, a momentous day." Dr. Jones wiped his lips with a cloth napkin and put it down. He looked at Celia whose smile hinted unexpectedly of shyness. "You see...I've asked Celia to marry me... and she has accepted."

Drew slapped the older man on the back, then offered his hand in hearty best wishes. Krisanne jumped up from her folding chair, tipping it over behind her, and rushed to kiss her stepmother on the cheek. In a moment, the two women were in an emotional embrace.

Smiling, Krisanne turned to Drew. "Tell them."

"You two deserve second congratulations," Drew told the happy couple, "because you're also going to become grandparents again."

Celia's eyes nearly popped, then became watery. "You're—"

"Pregnant." Krisanne grinned happily. "The baby's due in the fall."

Travis gulped. "Baby?"

"How would you like to have a little brother or sister?" Krisanne asked.

"I'm going to be a big brother?" The boy looked up at his father.

"Yep."

"Cool!"

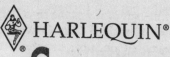

If you enjoyed what you just read,
then we've got an offer you can't resist!

Take 2 bestselling love stories FREE!

Plus get a FREE surprise gift!

Clip this page and mail it to Harlequin Reader Service®

IN U.S.A.
3010 Walden Ave.
P.O. Box 1867
Buffalo, N.Y. 14240-1867

IN CANADA
P.O. Box 609
Fort Erie, Ontario
L2A 5X3

YES! Please send me 2 free Harlequin Superromance® novels and my free surprise gift. Then send me 4 brand-new novels every month, which I will receive months before they're available in stores. In the U.S.A., bill me at the bargain price of $3.57 plus 25¢ delivery per book and applicable sales tax, if any*. In Canada, bill me at the bargain price of $3.96 plus 25¢ delivery per book and applicable taxes**. That's the complete price and a savings of over 10% off the cover prices—what a great deal! I understand that accepting the 2 free books and gift places me under no obligation ever to buy any books. I can always return a shipment and cancel at any time. Even if I never buy another book from Harlequin, the 2 free books and gift are mine to keep forever. So why not take us up on our invitation. You'll be glad you did!

134 HEN CNET
334 HEN CNEU

Name	(PLEASE PRINT)	
Address	Apt.#	
City	State/Prov.	Zip/Postal Code

* Terms and prices subject to change without notice. Sales tax applicable in N.Y.
** Canadian residents will be charged applicable provincial taxes and GST.
  All orders subject to approval. Offer limited to one per household.
  ® are registered trademarks of Harlequin Enterprises Limited.

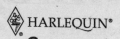

SUPERROMANCE

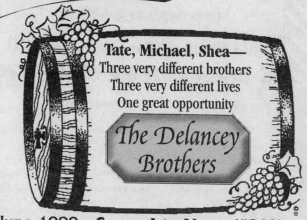

Tate, Michael, Shea—
Three very different brothers
Three very different lives
One great opportunity

The Delancey Brothers

June 1999—Second to None (#842)
by Muriel Jensen

What's a tough cop like Michael Delancey doing in a place like this? Mike was a hostage negotiator in Texas; now he's working at the Oregon winery he and his brothers have inherited.

Michael was ready for a change—but nothing could have prepared him for Veronica Callahan! Because Veronica and her day-care center represent the two things he swore he'd never have anything to do with again—women and children....

And watch for the third story in The Delancey Brothers series, Shea's story, *The Third Wise Man* in December 1999!

Available at your favorite retail outlet.

Makes any time special ™

Look us up on-line at: http://www.romance.net   HSTDB2

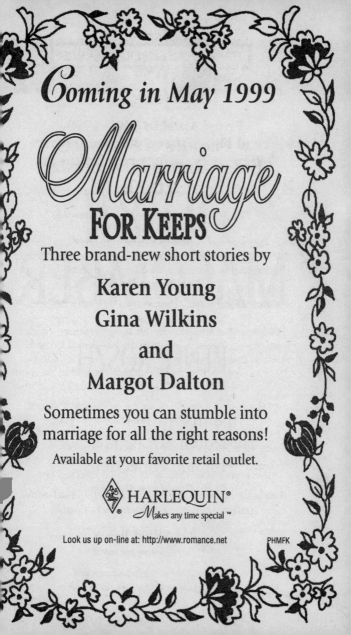

HARLEQUIN®

SUPERROMANCE

COMING NEXT MONTH

#840 IF HE COULD SEE ME NOW • Rebecca Winters
By the Year 2000: Satisfaction!

Rachel Maynard was rejected by her best friend's handsome brother, Nikos Athas, and now—years later—she's determined to win his love. Except that when she meets his older brother, Stasio, she realizes she's not in love with Nikos at all. Because *real* satisfaction can only come from being loved by a man of strength, passion and honor—a man like Stasio.

#841 WINTER SOLDIER • Marisa Carroll
In Uniform

When Lieutenant Leah Gentry goes overseas as part of a team that will provide medical care for those in need, she figures she'll spend long days doing fulfilling work. What she *doesn't* expect is to fall for Dr. Adam Sauder. *Or* to return home pregnant with his child.

#842 SECOND TO NONE • Muriel Jensen
The Delancey Brothers

What's a tough cop doing in a place like this? Mike Delancey was one of the best hostage negotiators in Texas. But he left it all behind to work in the winery he and his brothers inherited. He was ready for a change but nothing could have prepared him for Veronica Callahan—a woman with a *very* interesting past.

#843 TRIAL COURTSHIP • Laura Abbot

Life is a trial for nine-year-old Nick Porter. His grandparents make him eat broccoli and nag him about his clothes. Aunt Andrea's a great guardian, but she's always on him about school and manners and stuff. At least there's Tony. For a grown-up, he's *way* cool. Nick's seen how Tony and Andrea look at each other. Maybe if he's lucky, Tony and Andrea will get together and Nick'll get what he *really* wants—a family!

#844 FAMILY PRACTICE • Bobby Hutchinson
Emergency

Dr. Michael Forsythe's marriage is in trouble. He and his wife, Polly, have not been able to cope with a devastating loss or offer each other the comfort and reassurance they both need. It takes another crisis—and the unsettling presence of a four-year-old child—to rekindle the deep love they still share.

#845 ALL-AMERICAN BABY • Peg Sutherland
Hope Springs

To heiress Melina Somerset—pregnant and on the run—the town of Hope Springs looks like an ideal place to start over. Unfortunately, her safety depends on a man she met months ago when she was living under an assumed name. But this Ash Thorndyke is nothing like the man she used to know. She'd loved that man enough to carry his child. *This* one she's not sure she can trust.